Copyright

This book is a work of fiction. Any references or similarities to actual events, real people living or dead or to real locales are intended to give the novel a sense of reality. Any similarity and other names, characters, places and incidents is entirely coincidental.

Contact the publisher for wholesale orders @:
One Wheel Publications, LLC
P.O Box 6661
Hamden, CT 06517-9998
(203) 491-9896

ISBN: 978-0-9986156-0-8

Printed in the United States of America
First Edition printed in February 2017

Library of Congress Cataloging-in-Publication has been applied for.

Email: onewheelpublications@gmail.com
Website: www.onewheelpublications.org

Editing by Lori Stewart @ A Few Choice Words
Formatted by Dijon Wiggins
Book cover designed by Gregory Graphics

PART 1 OF A TRILOGY

BY

DANIEL "BOONE" MILLS

Thank You & Dedication

I'd like to thank the Poet/MC, Nas, for raising the bar with his classic song Rewind. That song's exactly what challenged my creativity for this novel.

This book is dedicated to my grandmother, Alese Mills, the strongest woman I've ever met in my life. I'll love you forever Gma.

7/28/1929-12/20/2016

Acknowledgements

Before anything, I have to thank God for blessing me, sparing my life many times over and over. Alese Mills, my last living grandparent for holding me down forever. I love you. (You were alive when I wrote these acknowledgements so it will remain). Grandad Mills (pops), Gma and Gpa Jones. My mom Brenda, I got you forever. My pops Burn Mills (Like you said at Gma's service," the blueprint is laid") and momma Pam, I love yau'll. My sisters Tanza, Tereze, and Arielle. My brother's Marqese, (Good look on the book cover for My Thoughts Become Things Bro), Russell and Jeffrey 'Rah Rah' Jones always. Crazy love for y'all. All my uncles and aunties thank you for everything.

To my kids. Mekhi, my first born. You impress and amaze me. Keep ya eyes open and remain a leader. Prince, my young Soldier. Daddy is lining everything up. It won't be as hard 4 you kidko. Dallas, my baby girl, my heart, I love you more than anything in this world. More than cheese pizza. No man, woman, or child will ever destroy our bond baby. Madison, my young dancing machine, I am so proud of you baby girl, I love you. To the mothers of my children Tasha, Aisha, and Leandrea. Thanx for these aforementioned gifts.

To everyone I grew up and hustled with on Congress Ave, Stevens Street, Liberty Street, and the whole Hill... Most of you are fake ones, but too many real ones to name. You know who you are. If you know anything about me, you know I don't front. Therefore, if I 'F' with you, then I 'F' with you. 1,000,000!!!

Definitely shout out my big Brodie Freaky Ty AKA FT. Haven't met too many dudes like you fam. Lenny, what's shaking bro. To the Ville, Tre, Island, and every Hood in New Haven, CT. 203 stand up! To the Teel family, Stevens, Harrison's, Beverly's, Penn, Johnson's, Silva's, Spearman's, Wiggins, Lester's, Jones', Hopkins.

Shout out to everyone who stopped by my barber shop to buy the first appetizer I put out, 'MY THOUGHTS BECOME THINGS'. I got a lot of love from CT, SC, all the way down to Florida for those couple short stories. Crazy shout out to Belinda Hunter and Adnileb Publishing for all the major networking down in South Carolina.

To everyone locked away in state and federal institutions. Hold your head, get in them books and get some rhythm in your cases for appeal. Them 365 boys showed it best. Shout out Johnny and 365 South, Leat, Darcus, and Sean Z. Peace Mo Diz, D nub, Lord, (fellow authors) Moody, my nigga Brotha John aka Junk (love u kidko), V Zok, and every good dude up North. My god bro Nate Johnson aka Great. My boy Roe in Fort Dix. Mainy-O, what up black ass. All my homies who kept it a buck in Fairton. Mello what up fam. Rich Porter what up rahsta man. Myyy nigga! My N.Y peoples Har, Stunna, Supreme. My B-more homies, what up Clark. S\O to my Boston, Jersey, DC, VA, SC peeps and everyone that kept it a thousand on their cases. All the Lifers, hold ya heads.

Rip my little brother Jeffrey 'Rah Rah' Jones. D lover, Bone, Shea Blizz, Pelly Pell, Jess Wess, Typer, Cow Head, and everyone lost to the streets. RIP Twin 'Big Boy' Lester. And my cousin Tyshanna Lester.

S\O to Big Rog and Germaine in SC. Bill, Kev, Rell (welcome home playboy). JB peace big bro. To two very special ladies, Poopie (Verdia Buie) and Pumie (Patricia Brown), I love y'all and Pumie you always have a son in me.

To my team at Head 2 Toe Salon over on 410 Blake St., New Haven, CT. OG Cleve, Cousin June, Dee Dee, Ty Bell and Riff. Stay loyal, when I eat my peoples eat. Definitely major love to my editor Lori Stewart for keeping it a million with me. Good looking on that contact Jug, my editor is the truth. Good luck with (Fly Contour) and all your endeavors.

To the small handful of men and women that reached out and showed love when I was away on my journey. You know who you are. Uncle Doug I'm forever in your debt of loyalty. However, my Cowboys gonna win the NFC East and multiple 'Chips' over the next 10 years with Zeke, Dak, and that young O-line. LOL.

Last, I gotta thank my lady, my rider, my queen, Dijon 'Didi' Wiggins. According to Webster's dictionary the definition of loyalty is "faithful to one's alliance". Well, you are the true meaning. Muah!

THE BACKSTORY

BY

DANIEL "BOONE" MILLS

Inspired by the Poet/MC, Nasir Jones', classic song 'Rewind', the story content of this novel will be presented in the same backwards fashion.

I now present The Backstory! Please begin your read on the following page.

THE END

Epilogue

Monty's State of Mind...

Neither Dionne Warwick nor Cleo the Physic could have told me my life would end this way. Ended by a single slug to the middle of my melon from the .44 Bulldog dangling from my wife's hand.

I've been in trap houses where the stick-up kids have kicked down the doors and tied us all up like in the movie *Paid in Full*. I even lamped in the projects while a hail of unannounced bullets interrupted our 20-man dice game. It seemed like everyone around me who was placing bets started dropping at a fast rate as the dice fell to the concrete with the numbers 4, 5, and 6 facing up. I had never been grazed, stabbed, or lumped up from a pair of brass knuckles during the hood fights we had at Central High School, as dozens of fists would get thrown quick. I mean, I'm not claiming to be Superman or to have immunity from hot ones, because me and my niggas have shot it out in broad daylight on numerous occasions where little kids and even pit bulls got caught in the line of fire. So no, I'm not a stranger to death. It's just that I had recently left the drug game completely, moving my newlywed wife out the hood to limit our exposure to the Vietnam-style murder game that went down in Bridgeport, CT.

I'm not a killer; however, I did go upside a few heads with the steel, plus distributed a couple of shit bags to niggas who thought it was sweet like pop tarts. So, because I was out the game, I thought it would be my past that caught up with me and got me murdered in the long run, if anything. I probably could've swallowed that outcome because I always held court in the streets. No sir, Lamont Lester's name has never been at the bottom of nobody's affidavit. Oh, hell no! I definitely believed in an eye for an eye.

The way this deranged wife of mines had handled the kick of the Bulldog that morning would have put a few shooters in the hood to shame. I noticed her improvement and how comfortable she became at the firing range a long time ago. Just think, I was the one who persuaded her to get the pistol permit when we first started getting serious. That was back when you couldn't tell me I wasn't holding on to her for the long run.

"I don't know, Monty. I shouldn't be getting a permit to carry a gun with this quick temper of mine," I could still hear her voice saying.

It was true. My baby was definitely a little firecracker. However, I knew how to put her flame out. I responded by letting her know that we wouldn't necessarily need to shoot anyone; the gun would just be legally available for our own protection.

I had a felony on my record; therefore, Tarahji's purse would be the perfect place to keep the hammer when we rode around in the Infiniti truck or any one of our V's. By all means, if shit went down and our lives were on the line, you knew damn well who was doing all the squeezing.

Moving on, what's crazy about this particular morning of my death is the way my wife crept into the room on some "shoot first-ask questions last" shit. While I lay on the floor with my life slipping away, I could somehow hear her voice asking me "What the fuck was I thinking?"

Yeah, I'll admit, I did some real fucked up shit to my wife but this bitch was the first to play foul. I know what you're thinking, but hold up this ain't no tit-for-tat shit. Both of us were very grown. Shit, I'm twenty-eight. And at forty years old she definitely should've known better. Trust me, I wasn't trying to be on no high school shit but Tarahji had shot my dog, so I had every intention on killing her cat. Sorry, maybe I should've picked a different one of her pets to slay. I'll start this story by explaining what I did to bite the bullet. I know everyone's going to say that I ain't shit, especially all you ladies who swear you're innocent.

Anyhow, Tarahji did some trife shit to me, too, and I didn't go pulling any pistols out on her ass like she did to me. As they say, men are like dogs and you know women cover their shit up like cats. That said, you would probably never figure out what she tried to get away with.

On a few guesses you'd probably say she tried setting me

up with the Feds so she could walk away with my plate; or maybe attempted to poison me, give me a disease, or something. Giving her pussy to another brother doesn't necessarily have to be the case either. But don't worry; I'm going to put you all up on her bullshit. Pay attention! You are going to have to start from the ending to get to the beginning. So, don't try to fast forward because in this story the ending just so happens to be the beginning. Only the rewind button works here. So, listen up, the backstory is this!

Chapter 20

June 24, 2006

L ala had been around Monty for a little over three years, so judging by the way he was balls-deep in her pussy for the past hour you'd think it was him who had been anticipating the opportunity to fuck her since the summer of '03. But truth was, he had never looked at her that way until eight days ago. The sex kitten Lala was young and very hot in the ass, so it was she who had been itching to ride Monty's dick from the very first time she saw him.

Tarahji had drawn first blood and all was fair in love and war. So not only was Monty cheating on his wife after just their first week of marriage, but he also decided to commit the sin right there in their very own bed.

Over the fireplace inside the bedroom was a picture of the two of them cutting the wedding cake just last week. Thrown over the Italian leather loveseat was the black sheer nightie that Tarahji had just taken off before going into the office a few hours ago. So, while her trifling ass was punching in on the company's clock, Monty was under their satin sheets working intensely on his second orgasm.

It didn't matter to him one bit if any neighbors were watching when Lala pulled up to the condo-styled home in the quiet area of Stratford. Monty wasn't really trying to hide his early morning antics. Besides, everyone in the neighborhood tended to mind their own damn business anyway. So, with those thoughts in his head, Monty had left the downstairs door open for the pretty young thing to walk right in.

Lala was twenty-three years old and had graduated with a bachelor's degree in criminal justice from Howard University one month ago. With long black hair and a thick hourglass-shaped body to match her sassy attitude, Lala had fit right in with the spicy hot girls in D.C.   They wore stilettos to class and were always on point just in case a music video director got behind them while waiting in line at Starbucks. Strip clubs and the go-go wave were therapy for all the dreadhead hustlers in the city.

With one-third Mexican descent in her blood, Lala had a unique look for the District of Columbia, so she found herself turning down offers to dance left and right.   Fortunately for her, she wasn't one of the girls who had to shake their tush in front of a gangsta to pay tuition.   If she did decide to pop her ass in front of a dreadhead, it wasn't for him to make it rain bands and it damn sure wasn't inside anybody's strip club. No! Lala would slide out of her thong and ride the dick inside her dorm room just because she liked to fuck, plain and simple.

She always blamed her Latin side for her sex addiction. It wasn't like Lala was fucking the entire D.C.; however, she made it her business to keep two or three benchwarmers on her roster at all times.   Just in case one of them was in some other pussy while claiming to be on the block, she'd always have another sturdy pipe on speed dial. As freaky as Lala's fine ass was, she made every last one of her partners strap up whenever she had sex.   TLC's song "Waterfalls" was her inspiration not to get caught up out there.

Meanwhile, it was now the end of June and Monty was lying naked underneath the forest green sheets in the middle of his and his wife's queen-sized bed. The central air unit was set at 63 degrees so the rooms in the house were extremely comfortable at this point.

Tarahji had decorated their home with all new furniture that was, of course, all her choice.   Monty had put his foot down, however, when she started throwing hints about putting pink sheer curtains around the posts of their canopy-style bed. He was drastically in love no doubt, but Monty was a true street cat.   He didn't want to start feeling like he was living in some sort of fantasy, so the female-friendly curtains that were supposed to go around the cherry oak poles were eventually put in the basement for storage.

When Lala walked through the front doors of the home, the newly-installed security system alerted Monty of an unannounced entrance. As soon as she closed and locked the door the ADT system pronounced, "Front door secured!"

Monty had been off probation for a while so he was blowing Grade A piff inside Bambu rolling paper. The thin Bambu sheets had the spliff burning steady and tasting superb. Everyone knows of BET's habit of killing the same rebroadcast shows, and at 10 A.M. on this morning, things were no different. Last year's *Hip Hop Awards* replayed, showing Killa Cam and the whole Dip Set running around the stage performing "Down 'N Out" from his *Purple Haze* album.

They were all dressed in red except for Killa who was dipped in mostly purple. Tommy guns, MAC-10s, and a bunch of other stage props were included to make their set look authentic. It's crazy because last year's event was actually the first BET awards where no drama had popped off since back when Tupac and the Outlawz faced off with Bad Boy in '95.

Monty shifted underneath the sheets and thought about attending this year's upcoming show in October. If his wife Tarahji didn't have it fucked up with him at the moment, he would've definitely taken her with him for a night out with the stars. However, all of Monty's daydreaming was put on the back burner when he watched Lala walk into the room wearing a loose-fitting pink summer dress with white Old Navy flip-flops.

"I've been waiting on you all week," the sexy twenty-three-year-old was saying with both hands on her hips.

Lala's inner thighs stayed moist, but it was probably the bulge forming between Monty's legs underneath the bed sheets that had her body temperature rising, because by the time he was fully extended she already had her soft cotton dress pulled over her head, craving the dick. It seemed like she moved in slow motion as the thin material rose above her toned calves and thighs. She wasn't wearing any panties so her small landing strip of pubic hair was exposed.

You see, there was nothing spontaneous about the scandalous shit that Monty was about to pull. Nah, he had put this ploy into effect the same night of his wedding; and if he would've skipped out on the honeymoon he could've been in Lala's pussy right after the reception that very same night. Yet Monty didn't want to do it like that. Certain benefits came with fucking Tarahji, and even though he'd been out the game for a couple months, he still relied on her peoples for his homeboy Bullet's sake. He was never able to fully trust his wife after their fall-out but you can just say that Monty was willing to stay married to the game.

At 137 lbs. with a 23-inch waist, the sexy brick house had two bottles short of a six-pack. Medium, but perky, breasts sat up top with rather large nipples that resembled Boston baked beans. The summer dress was thrown on the floor and the green bed sheets were pulled back to expose Lala's favorite male body part: a rock-hard dick. On all fours, she crawled up the bed like a feline and snuggled up next to Monty.

Monty had returned from his honeymoon two days ago with his new wife. Just like when they first met, he and Tarahji had spent 85% of their time fucking and making love on the Hawaiian island of Maui. While there, it was easy for Monty to fill her up with so much good dick because Tarahji was truly sexy. Yet on the other hand, the other half of his stamina had come from anger.

The newlyweds had formed an agreement between themselves to where once they landed on the island they were to act as if the mess Tarahji created the night before had never happened. Monty did a great job of suppressing the issue inside his memory, but she could sort of tell he was reneging on their agreement at times. For instance, when he was fucking Tarahji he fucked her like he was really trying to kill her. There was a knowing look inside her eyes as she hung off the edge of the bed while Monty came all in her, refusing to let her pull the other half of her body off the floor. When she asked for it in her ass, he purposely used the bare minimum lube before entering her. A part of Monty was trying to make Tarahji pay the whole time they were honeymooning.

Monty had prepared for Lala this morning by pretending to be drained when Tarahji tapped him on the shoulder for some loving before she went into the office. He could've easily shook one off in his wife, then cheated by popping a pill to surely fuck the shit out of Lala a couple hours later. But Monty wanted the young tenderoni to get the real him, without all the secret enhancements.

In spite of missing Tarahji's early morning rodeo show, Monty's pipe was now swollen to the max inside Lala's pretty manicured hands. While she rubbed back and forth in a very slow motion, Lala gave each of Monty's nipples a thorough wet wax. He laid back and finished off his joint while Young Jeezy, a hot new artist at the time, performed "Go Crazy" with Jigga to close off the BET Awards.

"Damn Lala baby," Monty whispered in her ear.

Lala made her way on top of him and boldly initiated a hot tongue kiss. Grinding her pussy down on Monty's dick, she smoothly intertwined her tongue with his. She was in a straddle position and every thrust made her dripping tunnel slide across the length of his shaft. There were a few times when Lala's strokes and thrusts were so long that Monty almost penetrated her sticky opening. As a result, only the head of his penis ended up covered in her vaginal juices.

Monty pulled Lala by the back of her head to push his tongue a little deeper inside her mouth. There was a fire inside of Monty's body that he had never felt before. With her being pressed up against his chest, he knew Lala could also feel the heat. BET was the furthest thing from his mind, but somewhere in the back of his head Monty could hear Red clowning Craig about getting fired for stealing boxes from the job. It was crazy because they just showed *Friday* two nights ago, and now the shit was right back on.

Monty couldn't get over how sweet Lala's tongue was. He wasn't trying to let her go. She had to fight to get away from his death grip to enjoy another part of his body. Starting at his ear, she slowly worked her way down to his neck, chest, and stomach; then looked up with a devilish grin as she played in the juice that leaked from the head of his dick. Monty's pre-cum had mixed with the fluid that was on his shaft from her grinding on him and it was like an invitation for Lala to quench her thirst.

He moaned instantly as his dick began to knock on her tonsils - being every bit of eight inches deep inside her mouth. He wrapped her long hair around his hand like spaghetti on a fork then started fucking her face in a soft slow rhythm. It was at this point when Monty knew for sure that Lala was a cold freak as she played in her pussy. Out of nowhere she spat his dick out of her mouth and licked her fingers free of all the cum that covered them. All of this just to take him back deep into her throat again. This bitch was in Heaven and she was bringing him along with her.

She took a short break from the oral so she could pull him more into the middle of the bed. They hugged and squeezed for a bit but it was only a matter of seconds before Monty was sliding in and out of her mouth again. The fact was Lala's head game was amazing. She had that fat brown ass in the air, smacking her own cheeks and creating a loud sound of thunder that echoed throughout the whole room. Then in a routine that Monty had never seen before, she started doing circles around his body like the long hand of a clock, all the while never letting his dick come out of her mouth.

She went around and around, never pausing, like the perpetual hand of a Presidential Rolex. Monty tried to lick her pussy each time she brushed pass his face but she was too swift and he failed on each attempt.

The unfamiliar motion of Lala's newly-invented blow job had Monty's balls tightening from such excitement. Once she felt his body tense up she made a sudden stop at the 12 o'clock position.

Right there in a sixty-nine, she massaged Monty's swollen sack as he pumped about a half-pint of jizm into her sizzling mouth. Monty couldn't stop squirting if he wanted to. Lala was rubbing the little spot beneath his scrotum that seemed to empty his pan like he was getting an oil change. She shook her ass over Monty's head and he suddenly had the chance to taste her love.

However, he couldn't catch his breath and he damn sure wasn't going to suffocate while trying to lick the pussy. She had fucked Monty up with her time-piece style head game. After she swallowed down the last drop, her fine ass hopped up and started taking little shots once she saw him discombobulated.

"Are you okay, Step-daddy?"

If you haven't figured out by now, the twenty-three-year-old Lala was Monty's wife's only child. Yes, she was his daughter-in-law.

Monty had peeped Lala jocking him the first time they met. Although he knew it was the ladies who really chose a man at the end of the day, he still felt like he had the green light to the pussy from the start. She would always flirt with him on the low. Lala had agreed to the shit too easily at the reception. She acted too thirsty and was head over heels about Monty. She would have sucked the lemon filling out of the wedding cake right then and there if he had asked her to.

Even though Monty wasn't planning to use this to cause Tarahji pain, it served him well just knowing that he fucked someone she was so closely connected to. In the bed they shared at that. The joy had nothing to do with the foul Tarahji committed. It was simply the person who Monty had chosen to use as revenge that had him salivating with satisfaction.

To be so petite, the Howard University graduate was extremely dominant between the sheets. She tried straddling Monty's dick raw, but he lifted her up and pushed her face first into the side of the bed that Tarahji's pillows were on. Getting aggressive himself, Monty slid his dick into Lala right from the back. It was just how she wanted it: RAW!

Without breaking rhythm, he snatched a pillow from his side of the bed and stuffed it under her pelvic bone. It gave him a much better path into her tunnel and he instantly started banging on Lala's G-spot.

Not one to back down, she tooted her ass up another inch or two and started bucking her hips into Monty's every thrust. Lala was biting down on her mother's pillows and tearing away at the sheets. Monty had a bird's eye view of his dick jabbing at the walls of her soaking love box. The shine from all the wetness turned him on even more. He didn't have to give Lala every inch to hit her spot in this position but every time he did she'd scream out like someone was trying to kill her. Monty couldn't help but slightly chuckle when he heard Debo in the background telling Craig how he would knock his ass out if he didn't get involved in the burglary of Stanley's crib.

Monty pounded Lala's ass out for another ten minutes before she came, sounding like an ambulance siren. Her body shivered as she released all her love down on him. Lala's infatuation with a stiff dick had become apparent to Monty when she fought to ride him backwards with her pussy still dripping from her first orgasm. Her sweet ass was hungry for more.

Lala was only 5'2", so most of her weight was packed in her ass and thighs. Her thirty-nine inch hips were spread over Monty's thighs and he realized that Lala had to be extra with everything she did. She didn't just ride his dick up and down like the average cowgirl. Nah, Lala rode in a circle, back 'n forth, and even leaned towards Monty's ankles and bounced her ass one cheek at a time.

In a matter of minutes, the former D.C student was yelling that she was coming again and Monty told her he was coming with her. He felt the milk circulating in his balls, and then run upstream towards the tip of his dick. His toes started spreading apart and he reached forward to grip Lala's fat ass and pin her pussy down on him. He was about to squirt all in her.

"Nigga, I'll fuckin' kill you mudda-fucka!" Tarahji shouted in her thick Mexican accent she only used when she was furious.

Monty suddenly knew how a deer felt when it was caught in a car's headlights. As bad as he knew he had to get the fuck up out the sack and grab his wife, he couldn't move any of his limbs except his fingers as he squeezed Lala's ass harder and filled her with his seed. It was like his brain didn't send the message to his body fast enough about how real the situation was about to get. On the other hand, Lala wasn't playing any games. She sprung up from his dick with the speed of light and started fumbling with the summer dress and flip-flops.

Tarahji was digging through her dresser drawer where she kept her panties and bras while Monty stumbled from the bed knowing exactly what she was looking for. The second half of his nut was still oozing from his dick. The bed sheets were wrapped around his ankles as he tried to lunge at Tarahji but fell a few feet short. He was then looking up into the barrel of her chrome cannon. Monty couldn't recall the last time his wife had come by the house on her lunch break. A pleading look had come over his face and Tarahji must have read his mind and answered his curiosity because she was shouting out the answer.

"While you and Bullet were in Vegas, I had hidden cameras put in every room of the house, you fuckin' bastard!" Tarahji yelled, full of rage.

"I'll see you in hell, puta," she cursed in Spanish.

One loud roar had echoed throughout the bedroom and it felt like a piece of Monty's head had flown off. As his soul started separating from his body, he could hear the sound of cheap flip-flops smacking the back of Lala's heels as she hauled ass.

"Oh, where you think you going, bitch?" Tarahji yelled out to her only child.

Monty heard four more roars of thunder then the sound of the hammer hitting the empty casings inside the .44's chamber. Time was of the essence. Heaven's light was right before his eyes and all the muscles in his body had threatened to release.

Right before Monty left the physical form he heard crackhead Ezel telling everybody that Smokey was in the backyard taking a shit. It's crazy because BET would probably play the same movie again later on in the night, but it's sad because Monty would definitely miss seeing all the re-runs on the network. If he had never found out what Tarahji had done to him first, Monty would still be able to catch all the replays. His life wouldn't have ended if he wasn't trying to get someone back.

CHAPTER 19

Monty's State of Mind...

My name is Lamont Lester but everyone close to me calls me Monty. I just turned twenty-eight a couple of months ago and as long as I can remember, my attraction to older women has been ridiculous.

I think it started back in '88. Around the time LL Cool J brought the *Rock the Bells* tour to the New Haven Coliseum. I was maybe nine or ten years old back then. My mother La'Kiya, who was a little fast, had given birth to me when she was just seventeen years young.

There was a fly red-bone honey by the name of Sandy who was my mom's homegirl. Mom and Sandy were dressed to impress on the night of the concert. It was the end of July so mom-dukes was wearing a skin-tight acid wash mini skirt with black fishnet stockings underneath. Up top she rocked a black tee on which she had used kitchen shears to cut slices into the shoulder and back areas. On the front of the tee was a juicy red strawberry that had a big bite taken out of it. The word "Delicious" was written underneath the berry. The outfit was capped off by a pair of fire-red pumps with a four-inch heel.

These were the days when girl and guy posses rolled deep and would all dress alike. So, it was natural for the two girls to be rocking the exact same get-up; a booty-hugging jean skirt, fishnets, and hooker pumps.

The only difference in the gear was the fruit displayed on the front of their black tees. Instead of a strawberry, Sandy had two ripe cherries that were connected by a stem. However, the red cursive letters had formed the same word, Delicious!

This shit may sound crazy but it is what it is. My mother was fine. She was a bad chick and it was pretty obvious that both these ladies were looking to get their fruit eaten that night. A young ripped-up Cool J would only perform topless in those days and he was just mastering the seductive art of licking his lips. Ladies loved Cool J and after that night so did I. Wait, that didn't sound right, let me explain.

Like I said, it was like moms and her girl Sandy were getting dressed for a music video. When I busted in the room without knocking, I caught Sandy in the mirror practicing her dance steps. She had on everything except the mini skirt. She stood there in a short tee, fishnets, and pumps. Salt 'N Pepa's song "Tramp" was knocking from my mother's bullshit record player. Mom was still in the bathroom freshening up and Sandy didn't notice me standing there in the doorway. Her yellow thighs squeezed out of every hole in the stockings and the high heels had her ass propped up like a piñata. My A-team pajamas had "I pity the fool" and a bunch of other quotes from Mr. T. written all over them. Getting a little excited, I pitched a small tent in the front of them. I was beyond ready to pin the tail on Sandy's donkey. She shook her ass to the rhythm of the beat and her booty clapped together in a way that would later become common in all the Atlanta strip clubs.

When Sandy turned around to drop it to the floor, she saw me standing there in the doorway, hard and wide-mouthed. My mother's friend bounced towards me before grabbing my shoulders, spinning me away from her half-naked body. Bending down to whisper in my ear, it sounded like she was singing when she said,

"Boy, you better take your ass to ya' room! But don't worry Monty, I ain't 'gon tell yo' momma."

Man, I hauled ass down the hallway with every bit of my three inches swinging. Laying in the darkness of my room, I couldn't shake the image of Sandy's juicy cherries. And you know damn well I don't mean the ones on the front of her black tee.

When I woke up in the morning I had to piss like a five-time champion Clydesdale, but you couldn't tell me my erection was from a piss-hard. I swear on a stack of bibles that I was still excited from last night's peep show. So, girls my age haven't been able to do nothing for me ever since. Rock The Bells!

I had grown to be a full-fledged man, weighing about 205, standing 5'10", with medium brown skin and dark facial features. It was plain to see how much I resembled my father. However, the one difference between him and me was that he was a bitch ass nigga and I wasn't. That's why I don't fuck with him at all. But that's a whole 'nother story that I'll get into later.

Anyway, my little sister and I took on our mother's last name instead of the deadbeat's. The Lesters are thick all the way from Connecticut to Fayetteville, NC. When visiting the Carolinas, I had to do a background check on the shorties to make sure I wasn't pushing up on a distant cousin. Bitches were in abundance and my up North swag had the spotlight right on me. It was crazy. Short, tall, young, even older women were on my dick.

My cousin Avery played running back for Ohio State and he took the Buckeyes to the Rose Bowl in his sophomore year, before being drafted by the Buffalo Bills as the third overall pick. Most people in the family believed that I'd follow in cuz's footsteps since I ran the ball with similar aggression in the Pop Warner League. No joke, I was punishing the linebackers and safeties who tried to square up with me. The same thing transpired on the field at Central High School. When the hood saw that I had a legitimate shot at going pro, all the drug dealers started buying me Avirex leathers in the winter and new Bo Jackson's in the summer.

I wasn't allowed to post up on the block for more than five minutes at a time. Pell, A-Love, and Typer were all aware that the Ds were liable to storm at any moment and my career would be over before it started once they found a few bricks of dope surely to be stashed in the parking lot. When shit like that went down, the Narcs played duck-duck-goose to pick the person they wanted to wear the drug pack.

Some time in my junior year at Central is when the temptation to hustle had won me over. It was a Friday night and I remember it so clearly because I had broken an old-school cat named Ricky Wilson's rushing record that night. The half- black and white high school standout could now be found panhandling anywhere from Stratford Ave. to Linden Blvd. in a dirty sweatsuit, but back in '83-'87 he had the green light to sex any one of the varsity cheerleaders. That nigga Ricky was a beast and posted a ridiculous average of 195 rushing yards per game over his four years at Central, with his career high for a single game being 250 against Fairfield Prep.

Well, on October 23rd, 1995, against a very stingy Crosby High School defense, I erased Ricky's name from the record books with a whopping 302 yards from scrimmage. My highlight reel from that game included a 99-yard hand-off that I took to the house untouched. We beat Crosby's ass and would go on to win the state championship that year. However, the celebrations from that night would definitely mark the start of my hustle game.

I didn't join the team at Famous Pizza after hitting the showers that night. Nah, I got up with my team from the projects for strippers at Pleasurable Escape instead. Unlike the bright field at Central for a big game, the stage at Pleasurable's was dimly lit and had only one pole. Women of all flavors took turns swinging and shaking their ass from one lap to another.

A bad white girl named Shannon was behind the bar and she made sure every drink was made proper and not watered down. Crews from every part of the city were posted up in their own respective corners of the club. Kush and different kinds of weed entwined with other clouds that lingered in every inch of the bar. Cigarettes, Black 'n Milds, and even a hint of dust smoke traveled through the air in thick circles.

Even though my forty-yard dash numbers were impressive, I had an addiction to the sticky weed that dated back to middle school. Ounces upon ounces of buddah and pepper-head bud had started accompanying the Bo Jackson's and leather coats from the boys in the hood. Although they knew it would affect my wind, I guess the older dudes were in denial because they kept saying that weed was from the earth. Either that or they were just like all the other niggas on the block; believing that trees made them do everything on an iller level. I don't know if there's any truth to the idea, but I was high as a muthafucka when I took the top spot from Ricky in that Friday night game.

One of the baddest bitches dancing in the club that night was a twenty-six-year-old Dominican chick named Kitten. She commuted from the Bronx every night with half of the other dancers who performed in Bridgeport. Kitten had a short cut like the singer Fantasia and her skin was the complexion of a manila envelope. Her natural titties were full like she had implants done and both of Kitten's nipples were always pointing north.

Her small waist gave way to round thick hips and she had an ass like two baked pound cakes. Little tattoos of kitty-cat paws trailed from her thigh all the way up to the area between her legs. Kitten was giving me a lap dance and from the way she moved on me you would think I had discreetly slid my dick out the zipper to let her pop her pussy on it. Her black stilettos were planted on the floor as she held onto the back of my chair while straddling me.

Moving nothing but her waist, the dancer's soft ass smacked the top of my thighs as the cream from her pussy soaked the bulging area of my Maurice Malone jeans. She breathed heavy in my ear as she came all over my denims, kissing and nibbling my neck, smelling like Lemonhead candy drops. B.I.G.'s remix to his song "One More Chance" thumped in the club and I was mad as fuck that the Hennessy and cold ones had me needing to piss at the wrong time. When I pushed Kitten up off me there was a long string of her juice stretching between her legs. I slid to the bathroom with a fat joint of pepper-head hanging from my lips. Yea, I was taught that good weed was better complimented in rolling paper, preferably Bambu. As I shook the piss from my tool, a cat who was two urinals down asked if I had another piece of pepper-head that I wanted to get off.

The OGs from the block made sure I kept pocket change on me so I was never hurting for cash, but I was smart enough to know to never turn down a dollar. We met up at the hand soap station and I took a small bud from the fresh ounce tucked in the inner pocket of my jean jacket. Dude gave me twenty-five dollars for the half-gram of weed and I slid him two sheets of Bambu paper on the strength. We quickly parted ways as I wanted to finish my business with Kitten and possibly sneak to one of the back rooms for a cheap shot of pussy.

After about fifteen minutes, the thick Dominican was able to double back to me once she wrapped up her lap dance with two lames from Danbury. As soon as Kitten sat that cake back on me the dude from the urinal approached me with two of his goons. My man Bullet thought I had static, so I peeped the razor fly out of his mouth and into his hand. Quan and Lord made a beeline from over by the wall and Y.G. was already fishing the .38 from down by his nuts. The dude from the urinal came out of his stupor in a hurry when he noticed all the movement. Seeing that it was about to go down, he threw up both hands, stating that he was coming in peace. The two goons who he was with spoke up over the music and announced that they only wanted to cop a piece of the weed.

Here we were about to overreact when all they wanted was to spend a few more dollars with me. Now mind you, I was the athlete of the crew. From Percocet to heroin, everyone around me sold some type of drug, but the weed had always been for our personal use only. Man, I put an end to that philosophy right then and there. I went back to the hand soap station and gave those fools several nice buds for $175.

By the time I left the club at a quarter 'til 2, I was holding $320 from the clientele inside Pleasurable Escape. I couldn't believe the shit because I was still sitting on about half an ounce of pepper-head. And that was after me and my niggas had blown about six sticks ourselves. I had definitely seen the light that night. And believe me, that shit was very bright.

By the time senior year had come I didn't want anything to do with Central High, let alone their football team. The records I now tried to break were held by dope boys in my projects. I was blinded by the Cuban-link chains and Buick Park Aves. In order to keep up with the Joneses, I had to switch lanes with a new product because the pepper-head money just wasn't cutting it.

The exotic weed went back to being for personal use only and I decided to join the big leagues. The real cheddar was in Monteca. That's right, Grade A heroin. I'm from P.T. Barnum projects, the West End of Bridgeport. I bet fifty that I could run down the names of at least ten niggas from my city who've seen a mil from the dope game. I can do it in five seconds flat.

The junkies banged needles in their veins as early as 4:30 a.m. where I'm from. There were more young boys in the hood with their noses running than you could imagine. Dope is on a totally different level from all other drugs. A kilo of coke was hitting for nineteen thousand but a good brick of heroin topped out at $80K.

Like crack cocaine, dope was highly addictive. However, the addiction to the much higher power would slowly turn into a medical need for the human body. Once a user was accustomed to the heroin fix, there would be days when the fiend couldn't make it out of the bed because his limbs wouldn't function. They called it being on "E." You'd be sick and in pure agony, shitting and throwing up. A dope fiend in this state would literally kill you for the drug. Seriously, they would push a long black hawk through your mid-section if you were fronting on their fix.

By going hand-to-hand between the alleys of the buildings, I got real familiar with my clientele. My work was a ten and I stamped my bags with a name I knew very well: "Touchdown!" Every last one of my customers felt like a starter once they hit my shit. They were all pro ballers, no one rode the bench. If you were short a few bucks on a twenty-dollar bag, it wasn't a problem at all. For the customers who relied on their everyday hustles and scams to get their fix, I would get them off "E." In return, they hustled hard and brought me new customers.

I learned the game from my man, Bullet. He got his lessons from dope-fiend Troy, an old nigga who was once a kingpin in his own right. You might not understand when I tell you that the dope money started coming so fast in the projects that I started getting scared. Those who played the game are sure to relate. I was clearing five Gs a day in no time. For regular Joes that punched a time clock, it would seem like I was rich. However, I was just a small fish in the pond. You had niggas in the Terrace Houses and Marina Projects seeing thirty stacks a day. But when you took my shifts into consideration, it was clear to see that I was a quiet storm. I made myself available three times a day. From 4-6 a.m., 12-2 p.m., and 5-7 p.m. My clientele was trained. When they saw me, they would cop what they needed for the day, instead of what they wanted for the moment.

We're talking three to six bundles at a time. I was eighteen and you couldn't tell me shit. I had a '92 Park Ave., a '90 MPV, and I was chilling on about seventy-five racks. The OGs had to accept that I turned down having a "future" in the NFL for "right now" money. Trying to look out, they started telling me that I should employ a pack boy to move my work for me.   I was on their ass and they knew it.   I thought they were hating on me.   Not listening to the wise was my first mistake in the hood.   If I had a pack boy moving my work, then a sale to an undercover wouldn't have landed me my first felony.

I was sentenced to five years suspended after three, meaning I only had three years to serve.   It was a non-violent offense so I was required to do only 50% before being eligible for parole.   I saw the review board in my fifteenth month and was granted parole for a date that was about four months later.   However, things would not be that easy once it became that short.   I had to beat the daylight savings out of a nigga from New Haven who was stuck on that "back in the day" shit.   His name was Head and he was a young wild nigga from the Elm City, around Howard Ave.

Head had put his paws on three different dudes in the nine months that he was down.   We were both about twenty years old but back when we were 14 and 15 there was a teen club in Milford called 302.   It was the place to be for young fly teens on Saturday nights.   It cost $10 to get through the doors, and of course, because we were minors they didn't serve a drop of alcohol.   The club's full bar consisted of Pepsi brand products only.   You could down cups of Sprite and Pepsi at the bar all night.

Well anyway, me and my niggas from the projects would arrive with E&J or gin already in our gut.   We were bent and ready to wild out, so we already knew the hood niggas from New Haven were on the same shit.   Young girls from all over were there in short skirts and acting grown.   There was always some sort of bad blood between Bridgeport and Elm niggas, so naturally the chicks that rolled with us bumped heads by law.

One of the rowdiest nights was when Smiff 'n Wesson from the Boot Camp Click was there performing their classic anthem, "Buck-Town."   Sway and Tech ran through their lyrics and didn't miss a beat when fists started flying and niggas caught buck-fifthies across their grills. There was a lot of blood spilled that night and a couple of shots even rang out in the parking lot despite Milford's police squad being deep and on deck. The shooters must have been pranksters because no one had gotten touched at all. That wasn't the first all-out brawl that went down in 302 and it damn sure wouldn't be the last. There must have been a secret contract that guaranteed the drama because it popped off every week between the 'Port and the Elm City.

While playing in a spades tournament in the day room of Enfield C.I., Head was talking real greasy about how he had laced the faces of a few niggas from Bridgeport that night at the club. He was popping shit and kept repeating that Bridgeport niggas were pumpkin pie.

This was Thanksgiving morning and we were all waiting for our unit to be called for chow. Me and my boy, Mega, only needed five books to advance to the finals in the spades tournament. My partner was giving me the look to fall back and not sweat the shit Head was screaming. He wanted me to just concentrate on bringing the $100 bag back to our lockers for winning first prize. I had a real soft spot for that fetti but my boy, Bullet, was doing really well out in the world so I wasn't hurting for cash while in the Bing. Mega didn't have much at all so I was feeling his outlook on the situation. However, I couldn't hold my composure when Head was popping shit and seeming like he was trying to stunt on me.

"Suck my dick, you bitch ass nigga!" I spazzed, smacking him with my last two cards, a jack and six of diamonds.

Head quickly squared up on the right side of my jaw and the blow only pissed me off. Anyone could throw a few combos but the other 50% of scrapping was being able to absorb a hit. Man, I went up under that nigga so fast, lifting him off his feet like light wind.

As soon as Head was flat on his back I ordered an eight-piece nugget and a soft drink for his dumb ass. I damn near killed that boy. The goon squad had to come in and pry me off of him. They took me straight to the hole and I kissed my parole goodbye. Mega had gone on and drafted a worthy substitute partner so at least he won a nice bag of commissary that was all food items.

My parole date was snatched and I had to knock down the remaining seventeen months, day for day. After a while I even considered it to be a blessing in disguise. Me and an ole head named Kwame became crazy tight and he introduced me to the lessons of the Holy Qur'an. I became humble and suddenly began planning with strategy. I was hearing that Bullet kept a cheese line of dope fiends inside the projects, but from Kwame I learned a system that would get our whole team out the hood. I started developing a crazy itch to get home but Kwame and the Qur'an were keeping me on my square. So, in short, I believe everything happens for a reason in life and this bid was all a part of the written history.

From Monday through Friday for eight to ten hours each day, Tarahji was strictly addressed as Ms. Valentine. It was her maiden name and because she had only been married to Monty for a week most people in the office had yet to acknowledge her name change. She was an Administrative Director for Bayer, the pain relief company located in Orange, CT. A new name plate had been ordered for her desk and door, but there was no longer a need for it.

Tarahji was a bigwig within the corporation and she enjoyed all the perks that came along with the position. A $140k yearly salary; a big enclosed corner office on the top floor; a ten-thousand-dollar yearly voucher to lease a company car of choice, which was usually a foreign model; along with three weeks of paid vacation time.

Tarahji was ballin'. She was very independent. If anyone insisted that she was with Monty for his money, then they were obviously delirious. To be quite honest, it was actually Tarahji who made Monty better. Broadening his horizons by way of her family ties was inevitable once he had gotten her to fall in love with him. So even though Monty was quite easy on the eye and had his own cash, those things had nothing to do with the reason she had chosen him.

Tarahji was thirty-seven years old when they met three years ago. Even at that time she was hot enough to strut stride for stride against any young runway model. By not aging a day since then, she could still balance the scales against Keri Hilson or any other sexy R&B diva. Her skin was flawless and Ms. Valentine's small waist led to a soft heart-shaped booty. She was bad and she knew it.

With Latin in her blood, Tarahji's frame was an exact replica of Jennifer Lopez's before all the rumored butt reductions and Hollywood diets. She was slightly bow-legged and when she dressed for work in her pumps and business skirts you would think she was going to do a photo shoot. There weren't too many women in the city who could fuck with Tarahji on a physical level. She could've long ago landed a rich bachelor from the single and free market, but Tarahji had her own. She was a lady that didn't have to ask the price for something she wanted to buy. Tarahji had class. She simply liked what she liked and knew exactly what she wanted. She was a cougar who was only sexually intrigued by young stallions. But not just any twenty-something-year-old was going to get chosen to be treated like a king. Nah, you had to have that "it factor" about you. You didn't necessary need to have Boris Kodjoe's features, but having a little sex appeal wouldn't hurt at all. For the most part you just had to be bright and strategic. You had to know the difference between an opportunity and a pipe dream. Tarahji was all professional but her man had to be straight gangsta in every sense of the word.

Not a dumb thug, just a gentleman who had common sense and moved well in the streets. If you were young and had that, plus knew how to lay the pipe down proper, Tarahji's only purpose in life would then be to cater to you.

Originally from Texas, Tarahji was born to a black father and a Mexican mother who moved the family to East New York when she was just fifteen. Tarahji's mother, Marisol, had installed old-fashioned morals in her only child from the moment she had stopped wearing diapers. She taught Tarahji how to take care of her body as a female, and cooking and cleaning were both part of the young lady's early home training.

Tarahji was taught that her grandmother believed a woman should be able to count all of her sexual partners on just one hand. Marisol had followed the old lady's tradition and even took it a lil' further because Tarahji's father Corey had been her first and only partner. Marisol explained to her daughter how important it was to have respect for your body and Tarahji had complied while growing up. But that was back in the 70's, so you have to realize that everything changes with time. Bell bottoms had played out in the mid 80's and afros had taken a back seat to perms and high-top fades by '88. Life's a cycle and yeah, everything tends to come back around, but women having sex with five people or fewer throughout a lifetime might be the one exception to the idea of traditions repeating themselves. Its chances are slim to none.

Tarahji lost her virginity to by a black dude from Queens when she was seventeen years old. He was a couple years older and didn't mind wining and dining for five or six months while waiting on her cherry.

By their third sexual encounter, Tarahji had started enjoying the love making and would get mad when he wasn't available to give it to her. The two of them kicked it strong for about two years until he and twelve others from his family had gotten indicted for running a profitable gun trafficking ring.

Very young and free- spirited, Tarahji wanted to live. She showed love by sending letters and flicks but other than that she wasn't around for doing a bid with a man.

Tarahji had gone on to have sex with two different Dominican cats from two different parts of Manhattan over the next year before spending a half-decade with a black guy from the Marcus Garvey Housing Projects in Brooklyn. His name was Jalen and he was four years older than Tarahji and seemed to be very intelligent and have a lot of upside.

Jalen sold two-for-five dollar vials of coke in the projects during the late night, but during the day Jalen drove the garbage truck around the city. He paid taxes and respected the game, never letting anyone rush him into making a move. Tarahji was impressed by the way Jalen milked the projects so discreetly. She asked her father to tie him in with the cartel on her mother's side.

Her dad, Corey, was already in direct position with the Mexican pipeline at the time. However, he didn't trust the way Brooklyn niggas moved so he never bothered to pay attention to his daughter's request. It turned out to be a good call because in the middle of the relationship Jalen started smacking Tarahji around until her father hired a bullet to calm his ass down. Corey knew how much his daughter was in love with the bully so he only paid for a flesh wound instead of a closed casket.

Whatever the case, the message was clear. Jalen went back to being a sweetheart with the quickness. Still, the damage had been done because it was during those three or four months of abuse that Tarahji had become vulnerable and fell victim to the comforting words of a total stranger. Tarahji and two of her closest friends were shopping on Broadway one afternoon when a group of four fly cats approached them on the corner of 145th Street.

Tarahji could tell from their accents that the crew was from out of town and probably on the strip looking for powder.

As she sized them up, the one with the most swag spoke up and claimed they were from Lenox Ave. in Harlem. He introduced himself as S-Class, and like Jalen, the Harlem cat was also a few years older. Tarahji's pussy got wet from just looking at his handsome ass. She had a thing for older guys and in the ten minutes she had known him S-Class had been saying all the right words.

They all decided to eat at a Dominican restaurant right there on Broadway. After peeping one of S-Class' boys follow a short Dominican guy into the rest room, Tarahji knew that her cocaine suspicion was confirmed. It was a whole ten minutes before dude returned to the table so smoothly. S-Class peeked over his shoulder as three new Latin customers entered the restaurant. He then focused on his homie that had come back from the restroom and informed him that he should start heading back uptown. S-Class and the two other guys had decided to stay with Tarahji and her two friends so the lone crew member gave his boys a pound then exited the restaurant in a hurry. Tarahji believed him to be Harlem bound and definitely holding the work from the way his walk had slightly changed. The six remaining friends had rented a penthouse in downtown Manhattan to enjoy drinks and a dip inside the heated pool. Everyone had a companion of the opposite sex and it seemed as if they'd been friends for years.

Once the straight shots of vodka worked into her bloodstream Tarahji became real emotional and started talking S-Class' ear off about how Jalen was doing her wrong. They sat arm 'n arm in the shallow end of the pool and S-Class was like a shark that smelled blood in the water. On beat, he hit her with a dozen different scenarios that all began with, "Well, if I was ya' man..." and over the next sixty minutes Tarahji rode his dick into three warm nuts.

Keep in mind that this was 1985, so a shot in the ass would cure anything under the sun with the one exception of herpes. They fucked until the sun came up. S-Class' dick felt like a boxing glove when she was through with him. They ordered room service for breakfast and by 10 a.m. the fellas slid out, leaving the girls a little cab money and fake beeper numbers. It ended up being a one-night stand and the only S-Classes Tarahji would see again would have sun roofs and leather seats. The funny thing is them dudes didn't look anything like them cats over on Lenox Avenue.

Jalen had taken a slug to the abdomen two days before Tarahji's sexcapade in Manhattan, so he didn't wild out and smack the shit out of her when he couldn't find her that night. Instead, he acted like a husband who worshipped the ground his wife walked on when he saw her the next afternoon. They cuddled up in his apartment and watched movies for weeks. Jalen couldn't do too much bending and flexing because of his wounds but his dick didn't have a problem with standing up every hour on the hour. Tarahji squatted down on it every time so it wasn't surprising when two pink lines showed up on the applicator of a pregnancy test three weeks later.

Latrice "Lala" Valentine was born in the spring of '86 and her father, Jalen, disappeared from the face of the earth two years later. He had started to become abusive again, and Tarahji's father Corey would deny that he had put a bounty on Jalen when she asked him about it. Tarahji held it down and waited for Jalen's return for the better part of a year, but when young Lala had started calling her grandfather "Da-Da," Tarahji knew it was time to move on with her life. She then met Greg from Yonkers and dealt with him exclusively for seven years. After Greg, she met Felix from Long Island for another five, and although Tarahji was already two fingers over the one-hand rule of her great grandmother, the fact that Monty would be only the eighth partner under her belt at her age was unheard of in the 20th century. And as for giving her cookies to S-Class, don't judge her. What grown woman hasn't had a one-night stand these days? The peculiar thing about this specific one-nighter is it just so happened to be the best she had ever been fucked in her life and she would never forget it.

Tarahji's father, Corey Valentine, was a natural-born country boy who stood out like a sore thumb when he first moved his family to Brooklyn back in '75. A diehard Dallas Cowboy fan, Corey looked every bit the part of a Texas bull rider. The plaid long sleeves and big suede hats would be replaced in the hot Brooklyn summers, but no temperature was going to make him come out of the pointy leather boots.

It took years for Corey to start losing his country accent and blend in with the New Yorkers. They had shown him love on the block since day one, especially the hustlers and users of all the recreational drugs. Heroin had been big since the war, but cocaine, and of course, weed was making a strong stance in the U.S. Through Tarahji's mother, Marisol, Corey was one of the biggest suppliers in the city. His only competition was two other cats from Harlem named Nicky and Frank.

Corey had an identical twin named Cameron. At 6'3" and built like linebackers, they were impossible to tell apart by anyone who wasn't an immediate family member. Like all twins, especially ones who were from one egg and identical, the boys shared an inseparable bond since birth. They would cry when the other one got beatings for misbehaving and would go as far as accepting the punishment for each other's actions.

The boys became stars within the Houston high schools. Having handsome features meant that catching females was never a problem area for either one of them. They flirted with their teachers, double-dated, and even made a habit of secretly switching off their partners for sex. None of their girls would ever be exempt. This was the exact reason why Corey was actually Marisol's second, and not her first and last, sexual partner in life.

Cameron was really the one who met and charmed Marisol at a Latin festival in Texas. He then passed her off to his twin once he got in her panties, and Corey fell in love with the Mexican beauty. So, when Marisol died in a fatal plane crash to Mexico in '86, she passed away believing that Corey was the one and only man she had ever been with. But either way you look at it, Marisol had still stayed within the one-handed tradition of her chaste female ancestors.

Before Corey's wife's plane crash, the cartel had already formed an alliance with both twins. Within two years they had niggas from New Orleans, Little Rock, and the whole south coming to Houston to buy kilos of Mexican heroin and fluffy white coke. Through his daughter, Marisol, the head of the cartel, Mr. Mendoza, was tied into two African American country boys who knew the skill of supply and demand.

Corey and Cameron had earned the trust of the family and it wasn't long before they had a tractor trailer loaded with weed and dope heading out to Houston just for them. It turned out that Marisol had introduced the family to two key figures in the States by getting pregnant by Corey.

With expanding to the East Coast on their agenda, the cartel had set things up for Corey to move Marisol and a young Tarahji to New York. It was the first distribution branch up North with Boston and Detroit to be next on the horizon. His twin, Cameron, was left in Houston to control the whole south by his lonely.

Business was booming and the boys' annual take was estimated to be between four and five million after fees and expenses. Due to Corey's internal affiliation to the family, he secretly received a substantially lower price on the shipments from his trailers. When the other twin discovered the favoritism, he was a little hurt and began feeling some type of way. Cameron's infinite connection to Corey wouldn't allow him to be envious of his brother, but Cameron was surely vexed at the old man. He always took care of his end of the cartel's business so now he felt betrayed. He was hurt and depressed. Cameron began banging the dope in his veins and over the next couple of years the money from the Houston shipments began to be funnier than Richard Pryor.

The murder and crime rate began to triple in Texas and sometime in the spring of '89, the driver of Cameron's trailer was hi-jacked and executed. The troubled twin wasn't on top of his game in the south and the Mexican family had grown furious. The truck had contained four hundred kilos of uncut dope, a thousand kilos of coke, and twenty-five hundred pounds of lime green weed.

Reagan and George Bush, Sr. had each declared a war on drugs and the prices for the two forms of powder had skyrocketed. The truck was considered a ninety-million-dollar loss for the cartel and it warranted death for the culprits behind the ambush. Fifty Mexican hit men were sent to Texas on the first plane departing the next morning.

After a million-dollar investigation, it was discovered that Cameron himself was behind the heist. The Mexican boss was heartbroken. He knew that he couldn't spare Cameron, but his love for the Corey twin had left him with one other ultimatum. Instead of the cartel killing Cameron in three different ways: by slitting his throat, chopping up his body, then feeding him to the fish; Corey was dispatched to end his brother's life quickly with one bullet to the back of the skull.

Corey was summoned to a warehouse in San Antonio that a friend of the old man, a lady kingpin name Jasmine, had owned. Corey's heroin-addicted twin was there being held hostage. Cameron was gagged and tied to a steel chair that sat in the middle of the old factory when Corey was given a .50 caliber, Israeli-made Desert Eagle. Mr. Mendoza didn't untie Cameron or give him the opportunity to plead for his life. Cameron was forced to only listen while the Corey twin asked for forgiveness for what he was about to do. Corey was making peace with his brother before having to murder him. It tortured him to have to pull the trigger, but Corey knew it was better this way. He knew their parents would rather bury their son's body in a closed casket, than not ever find him in the Gulf of Mexico.

As Corey raised the triangle-barreled rocket launcher to Cameron's head, it was natural for him to feel the pain of his twin's muffled pleas of mercy. As much as he knew it had to be done, Corey couldn't muster the strength that it took to pull the trigger on his brother. There were too many guns pointed at them to shoot it out with the Mexicans, but he knew killing Cameron was like killing himself.

So, with that said, Corey quickly pulled the barrel away from his twin brother's head and in one quick motion he stuck two inches of the monstrous cannon into his own mouth. Corey blew his head clean off his own shoulder blades. He knew firsthand how the cartel abided by all the rules of the game. He was 100% sure they would be satisfied with just one life. Although Mr. Mendoza wanted to kill Cameron in three different ways now even more, he honored Tarahji's father's decision and untied the dope-fiend twin. Cameron fell to the floor instantly grieving his brother's death. With Grade A heroin running rapidly through his veins, Cameron cupped what was left of Corey's head and rocked him as they both pissed and shit their pants.

By 2001, Tarahji had lost both parents and graduated from NYU. She had gotten fed up and left Felix, the unworthy hustler boyfriend, who strictly depended on her family ties for seven years. Tarahji took her daughter Lala and relocated to Stratford, a small suburban town outside of Bridgeport, CT.

Bridgeport was much smaller than the boroughs in New York, but was very fast-paced and still rough all the same. Tarahji had been involved with older men all of her life, so while at local gyms, church, and gas stations, handsome older men who dyed their goatees black would go above and beyond to get her attention.

She was the fresh face in the new city and quite breathtaking. Lip gloss and eye shadow were the only makeup ever applied to her skin. However, deciding on a change of pace from all the older men, the Mexican queen now looked for a young prince she could crown and transform into a drug king. It was a job given to her by her grandfather, the head of the Mendoza cartel. He needed new business opportunities throughout the tri-state area. But for Tarahji it would become much more intimate and personal than business.

CHAPTER 18

Monty's State Of Mind...

By the time our flight landed in Maui for our honeymoon, I had come to grips with the reality that I was just a "J.O.B." for the cartel from day one. Although I had already known this for some time because Tarahji had come clean about the mission once we fell in love, it had still taken me a minute to digest. Besides, she had sworn that the family organization now came second to the bond that we had built. Yeah, I'll be the first to admit that I had let my guard down for a minute, but I was back on that M.O.B shit for real this time. But business is business and it's never supposed to be personal, right? That's the reason I held hands and flirted the entire time on the eight-hour flight, enticing Tarahji to meet me in the rest room and join the mile-high club together. We had both agreed to work through the situation that went down the night before at the wedding reception. We wanted to enjoy the honeymoon and restore our friendship more than anything. She had done some real slick shit, but of course we were still in love. And why shouldn't we be? I mean, we did just tie the knot less than twenty-four hours ago, but I was now looking at this marriage thing more like being "partners", literally. Yes, modern day husband and wife - with business benefits.

Tarahji didn't have the heart to join me in the exclusive air club. In the back of my mind I started wondering if now as partners she would have a problem if the very sexy stewardess took her place in the sky. I may have been bugging, but I felt like the odds of her giving me some alone time to do my thing were now greatly improved. But as we exited the plane on the small Hawaiian island of Maui, there was no other pussy that I would rather been in than my wife's daughter, Lala. Just to remind you, we had it already set up since last night, follow me? She was just waiting on my return.

THE BACKSTORY

The June sun was bright and blazing on the exotic island and the beach was filled with some of the baddest women I had ever seen in my life. Yeah, my wife Tarahji is absolutely stunning, but you know how it is when you get used to something you've been around for a while. When you see another bitch as bad as your own, you feel like you missed out on hitting up a few places. Well, I felt like that the first five minutes in the Hawaiian airport.

I had been off probation for a couple of years and I would now blow a lil' weed on certain occasions. And this trip was definitely an occasion that I felt was worthy. Tarahji had gotten a half-ounce of purple haze past the security check by compressing it into two balloons and as soon as we were in our suite I used a double sheet of paper to roll a fat stick. Me and my wife were sitting side by side on the balcony of the tenth floor of the resort. We had an ocean view of the back of the hotel and hundreds of people were poolside, and also down below along the shore. I lit the fat end of the stick and a thick cloud of purple wafted up into the air. Tarahji was enjoying a small glass of Patrón on ice and I sipped slowly on a Corona Extra with lemon. All the drinks were complimentary from the resort's wet bar inside our suite. We gently clinked our glasses as we made a toast "To Life".

A half-hour had passed and we were both well under the influence so our conversation had begun to flow in a very peaceful, mellow direction. We politick'd about things such as adding a child to our family, relocating to a suburb near Atlanta, and getting his and hers matching Can-Am three wheelers. Tarahji bust out laughing about the time I threw up all over her on the Superman ride at Six Flags.

The Patrón had her eyes chinky and my baby was looking so sexy with her hair pinned up with a chopstick. I had to admit to myself that I was very happy about life. I mean, Tarahji did what she did, but I was going to get some type of get-back and that would be that. I'd be able to move on from it all. Don't get me wrong though, I would still be on that money-over-bitches shit 100%, but there was no way I was leaving my baby, not at this moment. But now that I knew she was slick I would just have to keep my mind on my money, that's all.

Me and Bullet saw over twelve million dollars of our own cash go through our hands as partners by fucking with Tarahji's family in the cartel. My wife and I had just bought a $285K home in Stratford and we had over a dozen rental properties throughout the city of Bridgeport alone. We also owned a twenty-unit building on Albany Avenue in Hartford. I drove four different vehicles; a barely year old all-white Range Rover Sport. From the exterior to the interior, the whole truck was the color of cocaine. I dropped cash for a brand new black Ford F-150 with the double cab doors. It's the Harley Davidson edition and the East Coast don't stand a chance with it. Then I had the CL63 AMG Benz with 22" chrome Lowenhart rims and the dual double exhaust making it a total of four pipes in the back. When I stepped on the gas, that bitch sound like a grizzly looking for its porridge. Don't let me catch you at the light in your lil' Benz with the lil' grill and wheels, because I'm going to make Tarahji ask if those are Bugle Boy jeans you're wearing.

On Sundays I would pull out the 2004 burnt orange Porsche Carrera and let the top down when me and my lady would go dining at Ruth's Chris or City Island. It's got 200 on the dash and it's a mean two-seater for just me and my baby.

But of all the jewelry and flashy toys, what meant the most to me was the 30ft. boat that I copped a couple summers ago. It's a speed, twin engine craft with a lower deck that boasts an eight-person capacity. To celebrate our engagement in August of last year, Tarahji and I had spent a Saturday night out on the water. We enjoyed a couple bottles of champagne over a candle-lit dinner. Back when I had met the ole' head Kwame, when they had revoked my parole, my brain had moved light years ahead of other niggas. I knew while I was in prison that I was coming home to take this shit to another level. I bought my mother her dream house and blessed my lil' sister Tyshanna when she graduated from UConn with her bachelor's in psychology. My gift to her was making sure her student loans had a $0.00 balance. As you can see, I take care of my peoples. And after living a grandiose lifestyle for the for the last three years, I still managed to be sitting on $4.7 million from the twelve-mil me and Bullet split down the middle. With all the legal investments I had in place, I'm sure it would be more than enough to last a few lifetimes. When I added that to the fact that I was deeply in love with Tarahji, it was more than enough reason to wash my hands of the game. My wifey supported my decision whole-heartedly, but I was met with a different reaction when I brought it to the cartel.

At seventy-something years old, Tarahji's grandfather looked like he was trapped in a fifty-year-old body. The exceedingly stubborn old man wasn't trying to hear my request to be done with the game. On my last trip to Nogales he made a subliminal threat, letting me know that the only way out of the cartel was to die out of it. Both our tempers flared and heated negotiations had gone back 'n forth over the whole weekend. Tarahji had given me the uncut version of her father's death about a thousand times, so when the old man seemed to be inflexible, Corey's decision was the only thing that kept coming to my mind.

At the end of day two, I made a suggestion that led to both of us being open-minded. It started with me putting my main man Bullet in my position as the head of the cartel's tri-state division. The family had never known that I was working so closely with a partner to handle my shipments. As Mr. Mendoza listened intensely, I explained all the little details of my program that the family wasn't aware of. It wasn't like I was in violation by working with Bullet in a 50/50 venture from the beginning, because the packages came in my care. So whether I sold or even sniffed the dope, I was the one who made sure the consignment money got to where it needed to go. So therefore, I did it my way. However, Bullet had never been told a thing about Nogales, Mexico or the cartel itself. In fact, I was a lil' pissed off when he figured that Tarahji was the one responsible for the connection. He was my man 50 grand, but it still wasn't how you were supposed to move.

The proposition of bringing Bullet on to handle the family's business seemed to lighten Mr. Mendoza's mood a bit. As he fired up a Cuban cigar I could see the gears in his head turning. The next question I was about to ask was "how soon did he want to meet my homeboy?" But right out the blue, I was cut off in mid-sentence. Just when I thought we were getting somewhere I was given his infamous ultimatum.

"Monty, you're my favorite grandson-in-law, but you have two options," the old man said in a voice as deep as the late great Barry White. "You either work and move all the shipments by yourself. Or you work and move all of them through this Bullet guy of yours," he said, with no room for any more negotiations.

The proposition of him meeting anyone was no longer up for discussion. The old man would not meet anyone and no one would meet him – period. The trailers would continue to come in my care and I would be responsible for all of Bullet's actions if that was the route I was taking. With the Corey twin still in my mind, I knew this was the furthest I was getting out of the game. I believed with all my heart that Bullet and I were cut from the same cloth, so I wasn't worried whatsoever about him getting on some Cameron shit. And because Bullet would be by himself, I had the old man lighten the load by cutting the tractor trailer shipments in half. I wouldn't be involved with none of the drug deals, but I'd definitely make sure Bullet was always on top of his shit. I would also make sure that he never got sloppy and started chasing the money because that's when mistakes were sure to be made. Forcing me to stay in the game at a minimal rate was one thing, but I knew the family would never want me to rush into an indictment.

It had been a few months since my boy Bullet had been on his own and he hadn't had any problems at all, so I was stress-free while away on my honeymoon. And since the packages were rather light, with just ten ki's each of heroin and coke, I came up with a plan to give Bullet only five birds of each product at a time. He was sitting on a few million of his own so I made him pay me the cartel's cut up front. So, he was basically buying his own work like real kingpins do. This way I was limiting my exposure to any liabilities that might come from fronting him the work. I gave Bullet the regular price that the old man gave me, and I never put extra points on the birds. As far as I could tell, Bullet had no plans on ever letting the game go, so this was my way of showing him my loyalty, and I figured out an even better way of how I was going to make him pay me back.

When Bullet would finish with the five ki' s of coke and the other five of dope, we'd repeat the program with the other half of the shipment. He brought the bread up front and cashed in on every delivery. He knew there was no rush and continued to take his time until every gram was gone. And when my boy was completely finished with the load, we agreed that he would take two months off between each flip. By doing it this way we would only be in the loop four months out the year. I explained the bind that I was in with the cartel and Bullet understood fully. The only details I left out were who, when, where, and how the shipments came in.

Since I had left the game and put Bullet in this position, his only method of moving the coke was wholesaling the birds. The going rate in Bridgeport during the spring of 2006 was twenty-four a brick for the average hustla. Bullet was beating everyone's prices at twenty-one and a half, but would give them to Y.G. and the rest of the crew for nineteen Gs. This way we took care of our own and the money flowed through the city the way that it was supposed to. He also wholesaled kilos of heroin to niggas who were really doing numbers. But he'd rather breakdown and sell the dope for $75 a gram, or $750 a finger, which was a ball of 10 grams. The price to come back to the cartel was $14K for the cocaine, and fifty stacks for the heroin. Of course, Bullet was making two out of each kilo of heroin, but he was leaving the yayo just the way it came. At this rate, he was seeing a profit of five hundred and twenty thousand come back for himself off every flip. The flips were now every three months, so he made a little over two-mil for the year. We were both already rich, but Bullet was really about to take off. I was cool with that and was willing to settle with the plan that I made for him to pay me back. And I wasn't asking for much.

My cut was only a kid-slice of the pie. Tarahji made a great salary and I already mentioned our numerous rental properties. I simply refused to get a job. I wasn't signing up to do shit. The income from our investments could easily handle our monthly bills. But after listening to Raekwon's first album one day I thought of another plan. With clearing two-mil a year, Bullet was about to run circles around my stash. So, I figured my wife and I should be able to live bill-free and enjoy our same lifestyle. And we should be able to do this while putting away every penny of our legal income. After crunching up some numbers, I figured Tarahji and I could live good with a thousand dollars a week allowance. That would be for the mortgage on our home that we reside in, the car note on her Infiniti truck and only my Benz and Range that weren't not paid for. Then you had our monthly utility bills, along with an occasional Hermès bag for her, and linen Armani shirts for me. With a "G" a week from Bullet, that would be fifty-two thousand a year. That was a small thing to a giant. And when I ran it by him, the giant had agreed.

Now as far as taking three months to send the money to Mexico for the twenty kilos, the cartel had to understand that it was now a one-man show. I mean, at the end of the day they were getting the money dollar for dollar, so they really couldn't complain too much. I was really hoping it would make the old man tell me to kiss his ass and cut me free. I guess it all depended on if he would tolerate this turtle pace for a whole year. Although I didn't know about Bullet's future plans in the game, I had everything I needed and was ready to be completely away from the life.

A million thoughts were racing through my head while away on my honeymoon: Mr. Mendoza, Tarahji, Bullet, and of course, Lala. I was totally aware that I had to play chess with each one of them. Tarahji had poured herself a third glass of Patrón and I was still baby-sitting the same Corona. I put the flame to another fat "J". At 3 p.m. it was the middle of the afternoon, and down below it looked like people had abandoned the resort's pool for the fresh water of the ocean. Sitting chest-naked on the balcony, I took deep tokes on the stick while admiring my wife's legs. We laughed as she did her Sharon Stone impression from *Basic Instinct* flashing her Brazilian wax while adjusting in the chair. She was dressed in a short summer dress that had a pattern of different sized circles all over it. She crossed her legs and dangled the Chanel sandal off her right foot. Tarahji peeked at me over the rim of her glass and I could see a sly smirk forming behind the drink. Whenever she was having nasty thoughts, it was this same devilish look that would spread across her gorgeous face. It would work every time and quickly turn me on.

Falling right into character, Tarahji pulled the chopstick from her bun and let her long black hair cascade over her shoulders. She shook the strands from her face like a cover girl, then ran her hand through the left side and tucked it behind her ear. She then placed her drink on the little square table and while biting down on her bottom lip she walked into the suite leaving me alone on the balcony. I knew this was a little game Tarahji was playing because she was looking back over her shoulder the whole time. I waited in the cut like a lion, acting as if I didn't want any problems. Then, being real light on my feet, I sprung from the beach chair as soon as she turned forward. I closed in on my prey and tackled Tarahji as we fell to the bed. Playfully, she screamed out in defeat as she realized she had been caught slippin'.

I roughed her up by pinning her shoulders down to the mattress and biting lightly on her cheek. Tarahji wasn't a weakling though. She worked out with weights and had skills. Locking her legs around my waist, she applied pressure and tried to squeeze the air out of my lungs. But I was in great shape myself, so even though her thick thighs were clamping down, my strong torso was solid enough to withstand the squeeze.

Wanting to abide by the rules of play fighting with wifey, I submitted to the pressure and rolled over so she could straddle me. Tarahji put her hands up in the air in a slap boxing position, then with Mayweather speed, she sent five or six soft slaps to my cheek. While crossing my fingers, I lied and answered yes when she asked if I gave up. We were engaged in a tongue wrestling match about one second later. Tarahji's dress was hiked up, as she slid her hips down deep, grinding her bare pussy across the bulge of my mesh shorts. She was a straight animal in bed and her competitive nature always drove me wild when we fucked. Both our bodies were on fire as the breeze coming from across the open patio doors only made it intensify.

At this point it had only been two hours since our plane

landed and it wasn't a secret that both our bellies were empty. But our appetite for sex overpowered any other desire. Why not? This was our honeymoon. I had passed out when we finally got in from the reception at 2 a.m., plus – for obvious reasons - I didn't even want to fuck Tarahji that night even though she had just become my wife. But now I needed to see how well she could handle the dick as Mrs. Lester. I could already feel the pre-cum starting to stick to my thighs. I arched up from the bed just enough to slide my shorts off. As soon as my dick sprung out it landed right on the money spot and started sliding in. Seeming to have a change of heart, Tarahji quickly jumped up from my dick and stood alongside the bed. I didn't know what kind of game she was playing, but the shit wasn't funny at all. I needed some pussy and I needed it now: and not just any pussy, my wife's pussy. I tried to rise up from the bed, but Tarahji pushed me back down and started sliding out of her dress. Her nipples were erect and her round hips led down to a pair of thighs that she worked hard to keep toned. She wore her buck-forty so well. It was in all the right places. She then stood in front of me wide-legged and I could see her ass from the front.

"Baby, we have six whole days on the island, let's shower and exchange one of our gifts before we head out," Tarahji said before adding on a "please?"

We had brought along six gifts to give each other, one for each day that we were spending on the island. I can't lie, the gift exchange was something I was looking forward to doing, but right now I was ready to jerk off if that's what I had to do to make the swelling in my dick go down.

After more pleas and a promise that I wouldn't be disappointed, I got up and joined my wife for a nice cool shower; she lathered all my parts and spent a few minutes scrubbing my back. Along with the soap suds, my vengeful attitude had started going down the drain. I became more focused on making sure Tarahji was smiling. I pulled her in for a soft kiss under the shower head. And when she went to hop out to dry off I gave her a firm smack on her apple-round ass.

Tarahji then proceeded to dry off quickly and she asked

that I give her five minutes before I came out of the shower. I could tell she was excited about the gift exchanging; therefore, I continued to be a good sport.

When she left the bathroom my swelling returned from thinking about how good she looked covered in suds. It took every bit of my willpower not to lather up my dick and rub out a nut.

When I entered the room, Tarahji was sitting on the bed Indian-style. She was only wearing a beach towel that she had packed from back home. I was also wrapped in a big white one that the hotel resort had supplied.

While pulling her hair into a ponytail with a pink scrunchie, Tarahji suggested that I go first with the gifts. I walked over to my luggage and opened up the duffle bag that I had carried on the plane. I made sure her eyes were closed as I fumbled around until I pulled out a long white rectangular box. I sat directly in front of my wife, and when I handed over her gift she began to smile instantly with excitement. Her light pull on the sky-blue ribbon gave entrance into the box and when she removed the top, the light from the chandelier bounced off the jewelry and sent sparkles throughout the entire room. It was a very thin 24K gold necklace that had a small, twelve-gram, solid gold teddy bear pendant. The bear had a rare red ruby that had been shipped from Africa placed in the middle of his belly. At a little under ten grand, it was the most expensive of my gifts, but was just a token of my love to my new partner for life.

Tarahji couldn't stop saying how beautiful the necklace was and after lifting up her ponytail so I could place it around her neck, she gave me a wet kiss on my lips then stood up from the bed. I was expecting her to go grab my gift from her luggage until I saw "that smirk" creep across her face. She let the beach towel fall to the floor and when she lifted one leg onto the bed I was staring face first at her dripping wet pussy.

My dick was fully swollen in under ten seconds, and as bad as I needed a nut, I was about to call Tarahji out. She had been playing a lot of games since we had arrived and I was about to let her know that she wasn't going to be dictating how and when shit jumped off on this honeymoon. She was the one to suggest we exchange a gift in the first place, so I raised my hand in the air and asked her where was my shit.

"It's right here baby. You get to eat this pussy," she murmured seductively, crawling on the bed to lay on her back.

Tarahji slid a pillow under her ass to give me a better angle. As much as I wanted to be mad, I couldn't help but to cup her thighs and bury my face in her tight tunnel. I parted her sticky lips then pulled back the mound to concentrate on her thumping clit. She had taught me exactly what she liked, so I wasn't surprised at how fast she was calling out my name. She started fucking my face, pressing hard against my tongue and demanding that I slide two fingers inside her. Her body's warm fluid was dripping down to her ass and my fingers easily slipped inside her while I sucked on her button. I came across a hard object when I slid in deeper, and with a little maneuvering I was able to grab a hold of it. I was in absolute shock when I held the object in my hand. Wrapped tightly in saran was a key to a BMW. I couldn't believe this girl hid my gift in her pussy. I laughed so hard with Tarahji before telling her the key better be to at least a 745. She asked if I would give her the best dick of her life if she told me it was to the 760Li. We both were starving, but you know I fucked her brains out. I had to. My baby! With four thousand a month coming from Bullet, paying the note on a new Beemer wouldn't be a problem whatsoever. Man, life was good.

Chapter 17

Bullet had been Monty's best friend forever. Ever since 3rd grade, when Bullet's mother moved him from their poverty-stricken St. Louis, Missouri neighborhood. A single mother of four, Bullet's mother, Karen, didn't have shit. Tyshanna and Monty's mother, Lakiya, didn't have much herself. Especially after the kids' father got indicted for racketeering and all kinds of conspiracy charges. But everyone in the projects always seemed to be there for each other to lean on. Pencil-written notes that asked to borrow sugar, milk, or eggs were common. Pride had no business in any of the run-down apartments.

Being the new face in the P.T. houses, of course Bullet was often singled out by all the young local bullies like Dante and Ro-Ro. These two knuckle heads weren't your ordinary eight-year-olds, and it wasn't surprising to see 5th graders cough up their candy money to the two bad asses.

One day, all the lil' kids from the projects were engaged in a game of tackle football in the park. Bullet was the odd-numbered kid left standing and it seemed like he'd be watching from the sidelines. It was nine on nine, and by doing the same scheme as always, Dante and Ro-Ro ended up on the same squad. These two dudes were little con-artists in the making. Bullet was always a little small fry and he was an inch and a half shorter than the littlest kid on the field this day. You would think that he made up for it in muscle, but he didn't. Determined to break him in and kick his ass, the two thugs gave the opposing team of pipsqueaks the advantage of having an extra body. The field was about fifty yards long from end zone to end zone.

On the thugs' very first possession, they capped off a four-play drive with a punishing touchdown run by Ro-Ro. 7-0. When the half-pints got the ball, Monty, already a young star, took the first two hand-offs about ten yards a piece. However, he was stuffed in the backfield for no gain on the following three plays.

The quarterback was Popeye, who was a clumsy little mess, and the thugs knew that Monty was the only one who had skills. So as soon as the ball was hiked, they decided to knock Monty on his ass whether he got the ball on a hand-off or not. So, Monty's team had punted the ball back to the thugs in no time. Still 7-0.

The game continued in the exact same manner and before you knew it the score was 21-donut. Bullet's little ass was playing wide receiver and whenever Popeye didn't get a chance to hand Monty the ball, the uncoordinated quarterback was popped hard by the thugs before he could launch a pass. The few pissy little girls that watched from the jungle gym were cheering the bullies on as they rang the quarterback's bell time and time again. His last play was a quarterback sneak and Popeye got hit so hard that he couldn't peel himself up from the grass. After his goofy ass got up and limped from the field, the thugs began to lick their chops as they saw the game was now even at nine on nine.

Bullet was the only one brave enough to play quarterback. After the ensuing kick-off, he called a huddle to draw up a play. Monty listened intensely as his second-string quarterback formulated a plan. Two of their other teammates were busy competing - pulling patches of grass from the field. This team was way worse than the bad news bears.

When the small fries lined up for their next play, Dante, Ro-Ro, and all of their little league thugs just knew that Monty was getting the ball. But when stuttering Jerry hiked it to Bullet, the whole team was drawn to Monty and Dante sniffed it out, knowing that Bullet kept the ball. He had intentions on sending Bullet's ass straight to the E.R. Running full speed at the nine-year old midget, Dante slid face first into the grass when Bullet juked left. The little lightning-fast quarterback then shot up the field for the longest touchdown run of the day. The whole team surrounded him in the end zone for a celebration as Dante pulled grass from his nappy ass head. The little cheerleaders smelled like piss, but none of the small fries seemed to mind as they spelled Bullet's name in a cheer. The underdogs ended up getting whupped that afternoon, 45-21, but Monty knew he had found a new speedster for a quarterback whom he could build his running game around that summer.

As Bullet came of age, he was eventually accepted in P.T. and all throughout Bridgeport. He became a pack boy at the age of twelve, hustling for OGs to put an end to his mother's Saturday morning notes. The dope and crack money always came at a fast rate, and his mother didn't ask questions as Bullet brought home at least five hundred dollars a night. He filled the freezer with meats, he kept the lights turned on, and he took his baby brother and two older sisters out of hand-me-downs. It got to a point where his mother was able to trade her food stamps for cash, and try to come up on the slot machines at Foxwoods Casino. Karen started balling. Section 8 had the rent at $25, and the gas tank on the Datsun was always at least 1/2 full. You couldn't tell that girl shit.

Bullet picked up his name by getting grazed by a slug in the back of his head when he was fifteen. The hot lead was meant for a cat named J-Rock who went around sticking niggas up with no mask. A caravan full of Puerto Ricans from the East Side had come through with handguns and choppers that could chip the bricks off the buildings. Bullet was conducting a sale for three bundles of dope when the wild Ricans started lickin' off. It caused him and the dope fiend to both haul ass into the alley. Only fifteen himself, the familiar barks from Y.G.'s .40 let Bullet know that return fire was being sent from the few niggas who were standing in the parking lot. Of course, none of them was J-Rock. His hot ass was nowhere to be found. The short-distance sprint had caused Bullet to bust a sweat. And when he wiped the back of his neck his whole palm was painted red. The nigga was so much in shock that he passed the fuck out and woke up in the hospital with the TV on *Family Matters*. His mother, two older sisters, and a few OGs from the projects were there calling him Bullet.

As the years passed, more money brought power, and an itchy trigger finger brought tons of respect. Bullet had a temper like Mike Tyson, and the smallest shit could make him go from zero to sixty in 0.2 seconds flat. As a known shooter, he was promoted from pack boy to lieutenant, then went on to buying and moving his own work. Bullet's stripes in the hood had given him the power to stamp his own name on his dope and pioneer buildings in the projects to pump his work from. With $20 bags of heroin, and dimes and twenties of crack that were so hard and white, Bullet's clientele led him to create his own crew. They stuffed their bags and put jumbos on the block to starve out all the other hustlas. Bullet didn't have to resort to gunplay to make the competition get down or lay down. He simply out hustled the other crews by supplying bigger and better product.

Bullet had learned all the tricks of the game from a washed-up kingpin who gotten caught up in the hype after trying a white line. Troy was from the Marina Houses and he's still considered the smartest nigga to ever do it in the city. Now fifty years old and washed up, he told Bullet every day how he was contemplating a comeback. If Troy could get out of his dope-fiend lean, there wasn't a doubt in the world that he could once again run the city. But as long as his face stayed in his lap, Bullet's spot as one of the top shottas was safe. He would continue to soak up all the game he could from the old head.

From Troy, the young boss learned how to cook coke in four different methods, by the way of stove, and/or microwave. But Troy's most prized wisdom came from showing him how to cut heroin and put A-plus dope on the strip. Bullet was taught that quality was always a key to success.

While Monty was knocking down calendars on his three-year bid, his childhood friend's power had continued to rise in the streets. Bullet was low-key and although he was sitting on about three hundred thousand he still rode in a bucket, like fuck it. He pushed a navy blue '94 Buick Century with light tints. When he did rent the big boy Suburbans for his team to attend Rucker Tournaments or the Puerto Rican Day parade in Manhattan, Bullet played the back seat with an expensive pair of dark boys over his eyes. He didn't want the fame. He knew the money lasted longer. And he sent his main man, Monty, a lot of it while he was away. Making sure his boy lived as comfortably as possible inside the can.

Besides a few bumps in the road, such as the connect not being consistent, and posting a couple of quarter million dollars' surety bonds for Y.G. and Lord, Bullet was still on top of his game when Monty walked out the gates of Enfield Correctional facility in the late months of '99. Bullet rented the new Grand Cherokee to take the one-hour drive from Bridgeport to scoop up his homey. Bullet stuck to the script and was sunk low in the back seats, but he didn't post his dark boy shades on this cold gloomy day. He secured the services of two bad bitches from Stratford with valid drivers' licenses to push the V8 truck up north past Hartford. Slightly older than Bullet, both girls were twenty-five and sexy as ever in their fitted jeans and Coach boots. Bullet had fucked Chrissy and Juanita together on a couple different occasions, so their job was to now give the twenty-one-year old Monty his first threesome. If there were any sexy lesbians when Monty first went to prison back in December '96, then they were all in the closet. But last summer, a groggy-voiced rapper from Jamaica, Queens, who was down with a label called Murder, Inc., had made it cool to pop ecstasy and have two or three bad women in the bed together. As far as the sex scene, at this rate there was no telling what would be going on by the year 2010.

When Monty walked from behind the gates, it was easy for Bullet to see the thirty pounds of muscle that his favorite running back of all time had put on. Both bitches up front were blinded by Monty's radiant glow. Chrissy used her middle finger to trace circles around the steering wheel. Juanita caressed the strap of her seat belt while squirming in her seat. Five thick cornrows and a neatly trimmed goatee had that boy looking like a well-done steak to them hoes. When he finally approached the Cherokee they all jumped out to salute Lamont Lester for keeping his gangsta so authentic for so long.

The ride back to Bridgeport seemed much quicker than the ride up, as the brothers from different mothers caught up on the street tales. Bullet was uncomfortable up front in the passenger seat, but he wasn't sweating it, he just wanted his homey to be extra-close to a bad bitch. Juanita was right next to him and enjoyed rubbing Monty's thigh the entire time the fellas were talking. However, when they reached exit 9 in North Haven, Juanita spoke up and asked Bullet if he would mind if she had some of Monty's time. Easily catching her hint, Bullet sat forward in the passenger seat and put in the L.O.X. CD. With twenty-four miles left to Bridgeport, Juanita quickly succeeded at gulping down everything Monty had in his balls with her heat-seeking deep throat.

"♫♫And just because you might see me in and out of her house, there's no way she can have a baby out of her mouth ♫♫," rapped Jadakiss on the new album.

Back in Apartment 21 of P.T. projects, Lord, Y.G., and Live were playing NBA 2K for twenty dollars a game. They worked as a team to polish off the fifth of Henny X0. Bullet had told them not to blow any weed inside the apartment because he knew they'd all be sitting around the table for hours. He didn't want Monty to get a dirty urine for catching a contact. So, complying with Bullet's orders, they took a blunt break in the hallway every thirty minutes, or between each game, whichever came first.

A fresh outfit with tags on everything was folded and laying in one of the kitchen chairs. It consisted of black and red A-Solo's, size 36 Akademiks, and an official Champion hoodie with the logo written in red. On another chair pulled next to it sat a 3-pack of underclothes that were Hanes brand, of course. Twenty-five grand, in all twenty dollar bills, was placed neatly on top of the table.

When Bullet and Monty finally walked through the door, the crew, now joined by Quan, and Ro-Ro, had stood to salute their childhood friend. Yeah, this was the same Ro-Ro who used to bully niggas. Unfortunately, his boy Dante had gotten himself smoked in the summer of '97.

Monty slapped fives and thug-hugged everyone in the room before being mesmerized by the graphics on the new game system, Dreamcast. When Monty had first gone away the original PlayStation had just come out. But before that Nintendo and Sega Genesis were the only choices. Now standing in front of the 50-inch floor model screen, Monty could see sweat trickling down Kobe Bryant's face while he stood at the line. Monty loved video games and wanted a piece of the action. There was a minute and a half left in regulation between Quan and Live's match. With twenty bucks at stake, Quan was up by six points. They both knew that Monty used to be the nicest on the joysticks, but that was NBA Live back in the Sega days. No doubt about it, the times had definitely changed. But still in all, Quan decided to disrespect Live by letting the fresh-out-the-joint Monty take over for him in the last minute and change. As soon as Monty got the controller, Live drained a 3-pointer and was now down by three. Trying to get a feel for the funny-shaped joystick, Monty was out of control as he made Kobe run straight out of bounds. Live then went down court and got sent to the line on a lay-up attempt. Scottie Pippen, who had restarted his career in Portland, had hit both free throws. Live and the Trailblazers were now down by 1 point. On Monty's next possession he killed a lot of time off the clock trying to gain coordination by passing the ball around. Then everybody in the room bust out laughing when he turned the ball over on a 24-second violation. There were seven seconds left and Quan was begging Monty to play good "D" so it wouldn't cost him $20. The pressure was now on and Live called time-out to advance the ball to half court.

After the time-out, Monty adjusted into the 2-3 zone on defense to prevent any easy lay-ups. He would rather die by the short jumper if anything. Damon Stoudemire inbounded the ball to Pippen, who took a couple of dribbles before giving it to Rasheed Wallace behind the 3-point line, that sweet spot where all his shots were suddenly dangerous at this point in his career.

Live pump-faked a three-pointer, making Monty jump in the air with Robert Horry, then Rasheed drove hard on the baseline to dunk it on Shaq and two other Lakers at the sound of the buzzer. The shot was good and cost Quan a dub. He called Monty a certified bum for giving up a six-point lead to lose by 1. But none of them knew that they wouldn't be able to fuck with Monty in 2K after a week's practice on Dreamcast.

Out of the shower and into fresh gear for the first time in thirty-six months, Monty had fit right in next to Bullet at the round table. The twenty-five Gs were a gift and sat neatly in front of him. Monty had leadership qualities ever since his days on the football field and it carried over into the streets after being turned out in the strip club that night. So, it didn't feel foreign for the whole crew to sit quiet as he went over a few ideas with them. And Bullet didn't take it personally when Monty said they were thinking small by limiting themselves to the projects. Monty congratulated the whole team on their successful takeover of P.T., but he insisted that now was the perfect time to expand their operation. There was money for the taking throughout Bridgeport, but Monty was thinking even further than that.

While being on lock, Monty had met and done pullups with a few real good niggas from Hartford, Meriden, and Waterbury. Although he had to beat the life out of Head's punk ass, Monty knew Kev and God Body were two of the illest niggas to ever come out of New Haven - Congress Avenue to be exact. Monty was fresh out, but every last one of the niggas he had met had already been on land for a minute now. The God had actually sent him a stack of flicks from this year's Freddy Fixer Parade. He didn't include a money order inside the envelope, but the two-page letter The God sent with the pics had made his struggles very clear. Monty understood his pain. Besides, the flicks had done something for him that a money order could never do. God Body had allowed Monty's mind to escape prison and live through him. Monty was physically locked in the Bing, but for a whole week straight he had visions of being at the parade in a coke-white bug-eyed Benz. It was real shit like that, that niggas respected in jail. The God never ratted on no one and was respected in Elm City. The days of the teen club, 302, and the beef between the two cities was now old news. The year 2000 was literally a few weeks around the corner. Monty wasn't trying to come off as the new boss, but there were definitely levels to this shit and his vision was extraordinary. The establishment of a true empire was on the horizon and Monty's promotion would eventually be inevitable. The only question was if everyone would play their position and not let their pride intervene. You know how that money do to most crews.

CHAPTER 16

The whole time while honeymooning on the Hawaiian island, Tarahji was feeling horrible about her betrayal of Monty. Being shiesty and back-stabbing really wasn't in her nature. The Latin side of her family had been built off loyalty. Tarahji knew there was simply no excuse for her poor choice. It's safe to say that lust simply took over. By all accounts, she was normally a shining star.

Tarahji was her grandfather's only weakness and the Mexican drug lord would grant her every wish, so she had never had to stress over finances. And she chose to go to college, refusing to depend on the cartel to make her life a walk in the park. Tarahji went out and got her own, so she never had to think about stealing from her sweetheart, Monty. She learned at an early age that every action had a reaction, especially since Jalen had taken a gut shot for treating her as if she was a punching bag. But still, as much as Tarahji regretted her actions, she never could have foreseen Monty shamelessly fucking her daughter inside the bed they shared.

She appreciated that he was a man who was very handsome and intriguing, and because he spent a lot of time out of state, Tarahji definitely suspected that he enjoyed his fair share of side pussy. She wasn't nobody's fool. She just wouldn't go looking for shit that would hurt her once it was found. And for his part, Monty knew more than anything to have respect for his relationship. He didn't leave condoms in the Range and then blame them on Quan. Bitches weren't putting up pictures of him on their Myspace pages or Facebook walls. He damn sure didn't make it his business to take a shit or shower with his phone like he was up to no good either. Nah, Monty had his mind on his paper and he took care of home. But when he did have a bad bitch dancing all over his dick, it would be out of state and there were no strings attached. He kept it to a minimum and wouldn't dare drop his seed anywhere. By continuing to read the Qur'an, Monty still strived daily to cleanse his soul. However, knocking off Lala was just personal; an act of get-back, not business.

Tarahji didn't have their Stratford home wired with cameras to catch her husband fuckin' another woman, let alone her only daughter. That shit wasn't even conceivable when she had the system installed two months ago. Whether traveling together, or away on solo trips, her and Monty were always on the move and spent a lot of time away from home. They used five different banks to hold cash amounts that were as much as six digits, but it was impossible to try hiding the millions that Monty had made through the cartel. They formed multiple LLCs, plus T & M, Inc. and when you threw in Tarahji's six-figure salary, they had an excuse to be rich. But being young and black with over four million in cash would be impossible for Monty to explain to the Feds. Even with all of his and his wife's business structures that were set up, he'd be indicted for sure. So Tarahji's initial intentions were to put a camera facing the false wall that hid the safe with the millions, but the security company talked her into wiring the whole house.

Monty was away on a business trip in Detroit when Tarahji had a private company come out and install the cameras. Jack Mack Securities was very thorough and reputable in the city.

Mekhi, the CEO, had personally assured Tarahji that he sent out a pair of guys that would get the job done quickly and soundly. The young CEO didn't have a foul bone in his body. Mekhi was just practicing good business skills when enticing Tarahji to spend a few extra dollars wiring the whole house. He topped off the deal by adding in a free bonus feature. By entering a five-digit code, Tarahji could watch live footage from her phone or any computer with internet access.

The cameras were pea-sized and placed out of view in spots that were completely undetectable. The only areas that were exempt were all the bathrooms and the laundry room. They had a lot of valuable possessions openly lying about the house and Tarahji wanted to be sure they'd catch any burglars from a number of different angles. As part of a crime family, the career woman knew she'd have to move very militantly and discreetly to outsmart any predators. Installing the cameras was a strategic move that she knew Monty, her then fiance, would respect and approve of. That is until she ran the news to Shameka Barnes, who was Tarahji's so called "best bitch".

Tarahji had known Shameka since her childhood days back in Brooklyn. Of all the girls from their neighborhood, these two had formed the closest bond. They had dozens of the same outfits. When you saw one, you saw the other, as they were always together. The only reason Shameka wasn't there when Tarahji had the one-night stand in Manhattan many years back, was because she was in Baltimore for a family reunion on her father's side. Meka grew up even more reserved than Tarahji, and if anyone could've stopped Tarahji from dropping her panties for a stranger that night, Meka was the one. She was sheltered by her parents and never given much freedom. But like a young pit bull who was fresh off the leash, Shameka didn't know how to act once she was set free.

Now at forty-one, Shameka was seven months older than her counterpart, Tarahji. With twenty-five notches scratched into the wall, there was a landslide of a gap between their respective number of sexual partners. Shameka had fucked over three times the number of dudes as her longtime friend. Once the biggest protester against one-night stands, it was now common for Meka to build chemistry with a guy at the bar and then fuck him in the same night. Married, recently widowed or divorced, no man was off limits. Shameka didn't see shit wrong with being the side bitch. Her one and only cardinal rule was to never fuck a man that one of her girls had been with.

At 5'6", Shameka was a couple inches taller than Tarahji when out of their heels. Although she didn't have as much booty as the Mexican and black honey, Meka's hair was just as silky and her face was actually cuter. Her father was black and her mother was Portuguese and Italian. Unlike Tarahji, Meka didn't have the heart to leave Brooklyn, and her salary was a couple brackets lower, but at $80K a year, you couldn't call Shameka broke. She had two daughters who were twenty-two and twenty-one and they both were in college pursuing medical careers.

Shameka, the gorgeous accountant for a printing company in Brooklyn, definitely had her shit together. Her credit was outstanding and Meka didn't have to depend on a man to pay her bills. She just wanted to be able to depend on his dick staying hard to make her cum three or four times. Being fortysomething, she was at the very tip of her sexual peak. It was cool if a dude had crazy swag, but it didn't matter, Shameka just wanted to be fucked. She kept it real with all her partners, never denying her prowess to think like a man. She believed that all niggas had some shit with them and she was just following suit. Meka just wasn't trying to be nobody's fool. And since Tarahji was her day one, Meka wasn't going to let her be nobody's fool either which is why she suggested that Tarahji keep the hidden cameras a secret from her fiance. She didn't agree with Tarahji doing it as a surprise gift. Meka told her friend that she was better off killing two birds with one stone; keeping an eye on the safe and the other one on her man when she left him at home. Meka ultimately believed that Monty was a good dude. She knew that he had the blood of a go-getta and was a great provider. Still she insisted that the cameras would allow Tarahji a much more in-depth look into Monty's day-to-day movements. Until he proved her wrong, Tarahji's fiance was cool in Meka's book. But cool or not, it didn't stop her from encouraging Monty's woman to join in on her bullshit at times.

Last summer the two ladies enjoyed a four-night stay on the exotic island of St. Troy. Meka's panties were soaked and wet the instant their plane landed. She couldn't believe the wide selection of men. Tall, dark, with abs bulging through their white tees.

Exclusive getaways were nothing new to the ladies, but it was the first time they visited the Virgin Islands together. The adventures on their voyages would usually consist of jet skiing, shopping, sightseeing, and looking cute by the hotel's pool. True to form, Shameka would never end a trip before finding a young boy who was full of rum to sex her down doggy-style. The guy usually had a friend and the night would always end with Meka renting another room for her scandalous fling. Tarahji would give the friend the cold shoulder before sleeping alone in the suite her and Shameka originally shared. This usually went down right before they left their vacation spot, so Tarahji wasn't surprised by the situation she found herself in the night before their flight left St. Troy. Three Long Island iced teas and a few puffs of sticky weed from the two teenagers had Shameka turned all the way up at a club called Coco Cabanas. The nightspot was full of young dime pieces with cute faces and curves. Dressed in different colored Dolce & Gabana skirts and Jimmy Choo stilettos, the two older women went head to head with the baddest twenty-one year olds in the club. Their toes were freshly done and their thick legs were oiled up with baby gel.

Tarahji and Meka's soft bootys wobbled out of control in their thongs while dancing to a hot new Barbadian artist's song called "Umbrella." Two local nineteen year olds had spent their time flirting with the ladies the entire night. It was clear that all the little girls who were acting stuck up weren't these young guys' speed. Tarahji's thick frame and Meka's seductive moves had "grown ass women" written all over them. One of the guys was dressed in an all-white short set and matching bucket hat. The other had on navy cargo shorts with a pink, white, and navy-striped, Polo rugby. Both guys were rocking all-white low-top Air Forces with no socks. The young island men had come forward and approached the ladies with celebrity confidence. Besides expensive watches, neither of them wore any jewelry.

The entire dance floor and club were packed elbow to elbow. After a little shoulder rubbing past five hundred amazing looking women and no less than three hundred other local jokers with liquor in their guts, the two young cubs made it to the outdoor patio with the cougars. Already feeling nice, Shameka easily agreed to burn a few sticks of green with them. Not wanting to be a party pooper, Tarahji didn't touch the trees, but she threw back two shots of rum from the outdoor bar. Tarahji was also the one to loosen up the conversation by flirting heavily with the boys. She knew there was nothing wrong with being friendly and having a little fun. Besides, the flirting was always as far as she'd ever take it. However, she honestly felt that both Bo and Jake were very sexy young men. She didn't know which dude her friend would choose to rent another room with, so Tarahji was careful not to distract the guy that Meka truly preferred. She played cool and prepared herself for the cue that she had gotten so used to when Meka was ready to mate.

Shameka's drunken gesture finally came around 2:15 a.m., but it wasn't exactly the normal cue that Tarahji had expected. Like every other time, Tarahji was looking forward to convincing her friend that she was in love with Monty and didn't plan to give herself to any other man but him. But tonight, Shameka approached the situation with a totally different spin. Meka knew her best bitch was stuck on getting married without any skeletons in her closet. So instead of peer pressuring, she asked Tarahji if she'd mind watching as her brains got fucked out by both boys. Tarahji knew her girl was a stone-cold freak but her facial expression still revealed total shock. She thought Meka was out of her mind, but yet and still, Tarahji agreed to hold her girl down.

The four club goers left Coco Cabanas with both guys holding on tight to Meka's trimmed waist. It turned out to be true that the young prissy chicks in the club weren't fast enough for Bo and Jake after all. Those conceited hoes were riding their brakes, doing 40 in a speed zone that had a 65-mph limit. The boys hit pay day because Shameka's rpm's were redlining.

Back in the room, Bo and Jake couldn't begin to believe their luck. The drunk and horny Meka wasted no time in attacking her prey. She ripped the white shorts from Bo's bottom half while tongue kissing Jake's handsome face. They were all rolling around the bed naked in a matter of seconds. A mouth was glued to both of Shameka's titties while her hands were wrapped tightly around two hard cocks. Jake seemed to be the more touchy-feely one as he took his free hand and dug two fingers inside of Meka's sloppy wet cave.

Tarahji was lying in the other bed watching late night re-runs of *In Living Color*, pretending not to notice the three brown bodies with entangling limbs. Jake then decided to swap Meka's left titty for an even sweeter body part. The more experienced boy pulled his fingers out of her wet center and made no attempt to hide the fact that he was doing a smell test.

After giving her a passing grade, he stuffed both fingers in his mouth before digging back between Meka's legs so she could taste her own love. It wasn't long before Jake had Meka's long legs wrapped around his teenage neck as he ate her pussy like a grown man had never done before. Meka fucked his youthful face while Bo's thirsty ass continued to nurse the same right nipple. Meka loved having her titties sucked but her mouth was starting to water itself. She dragged Bo by his dick until he was sitting directly on her chest. Meka opened wide while the teenager straddled her face, his surprisingly long rod hanging far down her throat. Bo humped Meka's jawbone in a steady rhythm as his partner, "Jake McNasty," moved further down south between her cheeks.

Tarahji's heart was now racing as she cut her eyes from the TV and Fire Marshall Bill, to the three-way action between the sheets that was so close to her own bed. Tarahji wasn't sure how much longer she'd be able to control herself. Meka had badly wanted Bo to quench her thirst but the Jamaican rum had him prepared to go the distance before painting her tonsils white. From getting her ass and pussy eaten, Meka had already come twice on the peach fuzz that Jake wore for a moustache. She then took Bo's muscle out of her mouth long enough to ask which one of them was ready to fuck her, causing them both to jump and speak at the same time for the opportunity.

Meka reached over and grabbed a six-pack of Magnums out the nightstand and the boys were still indecisive as to who would dick her down first. They had wanted Meka and Tarahji since first spotting them both walking through the club. Unfortunately, stuck with the option of only one woman, Bo and Jake huddled up in the corner for a secret compromise. Once everything was figured out, they both filled their condoms with well-developed hard pipes. Shameka had the "eye of the tiger" and didn't seem to care who was going first. This was her first time doing something of this nature and she was hard up on fucking the shit out of both youngsters. After the boys were wrapped up and protected, Bo took the initiative to lie back on the bed with his boner pointing towards the ceiling fan. He gently grabbed Shameka by her hand and pulled her on top of his young solid body. Meka reached behind her fat ass and guided the boy's muscle into her forever-tight vagina. Once slowly swallowing him up, she controlled her muscles, bouncing only her ass over his hips. The young island boy filled her cup to the brim. Meka's pussy was so wet that Tarahji could hear Bo's penis smacking as he slid in and out of it. Tarahji slyly turned the volume on the television all the way down so she could hear the soft moans that began escaping her friend's lips. The entire area under Tarahji's ass was now soaked and she couldn't help but use the pillows to sit up in the bed. Jake was rubbing his own dick back and forth while hovering over his homeboy and Shameka. He was staring over at Tarahji and she was now faced with a very tough decision. She couldn't seem to take her eyes off the head of Jake's dick while he enticed, waving his finger for her to come here.

From up under Shameka, Bo reached his hand around her ass and rubbed her pussy while still penetrating deeply. So much of Meka's juice was in his palm that Bo imagined it was lotion. With a plan of his own he rubbed it around the rim of Meka's asshole, his finger touching her rear, turning Meka on even more. Bo then grabbed her by the waist so he could fuck her at his own pace while he was on the bottom. Like an adult star, Meka just sat her ass still and took the dick like a pro. She turned her head to the left, and with a devilish grin on her face, she looked Tarahji dead in the eye from a few feet away. Jake, with his bone now harder than ever, had squatted down behind Meka's still cheeks and slid his throbbing cock slowly into her ass. Shameka knew exactly what time it was when she felt the pressure on her back door. She had only seen this done in porno movies, but Meka always dreamt of being on the receiving end of a double penetration. Her eyes rolled in the back of her head when Jake got all the way inside her anus. Both boys were knocking on her G-spot at the same time. Shameka felt like she had died and gone to Heaven. She ejaculated instantly with heavy spurts of cum, and oh what a feeling it was.

Tarahji knew she had seen enough right then. Her thighs slipped against each other from moistness and her round ass jiggled as she stood from the bed to do what any horny woman would do in her situation. That's right, Tarahji slid into her house slippers and went to the lobby in her PJs to rent another room. It was in this other suite where she rubbed herself into a gushing, pulsing rush of waves before passing out. After waking up the next morning alone, she didn't think anything was wrong with dreaming that both Bo and Jake were splashing in her ass and pussy that night also. Tarahji was absolutely positive that she would one day have to experience double penetration herself. However, it would definitely be a vibrating toy inside of her vagina, with none other than her fiancé, of course, drilling her ass.

Shameka and Tarahji's bond was still as tight as skinny jeans but the trip to St. Troy eleven months ago was the last one they had taken alone. Since then, Tarahji made it a point to bring at least one other girl along because she knew Meka would tone it down if she wasn't the only one who would know her secrets.

Tarahji knew that her so-called "best bitch" was an absolute freak, but she respected Shameka's cardinal rule of not fuckin' behind any of her girlfriends. And Tarahji actually believed that Meka could stick to her vow. However, now as a fortysomething year old woman, she would never put her man in the situation to test Meka's nasty ass.

A few years ago, at the tail end of Tarahji's relationship with Felix, the Dominican cat from Long Island, Meka had stayed the night with her girl after being too drunk to drive home. The ladies had called it a night around 2 a.m. and Meka was given the guest bed while Tarahji passed out in her own room. Waking up from dehydration, Meka went downstairs for some juice, half sleep. At 6:45 a.m., a mere moment later, Felix, the not-so-bright hustla, had just walked through the door from a bad business deal in Trenton, NJ. He had seen the light on in the kitchen and Felix's dick got hard the very second he saw Shameka's ass stuffed inside a pair of Tarahji's stretch pants.

In a very bold move, he came up on Meka from behind and rubbed his bulge on her ass while the glass of juice was turned up to her head. Hearing him trying to tiptoe behind her, Shameka wasn't the least bit startled, but she did turn around and push Felix before checking his ass.

"I don't fuck anybody that one of my girls done fucked," she said, snapping her neck.

Feeling cheap, the Dominican's erection went limp, and his uncircumcised dick began to shrivel up like it was getting lost inside a turtleneck. She placed her glass in the dishwasher, then came face to face with Felix to make sure she made herself clear. All Meka had was her word and she wasn't breaking it for nobody.

Truly sticking to her guns, she unbuckled Felix's belt and pulled out his reawakening muscle. Meka then fell into a squat and tried swallowing him whole. She sucked Felix's dick in a way Tarahji could only dream of. Her spit was beyond slippery and her accompanying hand job had sperm oozing out of Felix's extra foreskin in a matter of six minutes. Right there in the middle of the kitchen, Meka swallowed Tarahji's man's seed while her friend slept off the alcohol right upstairs.

It's a fact that what Tarahji didn't know would never hurt her. It's why Tarahji still called Shameka her best bitch for life, even today, while doing time behind bars for shooting Monty and Lala. Technically Meka didn't have sex behind her friend's back in those early morning hours. She simply sucked Felix off until he came in her mouth. Call it what you want but Shameka was still able to stand by her cardinal rule until this very day. And they'd laugh and reminisce about the good ole' times whenever she was able to visit her best bitch in the women's prison.

As far as Shameka's sexual appetite these days, well, some things will never change. She's still screwing other women's boyfriends. But hey, there's likely a Shameka in every female crew; and if it's you, then YOU GO GIRL!

CHAPTER 15

Monty's State Of Mind...

Even in afternoon traffic, the drive from Bridgeport to New Haven usually took the same time it would take me to blow a stick of haze; twelve minutes flat without ever leaving the middle lane.

Nicknamed the Elm City, New Haven had a lot in common with the 'Port. A small urban city which was famous for Yale University and a few other notable landmarks, New Haven was even more infamous for its outstanding crime rate. As soon as I exited 95 North on the Kimberly Ave. ramp, I was quickly reminded why it wouldn't be an upgrade to get an apartment in the Elm.

Bullet and I were sitting at the red light inside of a rented Expedition. There at the intersection of Kimberly Ave. and Ella T. Grasso Blvd., a crowded Mickey D's was to our right and an even busier Getty Gas Station was on our left. It was December 3rd and the mess from the state's first snowstorm made it quite difficult for drivers to move around. It was the reason we made the big Ford truck our top priority at Hertz rental car company yesterday. Bullet was behind the wheel of our V as I watched a small front-wheel drive Altima struggle to leave the Getty's parking lot. Every service pump was occupied, and there had to be at least six cars waiting to be fueled at the booming gas station. I sat silently thinking of how happy the Arabs behind the bulletproof counter must have been.

Our big monster truck was the third vehicle from the light, and right in front of us was a raggedy, rusted blue Ford Taurus. Bullet was laughing at the little Puerto Rican boy in the backseat of the Taurus wiping boogers on the rear window. When Bullet waved for the boy to stop being nasty, Lil' Pa-Pa stuck his middle finger up like he could do as he pleased. I'm thinking, he couldn't have been no more than six years old, When the light turned green, Pa-Pa sat forward as the blond-haired Latina eased her foot off the brakes of the Taurus. Mobb Deep's song, "Streets Raised Me," featuring Big Noyd off the *Murda Muzik* CD, knocked in the Expedition as Bullet pressed down on the gas.

In the middle of Prodigy's verse, our rear driver's side window flew into the backseat as it shattered into pieces. We looked at each other like, "What the fuck?" before I hit the power button on the stereo.

Over in the Getty gas station, there was a shootout between an old black Acura and a gold Beemer coupe waiting in line at the pump. A short dude wearing a North Face bubble coat busted out the front seat of the four-door Legend with a Ruger, while his man, wearing a hood over his head, jumped out the rear with a MAC-10. They unloaded on the 3-Series as the driver of the Acura tried to get around all the waiting cars. The BMW jerked in reverse and kicked up filthy slush that was left from the salt. A baby-faced teen who looked like he had just reached puberty hung out the window of the Beemer and fired back on his rivals. He had a huge black handgun that appeared to have an extended clip hanging from the butt of the gun.

Of course, my boy Bullet stayed strapped like seat belts, so as cars began running the red light, I could see him pulling the tan .40-cal from the left of his waistline. He kept one eye on all the traffic to avoid an accident. Bullet was pissed that our window was shattered and by the fact that we could've possibly been struck by a stray slug. And rightfully, so was I. But this wasn't our beef and we couldn't take it personal and start licking off shots. This was definitely some inner-hood shit and we just happened to get caught up in it.

The little booger-boy fell back in his seat when his mother kicked the pedal of the Taurus and it was our cue to follow suit. All four of our tires easily ate through the dense slush and got us up the next block of Kimberly Ave. We could still hear the barks of one of the cannons from down the street and it sounded like the big one with the extended clip that the young boy had. We were lucky not to be too far from The God's crib on Vernon St. I hit him up from my cell to make sure his front door was open in case the fuzz saw that our window was shattered and thought we were involved in the drama. It's crazy because it would've been a nasty way to get caught up with the strap we had in our vehicle.

Safe behind the confines of God Body's apartment that he shared with his shorty and their two-year old baby, The God and Bullet exchanged pounds as I introduced the two of them.

The couple had a beautiful little daughter that they nicknamed Tootie. It was unfortunate that the little princess was under the weather with a fever. Tootie had an ear infection. And with diarrhea, she had shitted up four pampers within the last half hour alone.

The God was a few years older than me and Bullet. Nikki, his beautiful brown-skinned wifey, was about the same age as him. When Nikki came home to take Tootie out of The God's arms, she gave him one hell of a strange look. God Body picked up on her vibe and met her back in the bedroom while Bullet and I small talked.

When my boy came back in the living room he had a look of defeat on his face. It was 5:01 p.m. and Channel 8 News was breaking the story of the shooting that had just popped off fifteen minutes ago. Janet King had jumped right in with all the details of the bloodbath while standing in front of pump #2.

There was yellow tape around the entire parking lot and the Asian-looking reporter revealed that two suspects had been killed along with an innocent bystander.

As the reporter pointed to her left, the cameraman followed Janet's direction and showed the bullet-riddled Ac Legend. Forensic techs and homicide detectives both fought for space as they snapped dozens of photos. As the reporter kept talking, the camera fell upon a body on the pavement that was covered with white sheets. Obviously, it was one of the guys who had been shooting from the Acura. I silently began to wonder if it was the MAC-10 handler, or the one controlling the Ruger. The Asian lady hadn't identified any of the victims, but she did report that dozens of witnesses saw a champagne-colored BMW plowing away from the scene.

"Live from the Getty gas station here on Kimberly

Ave, this is Janet King reporting from Channel 8 News with more updates to come."

When I turned back towards The God he was gripping the handle of a long-nosed rusty .38 with tears running down his face. Bullet had freaked out and started reaching for his own hammer while asking me what was up with my man. It was easy to tell that something was going on between The God and his lady. The first thing that came to mind was that Nikki didn't want us in the crib. My boy, Bullet, was still holding on to his gat tightly, but I could tell he felt a little more comfortable with the situation because it would've popped off already.

Without much of an explanation, The God said he was sorry for making me waste my time because he now had to handle something and wouldn't be able to politick with me and Bullet tonight. I had been around this dude for eleven months in the joint and had learned more about him than he could ever know. The God tried to convince me that it really wasn't about much, yet the nigga was posted in front of me with an ugly ass gun.

It took me to stand face to face with him for God Body to finally open up. His story would go on and pave the way to a relationship built purely off loyalty. Between Nikki and her man, they had five dollars and fifty cents to their names at the moment. The month's food stamps had been distributed forty-eight hours ago, but having misplaced her EBT card, and then with the office being closed the last two days due to bad weather, Nikki hadn't received her funds to take care of the household needs.

She had to contact the local office and they would then send out a new card by the next business day. The three of them had been grubbing on Oodles o' Noodles and grilled cheese sandwiches the past few days. Now with five slices of bread and two beef-flavored soups remaining, only Nikki and the baby would be having dinner tonight.

The five bucks and change could get them a whole loaf of bread and a few dollars worth of bologna, but Tootie needed children's Tylenol, plus she had just shitted in the last pamper. The God's back was against the wall and he was going out in the snow to rob a few pockets by doing a couple of stick ups. However, his first stop would be to Nauney and Dee's store on Congress Ave. to get his baby something for her fever. If need be, he already decided to let Tootie shit up his white Ts for the rest of the night. Now that the dark sky had fallen, God Body was ready to go out and find some victims. He knew he had to get a move on it before it got even colder outside and he missed all the good juxs and was left with liquor money.

Standing up, The God slapped fives with Bullet, saying it was good to finally meet him. He then asked me if I minded swinging back by his crib tomorrow morning. Now keep in mind, this was the same dude who took my mind away from the jail cell with over a hundred flicks of motorcycle gangs, pit bulls, and the baddest bitches from New Haven's annual Freddy Fixer Parade. And even though he never sent any money, he still took the time to write me a kite, sending his blessings and love. I guess The God felt bad that he wasn't in the position to send any cash with the pictures. Especially after eating from my locker his entire time in Enfield C.I. But on the real, I ain't give a fuck about none of that shit one bit. My team was on the streets eating and I kept at least a G-note on my account. So, my love for God Body and a few others up the way was strictly genuine. I wasn't looking for anything but realness in return.

By the time Channel 8 covered the sports, Bullet had put the pistol back on his waist and I could see a hint of admiration in his eye for The God. We could hear Lil' Tootie's wails coming from the back room and Bullet's eyes got watery when we heard Nikki telling her baby, "It will be ok."

I guess Bullet was remembering his own childhood and how his family would've starved if he didn't go out and get it by any means. It's the same mindframe The God was displaying right now. Bullet knew firsthand that early life struggles created the best hustlas. If you had never been through nothing you wouldn't know how tough you were. Right then and there, Bullet wanted The God to be a part of our team.

Standing up from the worn couch, Bullet slowly approached The God until the three of us were standing in a circle. Without anyone saying a word, Bullet stretched out his palm for The God to hand over the pistol. God Body's eyes were still puffy and his pain was clear as day. However, the love felt inside the living room was hard for The God to ignore. He felt demons and the weight of the world lift off his shoulders when he placed the rusty gun in the palm of Bullet's hand. I quickly pulled him in for a brotherly hug while Bullet sat the hammer on top of the coffee table. Honestly, we may have saved The God's life that night because that shit probably wouldn't have fired if he had to squeeze down on the trigger.

With knowing the feeling of having nothing, Bullet reached inside the pockets of his black Antik Jeans and pulled out a brick of cash. It was mostly twenties and tens, with only a couple of fives and one dollar bills.

Bullet peeled off twenty-two dollars and handed everything else to God Body. Turning towards me, Bullet smirked and said there was no way we were leaving New Haven without stopping by Sandra's Soul Food Restaurant. I then repeated my boy's move, but I didn't have any singles at all. Therefore, I kept a twenty and a five for the exact same reason. Man, Sandra's turkey-chopped Bar-B-Q dinners were famous in the Elm City.

Between the both of us, Bullet and I had laid over thirty-eight hundred on The God and his family. I still had a little over twenty grand left from my coming home cash, so the few dollars I gave up wasn't much at all. And Bullet was hood rich so you know he wasn't sweating it. The God was one of the few real ones left. He was the last of a dying breed; so, I saw it as Allah using me and Bullet to deliver a much-needed blessing to the man's household. Besides, from all the talk I heard while in the system about how New Haven was a gold mine, I knew we'd see that paper back a million times once we got in the loop.

The God had been released for a little minute now and made a couple minor moves, but for the most part he spent his time observing the movement on the streets. He enjoyed just chilling with his family more than anything. He wanted to give himself time to breathe instead of rushing back to prison.

Because together, we watched as many dudes make parole from Enfield C.I. in March only to come back in June or July with a list of new charges. They'd be right in time to order commissary. Of course, Nikki and Tootie needed The God out of jail the most, but now I was also depending on him like crazy. I, too, had a plan that he'd have a prominent role in.

Nikki had taken off in their piece-of-a-car to go around the corner to her homegirl's convenience store where she picked up the two most urgent items, the children's Tylenol and a small box of Pampers. I had gone outside to put a clear trash bag over the shattered window of the truck. She returned from the bodega in a flash, pulling up as I taped the last corner of the Expedition's broken window. Bullet and The God had stayed inside to watch the baby. I was planning on letting Nikki take the truck to do a much bigger grocery run, so when I gave her the keys she leaned in and handed over the small bag containing Tootie's things.

The white shopping bag had the name of Nauney and Dee's new establishment printed over it, A & S Variety Store. I told Nikki not to worry about the state taking two days to send her a new EBT card. She was to buy everything they needed and more from the grocery store with the money we had given them. I could see all the emotions building inside her big brown eyes and Nikki began to tell me how grateful she was.

She was very cute, but with a make-over of a perm and light shopping spree, Nikki definitely had the potential to be drop dead gorgeous no doubt. Most niggas would've played on her vulnerable state and tried fucking The God's girl, but I was cut from a very different cloth. The thought never crossed my mind. Nothing could hurt a grown man's pride more than him not being able to provide for his family and having to depend on the next cat to feed his kittens milk. All your dignity would be snatched away and you'd feel less than a man. But just imagine that same cat also tending to your wife's cookies at the same time.

Well, I was about to turn The God into a Don. And by always showing the utmost respect for his wifey, I knew they'd owe me their loyalty for life. However, before I could turn and head for the stairs to the back porch, Nikki pulled me in close and gave me a sisterly hug. It was nothing funny about it one bit. So, like a long-lost brother, I genuinely returned the gesture. Any neighbors who never saw my face before would've sworn on their S.S.I. checks that Nikki was cheating.

As I let her out of my arms and dashed up the porch, I saw The God standing in the upstairs window from out the corner of my eyes. He was peeking through the curtains with Tootie hugged tightly in his arms. Man, I was just hoping The God could see that I was truly the realest nigga on earth and had no interest in his lady whatsoever.

CHAPTER 14

E very successful drug dealer that studied the game and reached a certain level knew that coke droughts came and the prices tended to rise going into the month of December and the new year.

The cartel bosses and drug lords were regular human beings with families and other needs that they had to take care of. They would go on vacations for months at a time and some wouldn't return until the early spring season. The drug supply would become limited as all the under bosses tried holding on to the remaining product and stretch the work for maximum profits. And because heroin is now processed in the poppy fields of Mexico, the hard, brown powder is usually not as scarce as the fluffy white coke during the holiday months. The Colombians are largely responsible for the cocaine, and the head honchos of those families were dead serious about their vacationing. So, with it now being December 7th, all the signs pointed towards the mechanics of the game still being the same. Plus, Alex's fat ass, who was Bullet's connect, had forewarned us in so many words.

Alex was a fifty-year old, baby-faced Dominican who was border line obese. Born in the D.R., he was positioned right there in Bridgeport and had ties to the Washington Heights area of Manhattan. They were a large discreet group of young and older Dominicans who came from the island with only two things in common: They were stingy as fuck and well-aware that numbers didn't lie.

Just like all the other "Oye's" on the blocks in Washington Heights, Alex wore a couple pieces of jewelry, but his watch was never expensive. The Casio model with numerical buttons and a calculator was always the Spaniard's choice. Alex's English was broken but he understood numbers very well.

Alex and his people in Manhattan were tied into a gang of Mexicans who were stationed in Omaha, Nebraska. They had a major pipeline where ki's of coke would land in Mexico from the country Colombia. Then Nebraska from Mexico, only to finally make its last stop in New York City.

Alex would then drive to the Bronx and pick up the portion of bricks that had been set aside for him. From what Bullet, and now Monty knew, Alex's package had to be in the range of 25-50 birds every other month or so. They were able to determine that by calculating how many they bought from him, then estimating what Tito's crew was running through in Marina Projects.

Alex didn't fuck with too many cats in the city, but it would be ridiculous for Monty and Bullet to think that them and Tito's crew were Alex's biggest customers. You had niggas in neighboring cities like Norwalk and Stamford who were also getting real cheddar. With that being said, Monty thought it was safe to say that Alex had maybe four or five more people copping serious weight, because the plug wasn't the type to be dealing with just any and everybody.

The program that Bullet was orchestrating in the street had them running through a little over a bird of cocaine a week. Bullet would go see Alex twice a month for either three or four kilos each trip. Lord and the rest of the crew would then cook up a whole brick to supply the projects with dimes and twenties. Bullet would take one of the remaining squares and make it disappear within a week or so. The projects would do about $55K every ten days in those little dime and dub bags. Bullet would always wait until they had made back enough money to go and grab the same four ki order from Alex, only to be disappointed when he arrived for their meeting. It never failed that the big-boned Dominican wouldn't be able to cover four bricks on Bullet's second re-up for the month. The most the young hustla would ever be able to walk away with was two squares.

This actually worked because Bullet would still have product left over from his first re-up to throw with the two new ki's, but when he'd go see Alex fifteen days after that, there wouldn't be a crumb of coke left for anyone to grab. For the next three weeks Alex's phone would be forwarded straight to voicemail. You wouldn't be able to find him in none of the Latin bars or even at a red light in traffic.

Then a week or so later your phone would ring out of the blue and it would be his fat ass ready to let you spend your money with him. Bullet would be mad as fuck and shaking his head, but he would still haul ass and cop four more of them bricks. The crew was seeing money and being safe with the re-ups, but it was this reoccurring routine that made Bullet want to dump his hand and buy fifteen ki's a wop. He knew the objective was too never be without.

Alex's work was always fire, but he wasn't the most consistent at all. Monty was willing to bet Bullet anything that his connect wasn't getting hit off with more than fifty bricks. From everything he learned from Kwame, Alex wasn't what you considered to be a drug lord. The Dominican was good for the time being, but he was slowing up the process for what Monty was trying to do.

Alex's ticket for cocaine was twenty-one thousand per kilo for the average person. By Bullet rocking with him for over two years, plus the fact that he was buying four at a time, it made sense that Alex knocked a point and a half off each joint. So, at $19,500 per kilo, seventy-eight grand was always brought along for Bullet's first re-up of the month once Alex got his package.

Bullet had taken Monty to meet his connect the very next day after they had gone and seen The God down in the Elm. Looking out, Alex had hit them with some important advice when he tossed over the four kilos. After his tight ass had used the money machine twice to make sure they weren't short even a dime, Alex looked Bullet directly in the eye and suggested they sell the coke wisely. He didn't say much more but Bullet and Monty had read between the lines. It was a drought on the horizon and they were strategizing to take full advantage of it. It meant that Bullet wouldn't be able to take any of the ki's and sell weight to nobody on this flip. He would be supplying the competition by doing that. Monty felt that if you didn't have a direct plug to the work at this point and time your ass was to starve. It would only bring more baseheads to the projects to cop twenties from them. There was a much larger profit to be gained when moving the work in break down fashion. Limiting the suppliers would leave the fiends less options from which to score. It's where the saying, "You're only as good as your connect," comes from in the drug game.

Their plug Alex wasn't the most consistent with the weight, but Monty and Bullet's goal now was to be the main ones supplying breakdown bags throughout the drought. Instead of profiting a measly $6,500 off a kilo by selling grams of powder, the return would be over forty grand from cooking it and strictly serving fiends. The drought months were always a win-win situation for dedicated hustlas. The less cocaine around meant the more paper out for the taking. As soon as the boys left Alex's spot they started putting their plan in motion.

Knowing that Alex was usually low on the second time around, Monty and Bullet both agreed that they would have to see him sooner instead of waiting two weeks like usual. This was now overtime; the point in the game where you dug deep and scored as much as you could. After Bullet gave Monty the twenty-five stacks, he had exactly $264,086 in cash to his name. Two-hundred and sixty thou of it sat tucked inside the safe, with the four Gs and sneaker money left thrown around the house.

Monty agreed that Alex would definitely drop the price down to $18K a kilo if they spent the whole safe with him. It would leave them with eight thousand dollars after getting fourteen bricks at a total price of two hundred and fifty-two grand. It was funny, because Bullet and Monty both had on Casio watches, punching in figures to play with numbers. Monty thought it would be a good move if they waited three days for the projects to generate about fifteen more thousand from the breakdown bags. That way they could add a couple more dollars to the buy money

and walk away from Alex with an even fifteen kilos. Bullet just looked at Monty and re-enacted the Dunna Man's quote from *New Jack City*.

"P-p-pure, un-unadulterated, g-g-genius!" he stuttered.

They both cracked up and did the speed limit to go stash the four bricks inside the safe at the crib which held the work. The destination after that was to the 21 Bldg. in Bridgeport where

Monty had an appointment to whup Live's ass in NBA 2K.

When they got to the 'jects they saw the usual flow of traffic in the alleys. A few youngsters were catching crumbs from the fiends who tried walking past them in pursuit of Bullet's work.

The rules were: there was always to be two niggas from the crew posted up on the block with work. One would hold the hammer and play lookout, while the other one went hand to hand with all the customers. Bullet didn't have any heroin in the nine days that Monty was home, so Y.G. and Ro-Ro were in the alley with crack only.

Bullet said the dope that had been floating around was garbage, so he held back from investing over the last couple of weeks. When he and Monty jumped out the rental, they slapped fives with their homies before all walking up inside the crib.

Inside the 21 spot, Quan, Lord, Live, and a few chicken heads from Norwalk were popping ecstasy and chasing shots of Hennessy with Rosé. It was freezing out, so when they wanted to burn a blunt they would pile up in the bathroom and use the ventilation system to funnel the smoke outside. They also used wet towels to clog the bottom of the door. These steps prevented the whole apartment from becoming cloudy, so Monty didn't have to stress the possibility of catching a contact - giving a dirty urine wouldn't be an issue at all. When Monty walked inside the apartment with Bullet it seemed like all the girls wanted to jump his bones once he took off his bubble jacket. Their eyes squinted low and all you could hear were a bunch of, "Girl, I know that's right," being whispered in each other's ear.

Monty was wearing a cream thermal top underneath his North Face and because he wasn't wearing a wife beater or t-shirt underneath it, his pecs and traps showed like a WWF action figure. His glow hadn't faded a bit in the last two weeks. The whole crew was skinny and stayed intoxicated, so Monty shined like a bright blue diamond.

Bullet no longer smoked weed or bogeys and was only a casual drinker, so like his best friend, Bullet's skin was also radiant. However, at 165 lbs., compared to Monty's solid two hundred-pound frame, Bullet was very much light in the ass. He was a ladies' man no doubt, but Monty was sort of getting used to being the heartthrob of the crew.

By now you should have realized that Monty had a very competitive nature. It didn't sit right with him how he had blown a six-point lead and lost Quan's money to Live on his first day home. Therefore, over the past week he had done some light shopping with the stacks that Bullet blessed him with. Monty copped a modest 24K gold chain and a matching dog tag that read "R.I.P. TYPER" with his birth and death-date embedded in it. Type was a childhood friend who had passed while Monty was away. He and Pelly Pell used to hold Monty down with cash and kicks when the athlete once lived and breathed football.

Monty also bought a few Champion hoodies with a small piece of the cash, along with a bunch of different colored thermal tops. For bottoms, Monty was content with only three pairs of Roc-A-Wear jeans, two other Akademik denims, and four pairs of Polo sweatpants.

For footwear, he had two pairs of A-Solo boots and the all-black suede Timberlands that The Infamous Mobb Deep were known to rock. Those were classics. Shit, Monty was straight; he needed nothing more, nothing less. Going to clubs or tricking wasn't in his budget yet.

Monty also gave his mother and sister Tyshanna a stack apiece. The only other thing Monty spent any money on was a Dreamcast game system with NBA 2K and the new Madden 2000 that had just come out. He then wrapped twenty Gs inside a white shopping bag and stuffed it behind the dryer in his mother's basement. After Bullet dropped him off to the crib at night, Monty would spend a couple hours challenging the computer on the superstar level of 2K. He quickly learned all the buttons and signature moves while getting his ass whupped a few nights in a row. But a quick learner, Monty had been blowing them out by twenty points or more by selecting the worst team to use as his own. He kept this all to himself and never played at the 21 apartment again. But today he had every intention on redeeming himself against Live right in front of all the chicken heads.

The heat was blasting and the digital thermostat read 70

degrees inside the apartment. So as Live turned off the *Sugar Hill* DVD and started setting up the game, Monty came all the way out of his thermal before grabbing the Dreamcast controller. He was definitely showing off his physique and the girls started nodding like bobblehead dolls.

Monty told Live that he was letting him choose the worst team for him to use, but Live flipped out by saying that he would make him pay for trying to disrespect him. He then looked through all the team stats and gave Monty the bum ass Chicago Bulls - this was, of course, after the Michael Jordan era.

After Live picked his mighty Portland Trailblazers for him to run with, he looked at Monty like he was crazy when he raised their usual twenty-dollar bet to forty bucks. Monty did this because he wanted to get back Quan's dub, plus a dub for himself. With the game system now set up to play, everyone got comfortable and made their choice who to root for. Monty had easily won the jump ball before opening up the game with a 3-pointer by the one-guard, Jason Williams.

At the end of the first quarter Monty was up by thirteen points and had given Live the opportunity to tap out for $20. It was obvious to everyone that Monty had hustled him after mastering the Dreamcast system, but his homie's pride was in the way and Live opted to go the distance. The whole clique was getting money, so of course the forty bucks was nothing to either of them. In fact, Live usually put more cash inside a single Vanilla Dutch after calling the weed man.

With eight seconds left before halftime, Monty was up by eighteen points: 52-34. He took the ball out from the sideline and inbounded to J. Williams. After a couple of dribbles, he passed it underneath to a young Ron Artest, who was guarded by all of Portland's big men in a 2-3 zone. Monty took a few steps to the basket with Artest and dunked on Rasheed Wallace's head while drawing the foul from Jermaine O'Neal. The basket was good and only one second remained on the game clock.

Ron Artest drained the free throw, then Live called time out to advance the ball to half court. He was extremely thirsty to try and get off a quick shot before the buzzer sounded. They all knew the twenty-one by halftime rule was in effect and a blowout would warrant Live to pay up double.

Live inbounded the ball to Damon Stoudemire, who he used to launch a long 3-pointer; however, Monty blocked the shot with Drew Gooden to secure the blowout. The block got back Quan's bread plus some.

Up sixty dollars, Monty grabbed his thermal to get prepared for the night he had planned. Chrissy and Juanita were both ready to fulfill Monty's lifelong fantasy. Y.G. was trying to amp his homie up to pop an E-pill for the occasion. He told Monty the pill and a little Henny would give him the wings he needed to put both women to bed, but Monty passed on the E, settling for straight cognac.

After a little convincing, Monty did agree to try the small stimulant that Bullet had whipped out of his wallet. The pill was piss-safe for the parole officer and it would also guarantee him to get the job done in the sack. It was a shiny blue color, but not shaped like a dolphin or a G-lady. Monty popped the high-dosed Viagra tablet with speed and grabbed the keys to Quan's Dodge Intrepid. When he got to Juanita's crib on Ann St. in Stamford, he used his cell to call the girls and tell them he was coming up.

By the time Monty had put the vehicle in park and taken the key out the ignition his dick was harder than a bicycle frame. He had decided to take his mind off the money for a few hours and have a little fun. Everybody and their grandmother was talking about the thrills of a threesome and he just had to join the club.

Even though it had only been three days since they saw the connect, Monty still knew it was a chance that Alex wouldn't be able to cover their fifteen-kilo order. Hell, Alex couldn't even keep up with the three or four they would want after about two weeks. So, it was a long shot for him to be able to handle the mother lode. The worst-case scenario: they figured he'd at least be good for seven or eight squares considering it was a little less than 72 hours since they left his spot the other day. This mind frame they were in was the exact reason Monty and Bullet couldn't believe everything was gravy when they got back to Alex's spot. Alex had seventeen kilos left and he was ecstatic that they had come to cop so heavy. A lot of connects would have been leery, as if dudes were up to no good and trying to rob them all-of-a-sudden. It was the history that Alex shared with Bullet that made him not look at him and Monty funny. Every deal that Bullet did with Alex had gone down in good fashion and although he wasn't Alex's biggest customer, the chubby Dominican had told Bullet on more than one occasion that he was one of the smartest by far.

Alex loved how Bullet never came through the quiet neighborhood banging a Tupac song behind the wheel of a shiny new Benz. Alex knew that underneath the expensive jeans, Gore-Tex boots and fitted hats, was a very well-spoken twenty-something-year-old who knew what he wanted.

Alex was also impressed with how neatly Bullet would always have his money when he came to re-up. He never brought along any fives, tens, or ones, and all the bills would be placed together on the same side up. The Jacksons with Jacksons, Grants with Grants, and Ben Franks with Ben Franks. The cash would be in bundles of five thousand and held together by rubber bands. So, if Alex knew there was supposed to be $50K on the table, the first thing he would do is make sure there were ten bundles of cash there. Because five thousand dollars times ten is fifty grand, right?

The next thing the connect would do was program the money machine for whatever bill it was counting. Alex's only job would then be to make sure the machine beeped to let him know that every bundle was five Gs. Unlike a few of Alex's other people, Bullet never made the guy's job hard. And now with bringing two hundred and fifty-two grand, the only difference was that it took longer for the machine to run through the paper.

Getting the connect to drop the price to eighteen a bird was easier than expected. It made Monty and Bullet wonder if they should've negotiated for seventeen. It was like an auction; always start lower than you were willing to pay. They were 100% comfortable with their blueprint, but still walked away with a lesson in negotiation for any future deals.

This was the biggest flip ever and Bullet knew the profit

would fall over into the next bracket. Especially once the streets dried up in a couple of weeks and niggas were on a coke hunt. When Alex was going through the buy money the other day he went a little deep when discussing the drought. He admitted to being hip to Monty and Bullet's strategy and said they were bright for buying everything they could.

While the machine counted the last bundle of cash, Monty admired the 2ft. iguana inside the huge glass tank. The only thing Alex kept saying as he waited for the beep was how ugly the streets were about to get with the limited supply of cocaine.

The last five-grand bundle was over by $20, and the dub was sitting alone inside the slot of the money chamber. Alex brought it right over to the tank where Monty and Bullet were still fucking with the large lizard. It was only $20, and a lot of people wouldn't have sweat it if he had taken it. But a thief's a thief, and if it's not yours then you stole it. Although Alex was tight, he definitely believed in good business and didn't want any bad karma coming back on him. Bullet folded the bill, sliding it into his pocket, while asking Alex how soon would he be back on deck with work. The connect, wanting so bad to sound consistent, and not wanting them to search for a new plug, told a bold-faced lie when he said "two weeks." Monty knew - even more than Bullet - that Alex was bullshitting. It didn't really matter that much to them because the fifteen birds would last them a minute. Monty and Bullet were just looking for an honest answer to know how soon they'd be able to come back and cop more work. It took about a total of forty minutes or so for the money to be counted and rewrapped for the pick-up. When a minivan came and hauled it off, another one pulled up with the work about ten minutes later. They were the only three in the crib, but Monty and Bullet knew that a bunch of wild Latinos were always close by in case of a jux. The money and product separation was just an extra measure taken for robbery preventions. No disrespect to the stick-up kids, but Monty and his boy were certified hustlas and were only looking to "Buy" fifteen bricks of cocaine.

When Alex unzipped the duffle bag, Monty discovered that they had a little more than what they needed. For the first time in their relationship, Alex had decided to put something extra on top of Bullet's order. Alex only had seventeen birds left and he felt there was no need to hold the last two after such a heavy order. By getting rid of them on consignment to Bullet, Alex would eliminate the need of having to deal with one more person the next day. It was simple moves of this nature that separated the smart hustlas from the dummies in the game. Plus, if Alex's spot got raided later, all they'd find was mad empty duffle bags.

Alex would finish his shipment about two weeks early, but the most important thing is that he knew Bullet's face was golden with the credit. Alex saw it like having a nice piece of change just sitting in the bank. However, though he was willing to throw them something on the arm, there was a small condition that, of course, came with the consignment.

Alex wanted them to pay back twenty Gs apiece for the two birds he put on top. When you thought about it quickly it may sound like a bad deal, paying an extra two thousand for the ki's he threw in. But to a real brick layer it would be a no-brainer. Remember, Bullet's regular price was nineteen-five a ki, which was an incredible number in Bridgeport alone at the time, but it took them to come spend a quarter million on the re-up to get the ticket down to eighteen. So, by Bullet being accustomed to paying nineteen and a half, it basically meant they were only paying an extra $500 for the two kilos on consignment when he thought about it.

Monty personally believed the agreement would work for everyone. It was all profit and meant more free money for the team. It also meant another two birds in the upcoming drought.

You should already know the boys took the deal and exchanged handshakes with Alex before strapping their seat belts and driving slowly back up I-95. Monty also made a mental note to find a designated girl who could start transporting their work up and down the freeway. He knew he was there to be a partner, so he had to start making decisions as such. There was no room for error, and between both of their minds there would be no excuses for any. Too many nights were spent in Enfield thinking of ways to fool-proof the road to riches. Monty knew that niggas didn't get knocked for doing things intelligently, it was the dumb shit that brought along surety bonds and arraignments.

Bullet didn't think much of Alex's decision to throw them the two bricks, but Monty saw a bigger picture behind the choice the connect made. He knew that it was a test to see how maturely they'd handle their business. Monty knew that Alex was highly impressed; the admiration had shown all over his face. In this business, only a fool would want to deal with ten people when they could accomplish the same progress by only dealing with two. It was now just a matter of time before Alex would be trying to throw them five and ten bricks. Monty figured it was the perfect time to pioneer the spot in New Haven with The God. They had to turn it up a notch and get the forty thou to Alex as quick as possible. The connect was to get his money off the top, plain and simple.

Then Monty would watch with Bullet as the rest of the money would come back to the knot correctly. Bullet was caked up, but Monty believed that his boy should've risen a lot further in the three years he was gone. But he also knew that everyone hustled differently, so who was he to judge. Plus, he took into consideration the number of mouths that ate off this one plate. Every nigga in the crew had a lil' paper, but Monty doubted that any one of them had saved over twenty thousand of their own, besides Bullet.

Yeah, Bullet was the boss and Monty was clear on that, but he watched as Lord and them ran through the work, so he figured they should have at least fifty Gs apiece. His crew was under the impression that the game lasted forever, and that's where they had it fucked up. God forbid the Feds came or something happened to Bullet. Quan and Lord wouldn't have nobody to hold their hands; but truth be told, nobody should have to walk with them niggas anyway. It's a fact that there would be no Indians if everybody wanted to be a chief, but Monty felt like it was time for the Indians around him to man the fuck up. They had too many employees in the company and not enough jobs. And now with seventeen more ki's of coke, what better time to expand the corporation.

THE BACKSTORY

Monty did a lot of brainstorming on the ride to the stash house with Bullet. He shared most of it with his homie, but kept some things to himself. After arriving at the crib, they stacked the birds from the duffle bag into the safe along with the three that were left from the other day. With a total of twenty joints in their possession, you could say they were one flip away from being real kingpins. From just the projects' flow alone, Monty figured they could have Alex's money in seven days tops. But there were seven people in the crew and he knew that the forty Gs should be accumulated much faster. Monty was about to fix that problem and the shit was starting tonight. He watched as Bullet locked the vault, then he made Monty open it up to be sure he knew the code.

After it was opened on the first try they slid back into their North Face and headed straight to the 21 bldg. They needed a sit down with the crew now more than ever. And watch out because Monty's boy, God Body, would be next up to bat.

CHAPTER 13

Monty's State of Mind...

T he loud racket from Tyshanna banging on my room door the next morning woke me up a few minutes past 9 a.m. Upon my consent, she came in and informed me that our deadbeat of a father had done his once a year pop-up and was waiting on me in the living room.

I ain't give a fuck about that guy but I had a long day ahead of me and had to get up out the bed anyway. I wasn't gonna let whatever he wanted take up too much of my time. So, before I went downstairs I took a shit, showered, and got dressed to be able to head straight out the door after I dissed him.

Shaun Freeman was an old-school playboy type whom everyone in the streets knew as "Free." An ex-dope boy who earned his stripes on the Avenue, Free, along with three of his brothers and five cousins, were federally indicted on everything from the RICO Act to murder and drug conspiracy.

The Freeman family was thick and held a lot of weight throughout Bridgeport from the early to late '80s. All in their teens and twenties, the boys used to drive Saabs and new Maximas while rolling fat sticks of weed from out of little yellow envelopes.

A Jamaican drug lord would supply them with enough snow to ski on, and their murder game galvanized the blocks to move it all with speed. Free happened to be the most feared out of all the Freeman boys. He was the middle child of the brothers and a couple years younger than all his cousins. After developing a relationship with a local hustla name Pongo, Free got comfortable and began to trust him enough to front him dope and coke, telling him all his business. Well, after Pongo served an FBI agent ten ounces of powder, he was snatched up and given the opportunity to get down or lie down. Simply put, with their team, or inside the penitentiary, that is.

Pongo's bitch ass started wearing a wire and recorded

hundreds of conversations that would later be used as evidence in the indictment to prosecute the boys. But the biggest surprise would come at trial when Free was introduced, as the star witness for the government. In front of my granddaddy and grandma, who are his parents, and a host of aunts and uncles, this nigga rolled over and buried his own family alive.

Free testified about being present for eight bodies between my uncle, Man-child, and three of my cousins. He gave up the Jamaican and even told the government about the ten ki's in the floor of grandma's house. He tried to justify it by saying that he made sure her and granddaddy had immunity from all charges first. Grandma passed out when the jury came back with a guilty verdict on every count. Uncle Man-child tried to jump across the witness stand and choke the life outta Free until the marshals knocked him out. It was a straight mess inside that Hartford federal courtroom that morning.

Free was the only co-defendant to take the coward's way out. And after his 5K1.1 motion for substantially assisting the government, he was sentenced to 78 months in the feds. Uncle Man-child and everyone else got letters: LIFE, without parole.

Grandma had a stroke and died a year later and everyone in the family blamed it on Free. And why shouldn't they. Before he had become a stool pigeon, she was moving around, talking shit and tending to her garden every day. It was Free who brought on granny's sudden ill state.

Now after doing five-and-a-half years of his sentence, Free's maggot ass had relocated somewhere in South Carolina. He'd been home about three years and unlike grandma, he was fortunate enough to still be alive and pop up in CT every now and then.

Pulling a black Yankee fitted over my worn corn rows, I strolled into the living room where Tyshanna had been entertaining this bitch ass nigga until I was done showering. Free was smart enough to wait until my mother had already punched in to work before showing up unannounced. Tyshanna was the only one in the family to still have love for Free and tolerate him. But when I looked at him I could easily see how my mother could become so upset at times just by looking at my face. I looked just like this fuckin' rat. My sister and I both shared his big oval eyes and the same flat forehead. And it was plain to see that I inherited my charm from him honestly. Free was the definition of a ladies' man and I noticed his sense of fashion had correctly changed with time. Free was dressed in light blue denim jeans that weren't baggy at all and the Polo horse logo was burgundy on his cream knitted Ralph Lauren sweater. A pair of cream suede Clarks with the gummy bottoms adorned his feet. I saw a dark burgundy, waist-length leather thrown over the love seat, and Free traced the brim of a matching Kangol with the tip of his finger. Prison had definitely preserved him by keeping his figure trim and his clear brown skin wrinkle-free and tight. I wasn't there to admire him, so skimming past all the bullshit, I asked him, "What's up?"

Free said he had been in Patterson, NJ for a couple days visiting his girlfriend's family and didn't wanna be so close to home without seeing me and Tyshanna. He had left his girl, Phylicia, in Jersey for a couple of hours and drove her Honda Odyssey for the short ride to Connecticut.

After kicking the same ole' tired rendition of how he wished he could take back what he had done, Free changed speeds when opening up about what he was really looking for. He started licking his lips and rubbing his palms together like he was mackin' a bitch. A part of me wanted to text my lil' cousin Cracks, Uncle Manchild's eighteen-year-old son, and line Free up on his way out the hood. But he was still my pops, and as much as I didn't fuck with him, I wasn't ready to go to his funeral just yet.

With the same gleam that people have said would show in my eyes, Free lit up when telling me about the cocaine wave that he had created in Conway, SC. Conway was a small city not too far from the ocean's shore of Myrtle Beach, and the strip clubs and projects were in demand of powder and freebase, respectively. Free told me that even though times were changing in the south as far as the availability of coke in Charleston and Atlanta, Conway was stuck in a limbo and still charging $1,200 an ounce. And that was for a water-whipped ounce of base, or a yacked up an "O" of powder. He said the raw work that we pumped up North would turn the lights out in South Carolina. Free swore on everything that he could move four ounces a day by breaking down the work in dubs. He said he could sell about thirty-something hundred from an ounce in either form, soft or hard. To me, it seemed like he had taken his show on the road and was trying to bring back his 1985 heyday from Bridgeport. Free then pulled out his Nokia and showed me the numbers of ten different area codes, saying, "These are just some of the niggas looking to buy birds."

He started pulling out stacks from his leather coat, and with a fist full of paper, he said that he brought along fifteen thousand and was looking for me to throw him a whole bird. Knowing I had only been home a little less than a month, don't ask me how this nigga had figured I had access to a kilogram of coke. But then again Free knew I hung out with go-gettas so I guess it wasn't out of the question.

The proposition that Free made was he and I would be 50/50. We'd start with one ki, and he'd move it all in Conway to bring back top dollar. He guaranteed that he could move it all in twenties before a month was out. That would be about a buck twenty that we'd spilt, sixty Gs apiece.

He tried to sweeten the deal by saying he knew that I could get the bird for about twenty or twenty-one grand, and he'd be actually putting up more than half by giving me the fifteen thou he brought today. Free used to be cool with dope-fiend Troy, and it's a fact that he knew how to get to the paper like most ole' heads from the hood. I was sure he could have that $60K back here in my palms within the month like he promised, but it ain't no price at all on my freedom. How was I supposed to trust a nigga of Free's blood type? He put his own brothers in the pen for the rest of their lives, and son or not, I knew I wouldn't be exempt if it came down to saving the hairs between the crack of his own ass. Free was a coward who'd die a thousand deaths, and I could only die once. Plus, from all the shit I studied in jail, he could be debriefing with the agents every month and trying to line me up to get himself out of a new jam. Well, if his monkey ass thought I was a "get out of jail free" card, then he was just a silly ole' rabbit.

"Free, I've been home for about two weeks and I don't got

plans on going back," is what I said, shouting towards his chest like he was wired-up.

I mentioned that I had been looking all up and down Lordship Blvd. for a job and wouldn't stop until I was able to file a W-2 form next year. That nigga started licking his lips again, trying to see through my smoke screen with his menacing eyes. He could only know what I told him, and I was sticking to the script whether he believed it or not.

Free tried to penetrate through another avenue but I shut it down as soon as I saw the word "coke" form on his lips.

"Free, man, what da fuck I just told you? I'm done."

Free had a look on his face that said he couldn't wait for the day I would need him so he could shit all over me. But I don't know what the fuck he was thinking, because he was the last person I would ever call on. And before I gave in to the strong urge to text Cracks, I stood up and called Tyshanna to come finish entertaining her father. I slapped Free a weak five, then shot out the front door. I had business to handle and none of it was with him.

I noticed the Honda van that Free was driving out front and thought me and Bullet should cop one and get it outfitted to hold ten or fifteen birds. I had plans on us going to the moon and a stash box such as that would definitely be an asset.

By noon, me and Bullet had everything ready to go and see The God. There was a little mid-day traffic, and with the city doing construction on the highway, only one lane was open for a two-mile stretch on I-95 north. The roadwork put a decent delay on the usually short ride.

The meeting with the team inside the 21 bldg. had gone well last night. I could tell there were a few bruised egos from the way I was spazzing and singling out a couple of people, but my words weren't meant to be taken personally by any one of my niggas. I believed Bullet was too lenient on all of them and had grown comfortable with the set system. Well, I was now demanding more from everyone, myself and Bullet included. Lord and Quan were first cousins and most of their family was from around Main Street, over on the North Side.

THE BACKSTORY

There was crazy money over on that end and their job was now to wiggle their way into their peoples' hood and flush a portion of our work through the flow that already existed on those blocks. It wouldn't be wise to send them to try and take over that side of the city, but a small piece of the pie wasn't being greedy.

Lord and Quan's mission was to build a clientele that would move at least two hundred grams a week through the crackheads. That's only about seven ounces when referring to it in weight form. At this point, the average hustla in Bridgeport was bagging up about $1,800 off every ounce. So, you could imagine the size of the dime and twenty pieces inside the bags. I ordered Quan and Lord not to bag up more than $1,400 off our ounces. If they had to stuff extra rocks inside the dime bags that were already made to prevent going over that amount, then that's what they were supposed to do. I was willing to bag up the work myself to make sure they wouldn't try making extra bags for their own pockets. There was a strategy to the system that I needed them all to see. By sacrificing $400 from every ounce, it meant our dimes and twenties would be much bigger than the competition. In turn, a steadier clientele would be built on its own.

By taking two hundred grams over to the North Side, that would be about $9,800 we'd be taking from their hood every week -which was very small amount and was sure to be undetected on the booming blocks.

With Ro-Ro's connection to the Marina Houses through his homies Rattle and Po, it was another potential territory where we could move our work. But the way Po's projects were set up and the fact that everyone over there was already cliqued up, made their 'jects a little more difficult to infiltrate.

After we all gave different input into the debate, we decided that it wasn't worth the risk of going to war with all the "Stack Boyz", a gang of young goons in Marina. We had a lot of heavy metal for situations such as those, but our first objective was to stay low while getting silent paper. Being the boss that he was, Bullet came up with an alternative mission.

On an average, we were already seeing between four and six thousand dollars a day in our projects. And we were only outside from maybe 9 a.m. 'til midnight. Bullet was saying that the goal should be to move a whole bird in a week through the crackheads in our hood. He knew it would take major grinding, so he included the two hundred grams that Quan and Lord would push on the North Side as part of the kilo. That left only eight hundred grams to be moved through our own projects. While tapping numbers into his wrist, Bullet calculated the formula on the Casio.

At the time, we were bagging up the same amount from our work that every other nigga in the projects was bagging off his. But we weren't the average clique, so we couldn't get stuck doing average shit. Bullet suggested that we adopt the same formula that Quan and Lord were taking to Main Street and only chop $1,400 off every ounce for the projects also. He went a little further and demanded that someone be in the alleys as early as 8 a.m., and shut operations down – calling it a wrap - at two in the morning. Bullet figured the extra hours he implemented into our time of operation would bring a significant rush, and to a certain extent I somewhat agreed.

After Quan and Lord took the seven Os, it would leave twenty-nine that would have to move through the 'jects in a week. I could easily see it happening, but what my team was calling extra grind was just not cutting it. I got up from the round table, turned the stereo, TV, and Dreamcast off and spoke like a true boss. Every member of the crew then lowered their drinks and listened as I talked.

"Man, we gotta turn it all the way up, my niggas."

First and foremost, 8 a.m. wasn't going to get us where we needed to be as a crew. There was a basehead smoking crack every second of the day in Bridgeport and we had to be available to serve them twenty-four hours a day. We had no business letting those addicts down by not having somebody outside to get 'em right. Yeah, I know it was the month of December and Jack Frost was surely out, which is exactly why I came up with the next solution.

We needed an apartment in the 'jects that we could run money to and trap out of every second of the day. Bldg. 21 was strictly for chillin' and it would remain that way. I put this young chick named Tanya on task to get us an apartment in her name and she got right on it. We would put barriers behind the doors of the new spot and have battery acid close by to destroy the work if they raided. Only one person would be inside the spot at all times to serve the fiends through a hole in the door. This way it would be impossible to charge anyone with a direct sale. And on the flip side, if anyone did get arrested, it would only be one person and one bond to pay.

I knew it would be quite miserable being alone in the spot for six hours, but work was supposed to be work, it wasn't meant to be fun. That meant no weed, liquor, or bitches with you on your shift. Just cable TV, a walkie-talkie, and a G-pack.

They had a couple of empty apartments in P.T. and Tanya said there shouldn't be a problem sliding up inside one asap. To show the crew how serious I was about this shit, I even volunteered to work the very first shift as soon as she got the keys. This was no problem for me at all. It wasn't the first spot we kick-started and wouldn't be the last. So as far as the crew was concerned, last night we had covered all angles and were just waiting on the new spot. When me and Bullet finally reached exit 44 in New Haven, we got off Kimberly Ave. and automatically looked in the direction of the Getty gas station while remembering our last trip to the Elm. It was good to see that business still seemed to be booming for the Arabs, and that all the snow from the other day had cleared, so traffic at the service pumps was stop and go.

On the way down to see The God I was gonna have Bullet stop in West Haven and grab a quarter brick from the stash crib. But after an update from Ro-Ro, I made other arrangements. Ro-Ro and them had ten and a half ounces left from the original brick we had gotten from Alex, and those grams were set to be done in the projects within the next day-and-a-half. I knew I also had to set Quan and Lord up with the work for the North Side, plus, I wanted to start The God's program with a nice piece of weight. Maybe nine ounces, because there was no doubt in my mind that he was ready to hold it down.

The stash house was only for holding the mother lode and

you never wanted to make too many unnecessary trips back and forth there. So, when we went there to grab work, we usually took what was needed to hold us down and wouldn't need to make another stop there for a few days. We would take a whole bird and cook it in one shot, then whatever we didn't need in the projects would be held nearby at a shorty's crib on Central Ave.

Playing it smart, I took the 10.5 ounces from the safe on Central Ave. and was going to use it to jump start New Haven with God Body. Then on the way back to Bridgeport, we would stop by West Haven and grab a fresh ki to cook the whole chicken and be prepared for the projects and Quan's mission on Main St. This way we'd be on top of our shit and progress would be made with less moving around.

As a running back I had taken hand-offs in high school, and now without trying I had naturally started quarterbacking our crew. Not because I was a freak for power and wanted to be the boss, but because I just wanted to win. And I knew my vision was unmatched in the crew.

When Bullet and I stepped inside The God's apartment, we quickly noticed a few small changes. On the kitchen table, there was a big glass bowl with fresh fruit sitting next to a dozen beautiful white roses inside a shiny vase. The aroma of jerk chicken smelled amazing and four brand new pots covered the stove. Nikki had let us in through the back door and gave Bullet and me both a hug with little Tootie in one of her arms. The baby had a big pretty smile on her face as it was evident that the ear infection was long gone. Nikki was dressed in a crisp pair of fitted jeans and new black Air Max. She was rockin' the retro '95 editions. Her silky jet black doobie was freshly done and a small gold necklace with a pendant that said "GOD" hung down over her chest. Tootie was dipped in a Baby Gap sweat suit with a matching headband. A suede pair of little baby Timbs looked so cute on her feet. It was obvious that God Body did a lil' splurging with the stacks he was given and if I say I was mad, I would be using the wrong word to describe my feelings. But I'mma keep it real, I was feeling some type of way. I was half expecting to go inside the living room and see Italian leather sofas with big screen TVs and shit. We had given The God's family the money to do whatever they wanted, but I was hoping this silly ass nigga wasn't tryna "ball 'til he fall". Priorities and necessities were supposed to be the only thing on his mind. Times were rough and I wanted to be able to come back to New Haven and see The God's discipline. I never thought I'd be stuck in a stupor in the middle if his kitchen.

While standing over the steaming pots, Nikki looked back and told us to go have a seat in the living room until Germaine, which was The God's real name, came out the bathroom. At that moment, I contemplated grabbing Bullet and driving straight back to the 'Port, but for some reason, I just had to see The God's footwear and count how many diamonds he put in a chain. How hard I smacked the shit out of him was now depending on the size of the baguettes.

Surprisingly, the same living room set appeared when I walked around the corner and the modest TV hadn't been upgraded to an entertainment system with surround sound. To me it just meant more money The God popped off on a new watch. There was no way in hell you could tell me that boy wouldn't look like a rapper when he appeared from the bathroom.

After another two or three minutes, the door to the right of the living room opened and a chest-naked God Body came out shaking his wet hands while spraying Febreze into the air. He closed the door behind him quickly and had an embarrassed smile on his face when he saw us. I couldn't believe that this nigga had on the very same outfit he had on the other day. All black fatigues and scuffed Timbs. I was looking for the jewelry but all I saw was the same Walmart watch. If The God had on a shirt, I would've thought me and Bullet were having *deja vu* and had never left the nigga's crib. But he had on a new pair of red and white boxers and the reason I knew this was because I peeped the dingy white ones while he was holding Tootie the other day. I can't front, my boy had really shocked me. I found myself a little impressed by the content of his character, and when he told me about all the things he had done, I really had to tip my hat to him.

The God had put $400 into the raggedy Nissan Sentra,

and with a tune up, oil change, and muffler job, he had their vehicle now running pearly. The car was front-wheel drive and he only changed the two tires up front because the ones in the rear still had a nice tread. A ride to the Trumbull mall while Nikki's mother babysat had turned into a thousand-dollar shopping spree in the blink of an eye. Everything from Baby Phat, Polo, Coach boots, sweat suits, and seven jeans were rung up at the register. The crazy shit is that all those things were for Nikki and Tootie's upcoming Christmas. The God bought the baby a pair of pretty lil' diamond earrings from Zales, and the gold necklace that Nikki was sporting so proudly came from the same jewelry store as well. God Body then dipped into his bedroom and was all excited to show us what he copped for himself. The things he came back with had really let me know that he was cut from that other cloth I'd been mentioning.

This nigga pulled out five black thermal tops from a Walmart bag, then held up a black bubble coat like the one I wore to his crib last week. The only difference was my coat said "North Face" on the shoulder and my boy God Body's shit said "South Pole" on the back of the collar.

He ain't give a fuck about all the labels, and it was evident that The God was just grateful. A single tear slipped down his face as he recalled how good it felt to buy Nikki and his daughter all the nice things. He said he'd rather make them smile than walk around frontin' like he was really getting money. This was the same shit he used to say while we did laps up the way in the yard. And to now stick to the script while some bread was in your hands took a lot of discipline.

The realest shit ever was when God Body reached in his fatigues and pulled out the receipts to three money orders that he had sent up North to Mega, Dizzo, and Great. He was upset that it was winter time and he couldn't put any skin-flicks in the envelope, but he was hoping they understood and appreciated a letter and $50 apiece.

"I wish I could've sent more, but you know what it is with me, right Monty?" The God asked, hoping he didn't come off as a tight ass nigga.

That was all I had to hear, and I could sense that Bullet was feeling the same way. I was convinced that this nigga was the absolute truth. He filled the kitchen cabinets with canned goods, and the freezer with meats. And after all those other things, he still managed to tuck $1,800 inside his sock drawer.

"I gotta try and hold onto that, feel me?" he said sincerely.

Nikki had come from the kitchen with Tootie giggling in her arms. She told me and Bullet that she would feel disrespected if we turned down her jerked recipe for one of Sandra's dinners. We both agreed to the meal and after taking the baby from his girl's arm, The God was ready to discuss the real business at hand. He had activated a prepaid phone and over the last few days he got the contact numbers of six of his old customers. The God told all the fiends that he would give each of them a call once he had the work in his hand. On cue, I reached inside the inner pocket of my black Avirex leather and set the nine ounces of hard on the coffee table. Tootie was fighting, trying to get down to play with the crack as we continued politicking.

Nikki had brought in a plate, and of course, served God Body first, then me and Bullet were both grubbing a few seconds later. The baby went back with her mother as the three of us were finalizing a strategy over dinner. It would take dedication, but we all felt that this thing could blow. And sure 'nuff, another two hours at the Vernon Street apartment would start proving us right.

Using a new razor, The God chopped a few dimes off one of the ounces, then he called the six fiends to give them all a free sample. Two of the ladies didn't answer, but three other ones and a white guy name Tommy Gunz did. The God met them all a block away from his crib and gave 'em free dimes of base. They all gasped at the enormous size of the rock, and figured the catch would be that the work was garbage. But in the next thirty minutes, the little prepaid phone was ringing off the hook. The God had to run around the corner about six different times. He even met two new fiends who were walking together on Asylum St. They were on their way to cop from the boys on Syl-ville but when they saw the jumbos that The God had, they ended up spending eighty dollars with him.

When me and Bullet got up to bounce, it was 5:10 p.m. and just getting dark. Four hundred and thirty dollars had come through the phone and all of us were amped up. It wasn't enough to pay the rent but the potential was clear as day. All the signs were already there. This was how million-dollar blocks were pioneered. Me, Bullet, and even The God had seen it all too many times before.

When God Body walked us to the back door to see us on our way, Nikki must've heard us leaving because she stuck her head out the bedroom to make sure - for the third time that night - that we enjoyed our meal. Bullet and I again promised that we did, and before making it out the door I heard Nikki call out my name. Stopping me dead in my tracks, she told me how much she really liked my jacket. It felt kinda awkward but I managed to get my lips to say,

"Thank you, Nik."

When I looked over at God Body he sort of had a blank expression on his face. I thought back to him watching from the window as me and his girl shared a hug, and I would've given anything to be able to read his mind at this moment.

I slapped a five with my homie and gave him a thug-hug while telling him to be safe and to hit me if there was a problem. I then followed Bullet to the stairwell and when I looked back, I'll be damned if Nikki wasn't still jocking my Avirex. I could foresee a future problem but had decided to put it aside to get our asses to the stash house.

West Haven is a small, somewhat suburban city, that sits somewhere in between Bridgeport and New Haven. It's about three minutes from Congress Ave. and the Hill section of New Haven, but it's twelve minutes on the highway from my projects in P.T.

There was a nice community college and a lot of back streets where the cops would bust your ass for doing over 15 mph. It was a 50/50 split between blacks and whites, and the houses on most blocks seemed to have their own privacy. While I was in the Bing, niggas from New Haven would tell me how West Haven was the spot to steal go-karts and dirt bikes when they were kids. And snatching bags from white boys on Halloween was the norm. The girls were very easy and vulnerable, so in the summer time, or on school holidays, they would throw parties while their parents were at work. If you didn't pluck a few dimes from West Haven as a teenager, then there's a great chance you're considered a lame.

The small quiet city was so close to where the shots rang out, yet was still very secluded, and seemed so far. It's where all the dope boys from in town came looking for apartments to rest themselves on the low. Somewhere to quietly lay their heads at night after a long day of trappin' in the hood. And with it being a nice ride from Bridgeport, Bullet knew West Haven was the perfect place to stash work. We had all came of age and were no longer petty hustlas. We were buying cocaine by the birds, and had to stay a step ahead of the man, and the jack boys, amongst a few other people. These were just a few things that came along with the territory when you were playing this sort of game.

The stash crib was on a short dead end street named Glen Drive. There was a total of about twelve houses on the block, and they all were either single or two-family homes. Our address was 54, and with no one in the first-floor apartment, we were the only two to visit the house, let alone to have keys to it. We agreed to never bring anyone else there, not even a quick piece of pussy. We now had twenty kilos inside the place and didn't need any jealous bitches stalking the crib when they couldn't find us. The idea was to draw as little attention as possible to a place like this.

We hadn't needed to come by the crib in a few days but now we needed to cook a bird so we could handle our business. When Bullet pulled the rental into the back of the driveway, I could've sworn I saw something dart through the backyard and into the woods. Honestly, it looked like a big ass deer.

"Man, you should see the type of animals that come out in the summer," Bullet said, explaining the West Haven wildlife.

As we both hopped out the V and closed in on the back porch, we found it strange that the door had been left half open. At the same time our brains started thinking the worst. We tripped over each other trying to race upstairs. And when we got to the second floor, the apartment door was knocked off its hinges. I heard a low sickening moan escape Bullet's mouth. And as soon as we looked in the bedroom closet he couldn't hold back the tears. The 3 x 2, 100 lb. safe was gone. And so was everything my boy had worked so hard for. I suddenly thought of the possibilities of it being a dude I saw dash through the yard, and not a deer. I took the safety off the nine Taurus and ran wild through the dark woods. With no idea of whom or what I was looking for, I was ready to make the nine-milli bark.

CHAPTER 12

Staring at the ceiling, Monty laid in his bedroom inside the crib he shared with his mother and sister. He couldn't help but wonder if he was experiencing the same feeling that people in Vegas had after they'd gotten taken for everything. Granted, Monty didn't throw a dime inside the pot for the re-up, but Bullet had been his partner since 3rd grade. So, his loss was their loss. Monty had actually left Bullet a hundred grams of heroin before he went to prison. Bullet had taken a few losses back then and he only had an ounce of dope and a couple pounds of regular weed when Monty left, so the hundred grams of dope from his boy had really set him straight. Bullet did what a lot of niggas wouldn't have been able to do in crunch time. Without fumbling, he took that shit to the moon and never looked back. So, the stacks that were thrown Monty's way when he came home were really his from the start. Bullet always kept it on the up and up with his boy and Monty saluted him for that. It's why he was given 25 Gs and made 50/50 partner.

The two put together a list of suspects for the jux and when they got to a dozen names they knew it was pointless. Starting with the ones that were closest to them, every nigga on the team made the cut for the list. Bullet also threw in The God and a number of other niggas and bitches. Yeah, it's true that they never showed anyone the crib before. But just like they were on their job as dedicated hustlas, you had thoro stick-up kids who had master's degrees in their profession. They'd get the drop on you through other niggas you might be close with. Or even a bitch that knew you had chips and was fucking the both of y'all. While laying on you for days, weeks, or however long it took, you wouldn't notice a smooth jack boy on your heels three cars back. Especially with the stash crib being in West Haven, they knew the difficulty of detecting if it was someone close to them. Twenty kilos in a drought would shine like the bat sign through the skies of Gotham. It would take a lot of discipline for the average nigga not to show out with that type of bread. Even if it was a year from now, Monty knew the little weasel would eventually pop his head out the hole. And he and Bullet would be right there to see who could knock it off first. But Monty couldn't front; Bullet made him look at his boy God Body as the #1 suspect. He decided to watch The God closely. And if he was guilty, he promised to make The God watch while he fucked Nikki before murdering them all.

It was 3 o'clock in the morning and all Monty could do was think about the ideas that Bullet came up with. Robbing Alex was definitely pointless because he never had coke and cash in one spot together. And being straight up with the Dominican about what happened would get them nowhere. Being in the red for two ki's would kill all hopes of him frontin' them a couple more birds to get right. It took them to buy fifteen of them shits to finally get the two that they got. Alex would want his forty thousand, and that would be that. Monty and Bullet only had one choice and that outcome would either make them or break them. But they were real hustlas and Monty knew that there was only one way for them to go, and that was up. He knew one of the most important things in this game was how you bounced back after you fell.

They decided not to tell the crew about the loss at all. For one, they wanted to peep if they could see through any bullshit from any of them. The other reason was not to discourage anyone and make them start feeling thirsty. Bullet knew two other local Dominicans who were known to have good work. The only difference from Alex was that their prices were higher and the fact that they dealt with a lot of other niggas in the city. You never wanted to be tied into the loop with the #1 connect in your hood, because as careful as you might move yourself, his phone may be the Feds target line. And your voice would be intercepted with dozens of other co-d's.

Jose and Miguel both wanted twenty-two stacks for the birds. And because they weren't used to niggas coming to buy five or ten at a time, their price was set and wasn't going to budge. Monty and homie didn't have anywhere close to five-brick money, so the number on the yayo wasn't an issue anyway. Alex's coke was so pure that after they cooked up a whole kilo, a total of nine to ten extra ounces would come out the brick. This is what Grade A coke was supposed to do after you cooked it. It's how the crew still had about ten ounces left from that original ki from Alex. And, Monty had taken nine of those to New Haven for The God to jump off the new spot. So, it left only an ounce for Ro-Ro to take to the projects for yesterday. He had blown through the light weight and they were all pissed when Monty and Bullet failed to handle their end of the business and bring out the fresh bird as promised.

Mind you, picking up that fresh kilo was the only reason for stopping in West Haven on their way back from The God's crib. So, when Ro-Ro handed over cash from the last ounce, Monty held the truth from the crew and came up with some bullshit. The housing manager had agreed on a lease with Tanya for Bldg. 15, and the first and last months' security deposit was the only thing holding back the keys to the new spot. Plus, Lord and Quan had kicked it with their cousins and got the green light to bring a few grams to the North Side. Doing exactly what Monty had asked of them the night before, the whole team was now focused and calling for the ball. Able to put a cool look over his face, Bullet told everyone to fall back for the night and they'd all meet back at the 21 bldg. tomorrow at noon to start fresh. Ready to start trappin', Y.G. put up a light fight, but then decided to agree with the majority. All of this had only been a few hours ago, and Monty had been laying in the bed with a headache ever since.

Lucky for everyone, Bullet used a different place to stash the bread as the white crack rock quickly turned to green paper currency. It was sort of like how Alex moved when they did their business exchange. They didn't keep any of the cash in the same safe with the drugs. So, if one house got hit, they would always have the other to rebound from. The one lone ki that moved in the projects had accumulated exactly $46,800. That amount came from Monty and Bullet when they bagged up eighteen hundred dollars off each of those ounces, then they had split each ounce into two $900 packs. So, whichever crew member moved a nine hundred pack, they were responsible for bringing back $650 to the pot. So, that meant that $1,300 would come back to the pot off every ounce. When you times that by the number of ounces they had, which was thirty-six-and-a-half to be exact, they had almost forty-seven thou. And this wasn't including the ounces The God had in New Haven.

Everyone in the crew was either twenty-one or twenty-two years old, so a lot of street niggas were thinking that Monty and Bullet were pimping their homies. They figured that every grown man should be doing their own thing at that age. Well honestly, they should have long become a boss in their own right. However, everyone's not built to be a leader on the block. A lot of niggas would be fucked up if they had to find their own connect, cook up and chop the work, then be disciplined enough to bring the money back correctly so their re-up could double. Well, Bullet's crew wouldn't be able to get over the fourteen-gram hump. Definitely not Ro-Ro, Lord, and Live; but Quan and Y.G. would probably climb slowly to the top.

By setting a certain amount for them to bring back off the packs, it put discipline into the program and no one wanted to be spotted as the weak link by constantly coming up short. Although Bullet was the head, he didn't think the cash pot was all his. When he went out of state and splurged, they went along and got splurged on, too. Nobody had to bring so much as a dime of their own change for nothing. And no matter how high of a bail bond, an arrest couldn't hold any of them longer than five hours. Plus, when they all went to the car auction with Jamaican Dada, half the paper for their choice of vehicle would come from the cash in the pot. So no, this shit wasn't like the pimp game at all. They were a franchise and Bullet was just aware that he was in the position to lead the team to a championship.

The forty-six thousand and change was being kept over on Linden Blvd. at Bullet's favorite aunt's, Aunt Tiller's house. Aunt Tiller had her own money and she never even so much as smoked a cigarette. So, Bullet always knew it was the perfect place to hold cash. Plus, being close to the highway made it easy to get right on I-95 when it was time to meet Alex. Before Monty and his partner called it a night a few hours ago, they had stopped by Aunt Tiller's place to count all the cash. Bullet had also brought along the four Gs that he had laying around his crib to throw in the pot.

Originally on deck to do bullshit trickin', the few grand was mostly little bills, like tens and fives, with about two hundred dollars in singles. At this point, Bullet ain't give a fuck how neat the money was, or flooding the connect with dollar bills. His whole objective was strictly to now get as many grams as mathematically possible. They wanted to flip the coke a couple times before paying Alex his bread. They weren't worried about him calling for the forty Gs for at least another week or so. And when they had figured out the total that was at Aunt Tiller's, Bullet realized that they were still in a decent position. They just had to go super hard before Alex came around bitching.

There was $50,932 on the nose when the count was in. They both decided to let The God keep setting up shop with the nine ounces for now and collect the money when he finished. Bullet then reached into his pocket and threw two quarters and a nickel into the pot, too. He was all in. At twenty-two thousand a bird, he figured they'd at least get close to 2.5 of them, even if the greedy ass Dominicans wouldn't give them no play. Monty couldn't remember the last time he saw a fire burning so bright in his homeboy's eye. Their backs were to the wall and he wasn't leaving nothing on the table. Monty ran his hands over his thick cornrows and knew there was only one thing left to do. Bullet was his brother. And again, his loss was Monty's loss. Their motto was "united they stand, divided they fall." So, there was no way the twenty Gs behind the dryer wasn't getting thrown into the pot.

It's why the plastic shopping bag was now lying next to Monty under the covers. They were down for each other and had always believed that there were no ceilings as long as they stuck together. It's why Bullet had agreed to go Monty's route if things didn't pan out with the local Dominicans. Monty wanted to bypass them both altogether, but he was willing to try things Bullet's way first. They made calls to Jose and Miguel earlier that night and they both agreed to meet them at their business establishments the next morning.

At 8:30 A.M. sharp, Monty and Bullet pulled up in front of Jose's deli shop on Stratford Ave. Niggas were already on the block catching the early morning dope rush, and the bums had started their day with small bottles of cheap liquor. With burnt orange New York plates, they'd been in the same rental GMC ever since the Expedition was shot up. The young boys on the block had recognized the truck and started nodding their heads like "what up" as soon as Monty hopped out.

Bullet mentioned that he wouldn't be surprised if Jose was serving everybody on the Ave. That's just another reason Monty was happy about the way things ended up going inside the deli.

Jose's store wasn't busy at all this early in the morning and when they walked in Jose left a young Dominican girl to run the register. He shook each of the fellas' hands and immediately took them into a back room. Jose did his business right out of the store with only people he knew, so Monty and Bullet were prepared to make a deal right on the spot. They both had on big leather coats that were zipped all the way up. Stacks upon stacks of cash were thrown down the sleeves and backs of both jackets. They had walked right past a group of knuckleheads outside and nobody knew they both were holding thirty-five Gs apiece on their bodies. Bullet hadn't done any business with Jose in about two years, and after a warm greeting and a little small talk, they were shown a sample of the work.

The cocaine he put in front of them was fishscale. Soft shiny flakes that melted between your fingers with the slightest friction. It was exactly what the fuck they were looking for. Bullet told Jose that they were a couple of dollars short of seventy-one grand and were looking to get three-and-a-half ki's or as close as they could to it. A lot of big connects wouldn't break open a brick to serve someone half-bricks, but Jose was always one who would serve you dollar for dollar on the weight. It just so happened that he wasn't in the position to do it on this day. The nigga only had a kilo and two hundred and fifty grams on deck. And he told them that he wouldn't be back on until two or three days. The little bit of weight wouldn't do anything for Monty and his niggas' situation. They were trying to dump it all and spend their whole hand on the flip.

Jose started negotiating prices, even dropping down to $20 a gram for the last of his coke. But Bullet and Monty weren't trying to be shopping around and spending money with different people. The best deal in this type of situation would be to cop in a one-shot deal. So, they gave Jose dap and both said, "Peace." Jose definitely had fire on his hands with the fishscale, but he didn't have the weight they were looking for.

Miguel was ready to meet with them at 9:30 that morning. His Spanish restaurant was already preparing the *arroz con pollo* and other meals that would be ordered for mid-day's lunch. The up-tempo Latin music was playing low in the background from little speakers hanging on the wall. Sexy Dominican women were busy moving about and they all seemed to smile as Bullet and Monty walked through the door. Every waitress had on black pants with thick thighs and fat asses bulging underneath. As one of them asked Monty how could she help them, another one with a long jet black ponytail interrupted by saying that Miguel was in the back waiting for them. With a mesmerizing smile on her face, she led them through the kitchen area. Monty couldn't take his eyes off her juicy booty as it wobbled with every step. Miguel was an old school Dominican cat with long wavy hair and one gold tooth in the front. Maybe fifty-ish, his dark bronze skin was wrinkle-free and always oily. Growing up, Bullet and Monty both dealt with Miguel on more than a dozen occasions when they would buy grams of heroin and ounces of coke. Miguel hadn't seen Monty since he had been home, and stepping forward, he welcomed him with a hug. A whiff of cologne that an older woman would love, but was a little too strong for Monty, had caught him off guard on their embrace.

Miguel had always respected their hustle and made it a point to say that he still felt the same way. But then he went on to say how he got a bad vibe from Bullet calling him for work after nearly two years of doing no business together. It's a dog-eat-dog world, and Miguel had over thirty-five years in the game. He lasted so long because he always moved wisely. Business was always supposed to be business and never taken personal. Which is why Monty or Bullet ain't feel no type of way standing in front of Miguel in just boxers and socks. Rubber banded stacks of cash fell all over the floor when their coats were un-zipped. Miguel was satisfied after a careful examination and let both of them get dressed. Bullet and Monty knew the request was to look for a wire more than to see if they were strapped, which both of them definitely were. That was common because the handle of a huge revolver was also in plain view on Miguel's hip. Before sitting, he ordered that all cell phones were to be turned off, then they got down to business.

They quickly discovered that Miguel could cover their order, and to Monty's surprise he also agreed to go down on the price to twenty thousand even. Miguel was saying that he really missed their business and wanted to get back in tune. It worked for Monty and Bullet because at twenty Gs a ki, that was seventy stacks for $3^{1/2}$ birds. It was exactly what they wanted and the best thing about it was they weren't asking Miguel for anything on the arm. One of the Dominican mami's brought the work up from the basement and Monty and Bullet inspected the birds while she helped Miguel count the scrilla.

All of the bricks were white and soft, and even oiled up on their fingertips. But Monty and his boy both agreed that the coke had a funny smell to it. The ki's lacked that sort of gasoline smell and had more of a cake mix aroma to them. They were in a restaurant so a stove wasn't all that far away. And since business was never personal, Monty didn't hesitate with his request. Shit, they were made to stand half naked in front of a grown man, so there was no way in hell he was giving up seventy stacks without being able to cook the funny smelling coke in front of the owner's eyes. It would be no room for discrepancies that way.

Miguel didn't object, but he did try to persuade them that they would be wasting their time. He kept repeating that his coke was always premium work. Miguel didn't sell any cook-up at all, so his only condition was that if they didn't buy anything, they definitely would have to buy the work they cooked up.

Monty was ready to leave after hearing the suspect requirement, but Bullet insisted that they at least see what it was. So, they took one of the squares to the stove and after cutting through the tape, they weighed out a hundred grams of powder. They used a big digital scale that Miguel weighed his pork shoulders on. Monty suggested they only cook twenty-eight grams to check its purity, but again, his partner insisted they needed to put at least a buck in the pot to see it really perform. By this time, Monty was ready to give Bullet all the cash except for his twenty thousand and go his own way. But loyalty was everything and Monty's stayed with his boy.

An ounce of baking soda, little water, and a light flame was set to the Pyrex. When the process was complete, the digital scale read 91 grams. The work was definitely not an A+ with damn near losing 10 grams! Plus, it was still a little wet, so Monty figured it would drop to 88 by the time it fully dried. Monty knew the coke was bullshit from the minute they opened the bricks. It didn't have the shiny flakes that Jose's work had. Bullet was thinking he didn't cook it right and had kept it on the flame too long. But Monty knew his boy was just getting desperate and the denial was kicking in. Top shelf powder always came back heavier when you cooked it into freebase form. And it was obvious that the slick Dominican had used cut to stretch and recompress the bricks. But to make his boy happy, Monty broke another hundred grams off the kilo and cooked that batch himself. When the numbers on the digital scale stood steady, the work came back weighing an even 84.4 grams.

It all started to make sense after Miguel had a dumb *ass* look on his face like he didn't know why his cocaine was acting funny. Then Monty realized that was the reason Miguel's stingy ass had gone down on the price so easily. By buying this work for twenty thousand a ki, they would be taking another major step backwards. By the time they would cook up each kilo, it would only weigh eight hundred grams at the rate the coke was performing once it dried. Dope-fiend Troy schooled Bullet a long time ago to not get caught chasing the price of someone's cocaine or dope. He taught him to always be willing to pay for the proper work that he wanted.

Monty was mad as a muthafucka, but on that note he told Bullet to compensate Miguel for the weight, so they could get on with his plan. They cooked two hundred grams of Miguel's coke, so Bullet counted out four thousand dollars because it was twenty dollars a gram. Monty tapped a few figures into his Casio, and before Miguel could stick his greasy ass hands out, he took the cash from Bullet and peeled off six one hundred dollar bills. They may have cooked two hundred grams, but it only came back to a hundred and seventy-five. And by the time it dried, the work would be one seventy at best. So, at twenty dollars a gram, the price would now be $3,400. And that's exactly what Monty pushed forward while gripping the handle of the .45 on his waist.

Miguel pretended to be furious, but deep down Monty knew it was a front. Miguel just felt cheap that two young black kids caught on to his game. He didn't know that they received their lessons from one of the best that ever did it. It's funny, because on their way out, they could hear Miguel talking shit in Spanish while the sexy Dominican women acted busy in the front of the restaurant. Monty thought they all were in cahoots, and had believed that they had a pair of dummies to come and spend a grip with them this morning.

By being so focused and with his head clear, Monty was confident his plan would work. Something told him last night that things wouldn't go right with the local guys. That's why he was glad he thought ahead and played around on Tyshanna's laptop while he laid in bed.

As soon as they walked out of Miguel's restaurant he got the whole crew on the jack and everyone was notified to meet him and Bullet at the 21 bldg., pronto. He didn't give too much detail to the crew once they were there, but he explained how important it was to be on a serious grind over the next few days - even if he and Bullet didn't come around for a couple of days. Monty was depending on them like five-year-olds depended on Santa Claus.

THE BACKSTORY

They wouldn't have the deposit for the new spot in the projects for another week, but the plan was to immediately start beefing up the size of their dimes and twenties to get the money flowing right. Monty knew that word of mouth would get out to all the crackheads about how they were doing it, and by the time they set up the new spot it shouldn't be hard for it to be doing ten Gs throughout a twenty-four hours cycle.

Quan and Live were to hold off for a few days on the North Side move, but were told to be careful not to lose access to that other side of the city. Monty could sense a little worry in everyone's facial expressions, but he made them all poke their chest out when he said that the next few days would expose the weak link, if one truly existed. No one wanted to let the crew down, so Monty knew he had lit a fire under everyone's ass. And as for himself, man, Monty was determined to win. His boy Bullet had held it down, behind the wheel long enough. But Monty was making him pull over at the next rest stop because he was wide awake, focused and ready to drive.

CHAPTER 11

Monty's State of Mind...

For some reason, I believe that all stewardesses had to agree to model a bikini as part of their interview process because they all tended to be hot and have a certain level of sex appeal about them. Bullet had been on a plane over a dozen times, but with me being locked up since I was 18, this was my very first time flying the friendly skies. And just like the fine stewardess that Arnold Schwarzenegger kidnapped in *Commando*, me and Bullet were blessed to be in the presence of an incredible one on American Airlines flight #125 to Tucson, Arizona.

Her name tag said "Angela" and if I had to guess I would say she was African American. But Panamanian or Native American descent wasn't out of the question. She had her long black hair pinned up in a bun. It made it easy to show off her lovely facial features and soft baby hair along her neck and sideburn area. Angela looked like a doll. Her demeanor suggested that she was in her mid-twenties, but Angela's professional, yet very sassy demeanor easily said thirty-ish. I was thinking the Navy-blue blazer was maybe a small, but the hip huggin' skirt was more of a size needed to hold Serena Williams' voluptuous thighs. In a two-inch pair of black pumps, Angela sashayed up and down the narrow aisle, happily serving all the passengers with an enchanting smile. When she got to me, I kindly asked for a ginger ale, and if she believed in love at first sight.

If you didn't grow up like I did, and wasn't getting it how I lived, then you might think me and Bullet were traveling to Arizona as a change from the cold Connecticut forecast and to have some fun in the sun. But if you're a certified dopeboy, that go-getta trapstar, then you know exactly what the fuck I was flying out west for. The money travels west and all the drugs go east. Yeah, that's right, I was going to find a left coast plug for the yayo.

At first, Bullet was a lil' timid when I had my mother book two round-trip flights to AZ. But after realizing how much knowledge

I had on the situation he began to relax. See, my boy knew the game like the back of his hand, but we never really had to travel out of state to shop for connects. Besides the short Metro-North train rides to the Bronx or Broadway when we were sixteen, we had always copped the coke, dope, and smoke locally from low-key Dominicans.

I was tired of paying top dollar for average work on the East Coast. And even though Alex's coke was always fire, he could've also been steppin' on his birds and not giving it to me as completely raw as they came. He probably ain't cut the work to the point where it lost as many grams as Miguel's, but these Dominicans and Puerto Ricans knew all the tricks and trades to this shit.

Alex's cocaine usually jumped back with an extra seventeen or twenty-two free grams, but I wanted to get it from where *his* peoples were getting it from. Where the birds sometimes came with an extra twenty grams of powder packed on the side of the kilo. Yep, raw and untouched, handed over to me directly from the Mexicans themselves.

The idea of flying west and mailing the birds back to Bridgeport had come to me in prison while politicking with Kwame. He was the same dude who had introduced me to the Holy Qur'an, but Kwame was really known for being one of the most ultimate hustlas. Growing up in the Newhallville section of New Haven, Kwame and his little brother Macaroni had become rich by taking next level risks. These niggas flew to St. Thomas and vacationed for a month until they found a West Indian connect who would eventually be their direct pipeline for cocaine and heroin. With the lowest prices for the best product, Kwame and Macaroni were the people you had to see to get work in the Elm City. They received ki's through the mail and both got rich in the blink of an eye. E-190 Benzs and XJ-type Jags were only two of the models in their foreign fleet from the '80s. Between our lessons in the Qur'an, Kwame would entertain me with his coke-tales and give me the game for free while walking the track in the big Enfield C.I. yard. He told me he made over ten million for himself in his four-year run. And he would still be kicking ass if Macaroni didn't screw up mailing one of the packages. Kwame crossed all the Ts and dotted the Is while teaching me the foll-proof way to go 30 for 30 through the air like we watched Kurt Warner do for the St. Louis Rams on Sundays. Yup, without one single package getting intercepted.

The prison-converted Muslim had finished his Fed bid and was serving a consecutive sentence that the state of Connecticut refused to run concurrent. Kwame now had twenty-eight months left before he touched the streets. But his brother Macaroni had turned his fifteen years into life after killing another inmate with a sword-like shank in USP Pollock. I respected Kwame, because unlike my father, Free, his federal paperwork ain't have the letters 5K.1 typed on it. After the lessons on boarding flights to cut out the middle man, I began going to the library to study the world map. I take pride in the fact that I can point out every state in the nation without it being labeled.

Because it was such a small airport, we could not fly directly into TIA from Bradley International, and had to take a commuter flight from the nearby Phoenix airport. As we prepared for landing, the flight captain advised us that the temperature in Tucson was 72 ° on this December night. We were instructed to buckle up, and he brought us down for a smooth landing. We didn't check in any bags so we threw the small carry-ons over our shoulders and moved in a slow pace toward the exit. Angela was posted by the doorway along with another red-headed stewardess. They were thanking everyone for choosing to fly with American Airlines, and when I stopped in front of her she decided to finally answer my question.

"Yes, I absolutely believe in love at first sight. But I also believe that everything that's meant to happen will eventually happen," she said with her patented smile.

Moving through the Tucson airport was rather easy with our light travel luggage. And in a short period of time Bullet and me were behind the wheel of a rental Dodge Durango from Budget. Remember, this was the last month of 1999, so we hadn't yet come under the attacks of Al-Qaeda on the Twin Towers. Airport security was nonchalant and me and Bullet had over thirty Gs apiece taped to our waists. We wore baggy Duke University sweatsuits to hide the bulge of the stacks. After checking in to a modest hotel called "Rooms by the Boarder," we followed the plan that we'd created down to the very last little detail.

THE BACKSTORY

First, we needed two separate rooms on different floors to protect our cash. With a lot of vacant space in the hotel that wasn't a problem at all. Bullet had the key card to room #216, where he cut a hole in the side of the mattress and hid fifty stacks inside. I checked into room #423 and did the same with the sixteen thousand that was left on my waist. I kept a G-note to the side for me and Bullet to split for pocket change. It was what we would use to pop off at a few bars and night spots.

As soon as 8p.m rolled around, Bullet placed the "Do Not Disturb" tag around his door knob before meeting me in #423. He placed his small carry-on on the other bed in my room and then he took the key card to room 216 and slid it under the microwave. There was no purpose in carrying that room key around because we wouldn't need to get back in there until we found what we were looking for.

A few shorties who were hanging around in the hotel lobby told us that we should hit a nightspot called "Club Rolex." They all swore that we would have a lot of fun and it was only twenty minutes from where we were staying. They told us that the crowd was always thick on Thursday nights, and besides a scuffle or two, we wouldn't be amongst any gunplay at Rolex. But we were advised by all means to stay far from the Hot Spot, an infamous club on Allen Street.

Milli, Tara, and Sharice were all cuties and said that if they weren't dancing that night they would've joined us at Rolex. Milli, the redbone one with a heart-shaped ass, had come on strong to Bullet and told him that her stage name was Strawberry.

The girls said that we should stop by Cheetahs to see them dance after we enjoyed ourselves at the Thursday night hangout. After cell phones and room numbers were exchanged, Milli put a bright red lipstick print on Bullet's cheek. I found myself hoping that it would continue to be this easy to meet people.

Rolex was poppin' from the very moment we made it through the door at 10:25 p.m. It was hip hop night so most of the party goers were black and a few Latinos were sprinkled throughout. Our first instinct was to enjoy ourselves and scope out a few honeys to rub shoulders and more with, but Bullet and I had to remind ourselves that we were there to work.

Heading straight to the bar, we could easily feel all the eyes in the spot staring us down. We had changed into jeans and Polo rugbys, and our up North swag had its own place in the club. Sliding between two brown-skinned chicks wearing mini-skirts at the bar, me and Bullet ordered Remy VSOP and two cold ones. When I turned to my left to ask the shorty if I could buy her a drink, two goofy ass dudes basically came with handcuffs and pretty much dragged the sexy ladies away. Me and my boy just looked at each other and laughed. The first thing that came to my mind was what Milli and Tara had said about scuffling being the most that went down. That's when it suddenly hit me that we may have been ushered to the club where the cornballs hang out. Maybe the girls at our hotel couldn't see the thug in us - being dressed in the fly rugbys - and they just wanted us to be safe and have a jolly ole' time. No wonder different scents of perfume tackled my nose when I walked in, and not thick weed clouds.

Bullet suggested that we find spots where all the drama goes down. Where niggas be dumping shots inside the parking lot and putting weed in the air. He figured it would be where all the coke boys hung at. He was making a point, but that's when the bigger picture became clearer. I told him that we needed to type a few Mexican nightspots into the GPS and bypass all the niggas in hoodies and boots. Bullet agreed with my concept and we decided to finish our drinks before blowing that joint. Plus, what we saw next really verified our perception of Club Rolex.

The same two goofballs had met three other chumps in the middle of the dance floor. Me and Bullet just knew these niggas was about to get it on. They were muggin' and the two brown-skinned chicks who had gotten handcuffed were standing behind their two dudes just snapping their necks. I was willing to bet that those two chickenheads caused fights every week.

Dressed in a bright yellow cardigan sweater and brown leather Eastlands, the corniest of the two dudes got in one of the three guys' faces, and out of nowhere this wack-ass nigga started break dancing. I couldn't believe this shit at all. Bullet was just shaking his head at the damn fool. What took the cake was when the challenger grabbed his nuts like Michael Jackson, then started doing the snake all up in the lame nigga's grill. His two goons that were with him were handling the girls by doing the crip walk before raising the roof on them skinny hoes. Man, me and Bullet downed the Remy, but left half-filled Coronas on the bar before getting the fuck outta Rolex.

Two teenage Mexican girls at the Texaco gas station pointed us in the direction of the hottest Latin spot called "La Vida Loca." This former warehouse turned club was packed with mami's wearing tights and stilettos. And all the Mexicanos had red or black bandanas tied around their heads like Tupac Shakur.

Sticky green weed had thick blue-ish clouds circling in the air. The bass line from Don Omar's latest banger pounded on everyone's chest and I could feel it in the air that we were in the presence of hundreds of major cocaine cowboys. Little 5 ft. Mexicans were at the bar with big chains and Paco jeans. Every one of them had a bottle in one hand and a fat ass in the other. A few older Mexican guys were seen walking around with short cut fades and silk shirts. They chased glasses of tequila with long pulls on Tiparillos. From where me and Bullet stood it looked like we were the only blacks in the club. And just like Rolex, our gear stood out from everyone else's outfit.

We paid $100 apiece to club amongst the exclusive guests in the V.I.P. area. And after a half hour, me and Bullet were both mid-way through our bottles of Dom P. The bitches in the V.I.P. area acted way more conceited than the women on the floor. And the status level of the Mexican guys had also made an upgrade. Like Rolex, eyes were constantly staring in our direction, but me and Bullet were saucy from the alcohol, so we were feeling ourselves also. Unlike all the lames at the other spot, none of the Mexicans had brought their handcuffs to the club. So, me and my boy were running up on all the pretty ladies with no static from these dudes. Some of the guys were showing love by toasting their bottles in the air. Basically egging us along to try and score some pussy later.

But when me and Bullet sat and kicked it with a few mami's on the couches, it wasn't pussy that we zeroed in on. It was the lime green bud that one of the Mexican mami's put in a Philly Blunt. They all looked at me like I was weird after I passed on the weed when it came around to me. Shit, I was already hoping that the contact wouldn't stay in my system long enough to fail my next urine. There was no way I was getting violated like all the other dummies who just couldn't say no. I simply refilled my champagne flute and tipped it back while the girls puffed and giggled. I was kinda expecting Bullet to take a few pulls and choke to show the girls we weren't lame, but he also held back and concentrated on getting inside the intoxicated head of one of the mami's.

From out the corner of my eye, I saw a few of the guys paying close attention to us. I was silently hoping that our first impression was going good so far. Of course, Bullet's alcohol tolerance was a bit higher than mine, so after our bottles were done he ordered up another Dom for himself. I settled for just a double shot of Remy straight with no chaser.

By 1 a.m., the crowd seemed to get even crazier. Our entourage in V.I.P. had doubled. Being the only two blacks, we were a hot commodity. All the girls were pissy drunk and took turns sitting on our laps. A little thin one with big titties and a petite, but fat ass inside her skirt, was the one who finally opened the door I was trying to get in. While sitting her bony ass directly on my dick, Choo-Choo pulled out a little makeup kit and poured a small bag of fluffy white coke onto the mirror. Using her driver's license to make about seven thin lines, she then rolled up a twenty-dollar bill and dived in face first. Choo-Choo quickly passed the bill and the kit to her left where a thick pretty chick danced slowly in Bullet's lap. Without using words, Choo-Choo vouched for the quality of the coke by twirling her hands above her head and grinding down on my hard dick like she was trying to cum. A look of ecstasy covered her face as she leaned back into my chest. She was up in the clouds and I knew I had to get at her while she was flying high. The mirror had made its way back to the fourth girl, and the pretty Mexican brick house was now straddling Bullet's lap. She was busying herself by stuffing his face deep in her cleavage.

The V.I.P. area was dimly lit and had plenty of privacy. So, as I reached around Choo-Choo's thighs, I wasn't worried about too many people seeing me slide my hand up her skirt. When I parted her wet lips with my fingers, Choo-Choo moaned in my ear as she opened her petite legs just enough for me to penetrate her pussy. Everyone on the V.I.P. couches were high as a kite except me and

Bullet. So, I took my time and finger fucked Choo-Choo as if we were the only ones in the room.

I stuffed two fingers in that tight pussy and she was riding my hand. The whole time, I was in Choo-Choo's ear whispering that she'd better find me a kilo of the coke she was sniffing. Then, in rapid-fire speed, I would switch up and ask if she was going to cum. And when she'd nod her head "yes", I'd go back to the coke.

Once I felt Choo-Choo's buck-o-five frame shaking in my lap, I knew it was just the right time for me to bring this baby home. She couldn't hold back the orgasm any longer. And right when Choo-Choo's pussy started raining in my palm, I made her confirm to me what I basically already knew.

"You know where to find that kilo for Daddy, right baby?" I asked as her eyes were in the back of her head.

As the words were leaving my lips, I looked to the right and saw that Bullet's pants were pulled slightly past his hips, and the bad bitch whose ear he was in all night was slowly riding his dick up and down. There were three other girls engaged in a three-way tongue kiss, while the other two just laid back slumped in a stupor.

"Yes, Daddy, I'll get you whatever you need," is what Choo-Choo's horny ass was saying in my ear.

About 2 a.m., the girls' coke high had mellowed down enough for them to escort me and my boy around the club like they were showing us off. Bullet was still polishing off the second bottle of Dom. And by now, my second wind had kicked in so I ordered another one for myself.

While whispering in my ear at the bar, Choo-Choo cut her eyes at one of the biggest drug lords there in La Vida. The short stocky Mexican couldn't have been no more than thirty. We then shifted towards the left of the bar to get a lil' closer to the Don. Once we were in arms reach, Choo-Choo acted like she had just noticed him and stretched out for a hug. Never saying a word, the kingpin just smiled while returning the gesture. Still jolly from the unexpected nut that she bust, Choo-Choo pulled me by my arm and began to introduce me. She shouted over the music that I was an old friend of hers and was looking for a kilo. I straightened my face up the best that I could to show papi I was dead serious about finding a plug.

With the same smile he showed when he was returning Choo-Choo's hug, the little Mexican just started giggling, then walked away from the bar. While still never saying a word, he just held up the Corona with an expression on his face like I should probably try a cold one. Choo-Choo was pissed, but I knew the task wouldn't be that simple from the start.

This was a dangerous game we were playing, but I was very patient and down for the fight. Plus, Choo-Choo had cheered up and said there were thousands of kilos between a hundred different guys in the club. She then reached inside her purse and put a $100 bill on the bar for my bottle. I looked at Bullet to make sure he recognized my pimpin', but this nigga was on the other side of the bar tongue kissing shorty. I took Choo-Choo by the hand and drank straight out the bottle while we shopped the crowded club for a sturdy connect.

After being turned down by another dude, plus a tall dyke-ish Mexican lady, Choo-Choo saw a guy named Lou that she knew in the middle of the dance floor. The two of them tangled for two songs while I laid low in the background. From afar I was getting a good vibe from Lou by him smiling in my direction as Choo-Choo talked in his ear. In the middle of the third song she was waving for me to join them on the dance floor. Once I was in the circumference, Lou encouraged me to move my body to the Latin rhythm Choo-Choo then yelled over the music for me to flash a smile for the guy. The request kinda caught me off guard because it was a little awkward, but hey, I was like "whatever."

With the champagne having me tipsy again, I forced a crooked smile for what seemed like a job interview. Over Carlos Santana's smash hit, "Maria", Lou yelled out to Choo-Choo that I smelled like a pig. He then pushed out of her arms and jetted for the door. I stood stuck for a minute, wondering how he could think *I* was a cop. That shit made me sober up. I located Bullet against one of the walls in the back, where I had to snatch his tongue out of shorty's mouth. I was ready to call it a night. Plus, the DJ had yelled in Spanish that it was last call for alcohol as the club was now closing.

THE BACKSTORY

Me and the entourage that now consisted of just Bullet and both girls headed for the exit, and became wide awake in the cool breeze of the parking lot. Only a third of the club hoppers had made it outside so far, and as me and Bullet sat in the front seats of the Durango, our two senoritas were leaning their heads inside the windows. I was behind the wheel, so Choo-Choo's head was in the driver's side window. Her small round ass was tooted up outside the truck. We were making plans for the girls to follow us back to the room and spend the night. I knew Choo-Choo was my way to the yayo and I had to keep her close. Even though we ain't score tonight with finding a plug, it was obvious that she knew people and would eventually lead me to the powder. Even if I had to let her make the deal in my absence.

I think passing on the blunt and makeup kit in front of all the kingpins was a bad look for niggas who were searching for a bird. Everybody in that muthafucka had probably felt like Lou, and had thought we were Feds. We went about it all wrong and I couldn't help but to laugh about it now. However, as soon as I started to crack a smile, with Choo-Choo reaching inside the truck to rub my dick, I heard the shots ring out.

They were coming from my side and I saw the first one rip through the side view mirror. Choo-Choo's little fat ass was still in the air. I looked over her shoulder and saw Lou in the passenger side of an Impala with an army gun. The second pineapple from the chopper knocked off half of Choo-Choo's butt cheek. She fell directly to the ground as I shifted the truck into drive. It felt like a little speed bump when I ran her ass over with the back tire. We made it to the hotel in ten minutes flat and me and Bullet knew that Budget would cancel our ass for sure this time. Renting trucks from their company had been bringing us bad luck lately.

I felt like dawn had come around as soon as we closed our eyes for the night. The winter's sun was peeking through the room between the narrow slits in the tan window blinds. I got up and pissed about a half-bottle of champagne before squatting down and shitting the other half. A long hot shower then brought me back to life, and I sat on the edge of the bed in my boxers and slippers. MTV was airing a new episode of "Cribs," and the boy R-Kelly was walking the camera man through his indoor rain forest. The R&B king was definitely living the life.

At 8:40 a.m., the hotel phone started ringing and caused Bullet to start awakening out of his sleep. I picked up the receiver to hear Milli's southern voice saying good morning. She invited me and Bullet to come to a local diner and join her and her girls for breakfast. She offered to treat, plus show us around the city for the day. She figured we wanted to do a little shopping at the mall or outlets. I wasn't planning to spend any money, but decided that it was probably a good idea to go with them and see what we could stumble upon. I kindly told Milli that we would meet them in the lobby in thirty minutes. And as soon as there was a dead quiet moment on the phone, Bullet rolled over in the bed and farted loud as fuck. Milli yelled "EWWW!" and was calling me nasty. Before I could blame it on my boy, she told me to wash my ass and meet them downstairs. Then her phone line went dead. And the nigga Bullet had the nerve to look at me like I did the shit.

"Auntie's Kitchen" was black owned and managed, so all the cooks in the back looked like their names could be "Auntie." The turkey bacon had a just-right crisp, the grits were lump-free, the eggs lightly scrambled with cheese, and the thick fluffy pancakes tasted like warm vanilla wafers.

One of the Aunties came out with a big pitcher of freshly squeezed O.J. She made it her business to ask if we were okay every six minutes or so. Auntie's kitchen service was unmatched by any diner I had ever visited. And when the bill came I found myself even more impressed with the business. All five of us had "got right" for about $38. Tara paid the bill in all singles and Bullet slapped a dub on top to cover the tip. We were in the smoking section, so Sharice and Milli wanted to enjoy a Newport before starting our day. I told the girls about how they started shooting at the Mexican spot last night and Sharice updated me with the latest news. She said the twenty-three-year-old female was expected to recover after being shot in the ass and suffering a broken collar bone. Milli asked why we didn't follow their advice and stick with Rolex.

Tired of all the bullshit, I decided to keep it one hundred with the girls. I told them that we partied with the Mexicans because we were looking for coke. Sharice blew a long swirl of smoke out the side of her mouth, while easing her head into a "yes" nod. She kept it all the way raw.

Dressed in form-fitting jeans, black leather Dolce boots and a thin jacket, the brown-skinned pole dancer said she knew what time it was with us from the very beginning. She said that's why they sent us to Rolex. I told her that Rolex had put me in the mind frame of an Usher Raymond video and we were looking to deal directly with the Chicanos. Milli chimed in and explained that the Mexicans didn't work like that at all. She said that the drug lords would only interact with people they knew.

With perfect timing, Tara laughed and asked if I was willing to bet that there were more coke boys in Rolex than we would ever believe. With that, she flipped open her Motorola Sidekick to call up her brother - not only to see if he had hit up the club last night, but also to see if he could give her new friends some assistance. After almost geting murked last night by a wild ass Mexican, I couldn't believe how this shit just fell into our lap. Me and Bullet both sat in the booth trying to hide our excitement. JACK POT!!!!

CHAPTER 10

Like any corporate organization or professional team; will, discipline, and endurance is what really built your status. Take President Bill Clinton and the Democratic Party for example. He, Hillary, and the whole committee withstood a tough challenge from the Republicans during the Presidential race. And when Clinton came under fire for a sex scandal, his wife overcame the backlash and absorbed all the blows to her chin. As an outcome, the President succeeded in most of the challenges he faced. And he's considered a hero and a stand-up guy, especially in the hood.

The same goes for Bullet and Monty's campaign party of Lord, Quan, Live, Ro-Ro, and Y.G. Although the crew had been kept in the dark to the steamin' pressure they faced, when they were asked to each play their position in crunch time, everyone strapped up and put on their game face for war. As a result, the team was able to move strongly to the next phase as a unit.

Without seeing Bullet and Monty since Thursday night, Y.G. and the crew felt a big relief when their general, Bullet, had showed up at the 21 bldg. Saturday night. The six and a half ounces that were left to hold down the projects had been finished since about 10 a.m. that Saturday morning. By following the blueprint that Monty had laid out before they left, the clientele from Bridgeport and all the surrounding little towns were knocking down barriers to cop the dimes and twenties that the crew had put out on the strip. Their product had always been a ten in quality, but doubling in size had the P.T. projects booming about an hour after Monty and Bullet had left for the airport that day.

Whiteboys in F-150 pickups, Puerto Rican fiends in RX-7's, and black zombies on ten-speeds were all coming through to cop work. Quan and Lord had put their North Side mission on hold. So, what they did was ride around the city picking up all the baseheads to show them the bags they were giving up. And after dropping them back off at their desired destination, Lord told them that they would get a free dime for every new customer they brought through. Quan boosted the deal by saying that every five bags they copped would also earn them a gift-rock.

The marketing plan had proven to be a brilliant gimmick. Every rock star with a glass dick was making it their business to go out and find new smokers to take advantage of all the crack that the crew was offering for free. In hindsight, the word of mouth would spread fast and the wave of fiends bringing new customers would fizzle out in a few days. Nobody would be waiting on other people to bring them to cop once they heard for themselves that the boys in P.T. had jumbos of hard white; the boys who were sitting inside parked cars around Bldg. 21 to be specific.

The fellas felt comfortable being designated in one spot for the weekend, so while Quan and Lord played taxi in the December cold, Ro-Ro and Live sat in an idling Monte Carlo with the car heat on hell. Y.G. played Quick Draw McGraw and held the gat a few cars down. He watched Live and Ro-Ro's back while they took turns pumping the bundles in and out of 30° temperatures.

One was taking the money while the other pitched the work. They sat inside the V and blazed blunt after blunt, while twisting the top to warm bottles of expensive cognac. No drugs were kept on their person and one bundle at a time was stashed inside of a black tennis ball that had a slit in it. So, getting run up on by the jake while playing sitting duck wasn't going down at all. Of course, none of the customers would peep where the ball got stashed. And if shit got real while making a sale outside the car, the little tennis ball could be launched over buildings and never found in the dark.

Until Tanya was able to get the keys to the new spot, it had been suggested that someone play the alleys 'til at least 2 a.m. But since Bullet and Monty had been gone, the coke rush wouldn't start dying down until the sun was about to come up. Then it would start all over again until it was about to go back down.

Ro-Ro and Live had held it down with minimal sleep and six or so O's had vanished in a day and a half. After paying the runners who brought the new fiends through, $7,800 came back from the work. Now the guys have been waiting around the 21 bldg. all day since that last twenty had been sold.

Now sitting at the round table with the crew, Bullet was sorting through the cash while catching up with the block politics. While Y.G. explained the business, Quan and Ro-Ro put new razors to the fresh hundred grams that Bullet had pulled out of his army jacket lining. Not knowing that they were all just in a bind, neither Ro-Ro nor Quan had noticed how much harder or glass-like the new work was from all the other batches.

Bullet watched as pieces of rock flew across the room as it got chopped by the blade from being so solid. Those are the signs of the product being straight drop. Pure crack, cooked and purified with the minimum of baking soda and water.

As Quan stuffed boulders inside the 58/58 sized bags, the whole crew's hearts had stopped when they heard the banging on the door. The knocking was in a way that only the police did. Lord tiptoed to the door and stuck one eyeball into the peep hole. When his vision became clear, he couldn't believe the shit he was seeing. There were five baseheads posted up on the other side of the door. The shortest one was stretching up on his toes to see if he could peek into the apartment from the outside-in. Live had read Bullet's mind and quickly explained that they didn't serve anyone directly from the crib while he was gone but had been telling the fiends that they would be back in the alley with work in a couple of hours. Ro-Ro threw in his two cents and complained that Bullet and Monty's phones had been going straight to voicemail all day.

Well, tired of all the fucking around, the baseheads were ready to smoke crack. And they were bringing their wild habit straight to the doorsteps where niggas chill at. Crackheads ain't respect shit. But it was definitely a violation and Y.G. jumped up from the table to check their asses.

"Who the fuck told you to knock on this door, Turtle?" Y.G. barked when he snatched it open, making the small-headed zombie damn near fall into the crib.

Shirley Ann, Mike-Mike, Nuney, and Wee-Wee all tried to look innocent - like Turtle had put a gun to their head and was holding them hostage on the stoop. Dope-fiend Troy was also in the entourage, and being an ex-kingpin, he already knew he was in the foul. Dressed in a full jean jacket with fur on the hood, the strung-out legend tried to tuck his head and ease off the porch. The kitchen table with the crack on the plates was around the corner and out of sight from all the wandering eyes. Looking around on the floor for God knows what, Turtle managed to unlock his jaw and said some ole' fly shit.

"Man, I got this white bitch ready to suck a dick and y'all been playing games all day like y'all don't want this money," he said while flashing two crisp hundred dollar bills like he was a boss.

By this time, dope-fiend Troy was a few buildings away and the long tail of his jean jacket was flapping in the cold air. Mike-Mike and Shirley Ann had already decided to spend a couple dollars with a young sixteen-year-old who was hungry enough to still hug the block at 11 o'clock at night. In a clever chess-like move, Y.G. calmly told Turtle and Wee-Wee to go wait in the alley for a couple of seconds. All excited and finger-fuckin' the two $100 bills, Turtle looked at Nuney and Wee Wee and said,

"See, I told y'all this was the spot," before turning on the heels of his borrowed Bo Jacksons.

The same orange and blue ones that Nore rapped about last summer. Lined up like three stooges as they walked off the porch, them niggas fell like dominoes when Y.G. kicked Turtle dead in his ass.

"I told you earlier today that if you don't see us in the alley or sitting in the whips, then that means we ain't on, you silly mutha-fucka. I'mma knock yo' ass out if you come to this door again," the Young Gunna riffed.

It wasn't exactly what Bullet wanted to come back and witness - meaning customers coming to get served from the spot where they chilled. He peeked his head out into the projects and could easily see a welfare line of baseheads starting to point at 21. Ro-Ro spoke up and predicted that P.T. and their bldg. was probably in a position to do about ten Gs a day. He said they easily missed about six stacks by being out of work since earlier that morning.

Ro-Ro totally agreed with Monty that no fiend shouldn't be able to beam up to Scotty at any given moment. Bullet did a "yes-nod" to Ro-Ro's analogy, but he knew they needed to slightly tweak the plans they had made. He didn't like the fact that Turtle and the other fiends knew exactly which building they sat around the table at. So, whenever Tanya did get the keys to the new building, it would no longer be pioneered to become the trap spot. Instead, it would be the new headquarters for them to sit around and politick.

The 21 bldg. was stationed in the back of the projects, so it made sense for it to be the crack house. Lord thought it was a no-brainer, so he shot for the door to be first to set it off. Mike Mike and Shirley Ann's tail-lights were seen leaving the 'jects, but the three stooges had the young boy surrounded like they were about to rob his ass. Dope-fiend Troy was standing under the street light in his full-length jacket like he was Kool Moe Dee in the "Wild Wild West" video. The fur around his hood looked like a wet lion.

Lord did their projects' "bird call" and all the fiends necks snapped back like elastic. Standing in the doorway, he waved for them all to come towards 21. In the narrow hallway of the apartment, Lord explained to every one of the geek-monsters that the crib was now the Mickey Ds of the projects. They would be able to get served 24/7, 365. Y.G. pimped around the kitchen corner with a handful of fat dimes in red bags. Even bigger $20 rocks were stuffed in clear ones.

Turtle must've thought it was another set up, because he flinched when Y.G. reached for his $200 like Red did in the movie "Friday." He thought Y.G. had just made up an excuse to knock his ass out like he had promised. But when he saw the big oily looking rock shining through the small clear bag, Turtle slid his head out of his shell and started picturing the red-headed snow bunny deep throating his dick.

Wee-Wee and Nuney also bought a few of the dubs. As soon as the traffic left the team sat around the table and bragged how they were about to be rich. They sounded like one person in unison when everyone at the same time asked Bullet where

THE BACKSTORY

Monty was at.

Monty stood over the stove while the second batch of two hundred grams cooked over minimum heat. What he was doing was trying to figure out the best calculation and method for the Arizona cocaine to exploit its full potential. The couple of times that he put only a hundred grams in the pot it came back weighing 147 and 151, respectively. And if you know anything about cocaine, then the purity of these birds was self-explanatory.

Sometimes when transforming powder coke to base form, you would make out better when you put more grams in the water to be cooked at one time. But you wanted to be careful and not overcrowd the pot, holding the yayo back from showing off how potent it was. Some dope boys are known to throw a whole kilo inside the glass Vision Ware pots that their grandmothers used for baked mac' n cheese.

Slamming it all like that, the thirty-six ounces in a ki may then come back with twelve free ones in the one-step process. Or in places like Hartford, CT, and some places in the south, it's amazing what them niggas do with a bottle of Poland Spring and a fork. Them boys would whip that raw bird into two chickens and a quarter by getting the base to retain all the water inside the middle. The work would burn clean, but all the suppliers would be getting rich off selling you Poland Spring.

But in most poverty-stricken cities where the fiends are crackheads, and not just casual smokers, man, them muthafuckas wanted that hard clear-like white that was damn near see through. That work that had Ray-Ray peeking out the window like he was brother Malcolm X. Or strung-out Lorraine trying to sell her two-year-old daughter. You know, that straight drop rock.

The first batch of two hundred grams that Monty dropped in the large Pyrex had come back with the numbers 318 displaying on the digital scale. This clearly showed that the coke had performed better when cooking more than a hundred grams at a time. Because when you split three hundred and eighteen grams in half, it was one-fifty-nine. Eight grams more than when only a buck was in the pot.

When Monty saw the coke oiling up in the Pyrex and sticking together in a glob, he knew that the latest batch was ready to be shocked with cold water. With the temperature quickly changing inside the boiling glass, the sticky glob locked up and swelled to be about an inch and a half in thickness. After fishing it out of the water, it looked like a big round rice cake while drying on yesterday's copy of the *Bridgeport News*.

Letting most of the water drain of the crack-cookie, Monty reflected on how being inspired by Kwame and studying the U.S. map had made the risk of traveling west pay off with huge reward.

Monty and Bullet couldn't believe who walked in through the door of their hotel room. Tara's brother was none other than the challenger on the dance floor at Club Rolex. The one who was grabbing his nuts while doing the snake. You know, the cat whose back up dancers were raising the roof on them skinny hoes. Besides having only Tara in the room to make the introduction, her older brother Rudy came all alone to the hotel to see what the business was. Although his swag was on negative zero, and Club Rolex had closed over twelve hours ago, the fact that Rudy was still flanked in the threads from the night before had proved that he was at least a little bit ghetto. He was rocking a brown and green knitted sweater like Bill Cosby would wear, tan khakis from the Gap, and doo-doo brown Rockports. Monty thought this nigga was a 100% herb.

At twenty-nine, Rudy was six and seven years older than Bullet and Monty, respectively. He was only fifteen months older than his little sister, Tara. As much as Rudy looked like a computer geek, he had dropped out of high school in his sophomore year to help the Mexicans carry bricks of coke and dope across the country's border. Not necessarily a mule, Rudy was more of a decoy toting large bookbags and luggage while the real suspects walked over with thousands of kilos. Now with thirteen solid years with one of the strongest cartels, Rudy was honored, trusted, and considered to be a made-man by the family in the small city of Nogales, Mexico.

Rudy explained how the dance competitions at Rolex were similar to how the king of the jungle pissed on the female lions to sort of mark their territory. He then let Monty and Bullet both give their story of where they were from and what they were looking to accomplish. Of course, this all came after questioning if they were officers of the law, or even working with them in any way. For the moment, Tara's sexy ass was just sitting on one of the beds with her legs crossed like a lady. She was pretending to do what her brother had asked her in seeing if she could sense anything suspect about the two. In the back of his mind, Bullet had silently decided that he would be the one to fuck her until she gushed that pussy juice as a reward for turning them on to a good plug. And Monty was thinking the same thing to himself, before Rudy started discussing prices.

Rudy said that he had always wanted to get his foot through the door in one of the East Coast cities that was close to Jersey or New York. And he was ready to do business on the up and up with them, if they could prove their loyalty. He told them that the Mexican's price was twelve thousand for a ki of cocaine, and fifty for the heroin. Rudy told them that at this point and time in the relationship there was no way he was going to assist them for anything less than two and five thousand. Meaning he'd give them the coke for fourteen and the dope for fifty-five stacks. He followed up his discussion of all the prices with guaranteeing that both drugs would be raw and uncut. Unlike how they were after the slick ass Dominicans up North got a hold of them.

Bullet ain't have to tell Rudy this was a major issue on their end, because Rudy's corny ass was truly connected and knew the game for real. He even offered to sell them the "trade" for twenty-five hundred, and teach them how to cut and re-rock both drugs back to a kilo like the Dominicans were doing to them. Seeing the future benefits of the knowledge, Monty and Bullet both agreed to the course at a date in the near future. But for now, they were just concentrating on establishing a relationship and making sure this first deal went down with no problems whatsoever because there was no room for any - with them playing with their last bit of cash.

Being cautious, Monty told Rudy that they were prepared to only buy a ki for starters. But he told them that they were in position to have the bread for four more sent in overnight mail if the yayo was right and he'd do the deal for thirteen a ki. Rudy had already figured they were planning to use the postal service to get the blocks back East. It didn't bother him at all because that's how most people were transporting coast to coast these days. He knew if they started off with five of them thangs, it wouldn't be long for their numbers to be up in the twenty or thirty kilos. And if he had to drop down and do the deal at thirteen a ki then so be it. Shit, Rudy had figured that the quicker they got rich, the richer he'd become. Besides, Rudy was really getting the blocks fronted to him for ten thousand by the Mexican family anyway. The price game that he spit at Monty and Bullet was just a part of the hustle he had picked. up along the way.

Using the hotel room's microwave, an emptied mayonnaise jar, and a piece of a wire hanger, Bullet whipped up a buck of the bird that Rudy had Milli drop off to the room. The coke cooked fast in the microwave and you couldn't really play the way you could on a stove, but Monty and Bullet's only objective was to make sure it locked up and didn't lose grams. It passed all the initial tests when they unwrapped it, but you never knew what you were getting until you gave the bird a bath. There were ways to get around the smell, taste, and touchy-feely test. But there was no way for a connect to get his cocaine to trick you by locking up to a solid, then melting into mush after he got paid and jetted. That shit would either cook and lock up, or not.

Since the mic had the cocaine ready in a New York minute, melting down, then locking up wasn't a problem at all. And after weighing a dollar bill on the digital scale and it reading a gram, it was also proven that Rudy's digi wasn't rigged either.

The big hard boulder smelled like a jar of peanut butter and it weighed an impressive 126 grams. Monty Knew that Alex's coke came back weighing similar numbers, but he took into consideration to the fact that they had just used a microwave, opposed to slow cooking it on the stove. Monty believed that Rudy's work would shit on Alex's coke over a stove's low fire.

The 126 of base and 900 grams of powder that was left from the ki was vacuum-sealed and Rudy suggested that Monty and Bullet rent another room after he and Tara left to store the Brick until the cash was sent overnight. He said that it wouldn't be appropriate for him or his sister to know the room number and it would be better for them all. Rudy didn't know that they already had another room and were one step ahead of him anyway. However, Rudy did insist that they all go out and enjoy the city for the night especially after being clapped at by the crazies the night before.

Monty had done the math in his head and knew that they would only have fifty-two Gs left after giving up fourteen for the bird they just bought. That's why he made Rudy agree to do the last four bricks for thirteen apiece - at that price the four ki's would be fifty-two stacks even.

After ballin' on a budget in V.I.P. last night, Monty only had $125 left in his pockets from the G-note that he split with his partner. And with $146 in his polo pocket, Bullet wasn't doing too much better himself. So hanging out and poppin' a bottle wasn't an option for them at all tonight. Their round-trip ticket was already paid for and they had just enough paper to pay for the five bricks and have them shipped back home through the mail. A super-express delivery would have the package meeting them after landing.

Rudy wasn't taking no for an answer on his invitation and he wanted to celebrate the start of a beautiful thing. After Monty counted out fourteen stacks from the sixteen thousand he had in his room, Rudy, in his Cosby Show get up, told both guys to be ready to make it rain at the strip club later that night. He said for them to not even think about bringing so much as a dime of their own cash. Shit, them niggas sounded like Doublemint Twins when they asked Rudy what time he wanted them to be ready.

About 11:20 p.m., the three of them rolled up in front of Cheetahs in Rudy's silver 1998 GS 400 Lexus. It was a Friday night, and judging by the parking lot, the strip club was on pace to have another jumping weekend. Range Rovers, Benzs, and Caddys sat on oversized rims and were lined up bumper-to-bumper in front of the club. Rudy had even changed his style for the night to a professional businessman's attire in a charcoal gray three-piece Armani suit.

Still not fully adjusted to all the fly labels of the free world, Monty kept it hood in Roc-A-Wear jeans, burgundy suede Timbs, and a matching Champion sweatshirt. Low key, in his usual comfort zone, which was the back seat of the V, Bullet hopped out in cream slacks, and black leather Mauri's to match his black and cream silk Versace shirt. Rudy easily got them past the thick security at the door and them niggas started ballin' as soon as the first thong was in eyesight.

Rudy got a thousand singles for each of them and ordered three bottles of Cristal along with a fifth of Hennessy to be put on a bucket of ice in their booth towards the back of the club. Totally naked, Tara and Milli were over by the stage entertaining a table of go-gettas. Not wanting to be in the presence of her brother and cramping the boys' style for the night, Tara and Milli sent over five of the baddest bitches who were in thongs and stilettos. Two exotic looking Mexicans, Lee and Traci, were built like race horses. Renee and Farrah were the thickest black girls that Monty had ever seen, and a bad white bitch named Lolli Pop had an ass like Deelishis from "The Flavor of Love." Bullet was tongue kissing her in a matter of minutes. Them niggas got pissy drunk, made it rain, and got their dicks sucked all night by different women in the back rooms that were for private lap dances. Rudy ordered another three thousand singles before they threw it all in the air and called it a night at 4 a.m. The business relationship had been solidified and Rudy believed that he had accomplished his main objective which was to let his new East Coast contacts know that money wasn't a thang to him and they were really about to eat.

THE BACKSTORY

The next day around noon, Rudy had no problem believing Monty and Bullet's story that the fifty-two Gs had been flown in overnight. His only concern was if it was all there. Also, for them to make a habit of putting their safety first going forward. Rudy explained how he never did a deal in the manner in which they had done it yesterday, with having the cash and work exchanged at the same place and time. Bullet was all too familiar with what Rudy was saying from being used to Alex's system. But the problem with Rudy requesting the method was that their relationship was all new. So, he and Monty weren't trying to let him leave with their paper at all. True, they did witness Rudy deliver a Grade A kilo the day before, drop ten Gs in the strip club last night like it was nothing, and he even treated the big boy Lexus like it was a bucket over the deep pot holes in the city. But Monty knew from his younger days of going to Manhattan that there was no limit to the con game.

Rudy was not trying to bend and go against his style of business for the second day in a row, but after seeing how much they were really trying to protect their assets, he chose to meet Monty and Bullet halfway with a compromise. He was willing to take half of the boys' money and leave the other half, along with his baby sister Tara, at the hotel with them until he came back with the four blocks of coke. He also suggested that they do business at one of his many homes going forward. Everyone, including Tara, had agreed and Rudy quickly left the room with twenty-six stacks. He promised to bring back four of the rawest birds that they had ever seen in their lives in forty minutes tops.

Thirty minutes later, Rudy was knocking on the room door and Tara was in the process of fastening the last button on her blouse. No, she didn't give Monty or Bullet any pussy or even suck their dicks, but she did entertain them with a very hot strip tease while her brother handled his biz.

Monty thought it was cool to cut a small slit in different parts of every kilo to do a taste, and smell test. But he only felt it was only necessary to cook a few grams of just one of the birds. That way, they would be easy to repackage and hide the smell because the kilos already came wrapped to protect a sniff at the postal service.

This last cook came back with twenty-four extra grams and everyone was happy and satisfied with the deal. Bullet and Monty's flight was in a few hours at 4 p.m., so they had to quickly get their package together and ready to be sent super express. They thanked Rudy for a live night out on the town, and even more for the good blocks of raw. Monty then promised Rudy that he would pay homage to their grind over the next few months. In turn, Rudy promised them that no matter how ugly it got in the upcoming drought, he would never be without work for them to come pick up. And he guaranteed that their price wouldn't fluctuate one bit. Rudy had them locked in at a rock bottom thirteen grand a bird. The fellas exchanged daps and half hugs, and Tara gave kisses on the cheeks before they all left the hotel in its entirety. Monty and Bullet couldn't believe their luck. They had no idea that Rudy would become the best connect that they would have for a very long time. Monty had always been a good judge of character and he felt that Rudy had proven to be sincere and strictly about his business. He and Bullet were able to rest peacefully on their flight back home.

"Damn, this shit jumping out the gym!" Monty shouted to no one but himself when the scale showed the numbers 330.

Bullet hadn't returned from taking the work to the projects yet and Monty was still at the stove trying to finish cooking the whole bird. He was amped up when seeing this last batch gain an extra 130 grams. Monty knew that two hundred grams at a time was definitely the recipe. At the rate the cocaine was jumping, they were liable to get as much as a free six or seven hundred grams off every brick. And this was the coke doing this on its own: without all the wrist tricks known to man. This was the cocaine that the Dominicans were keeping for themselves, or smacking all around before giving it to niggas. While putting the work into sandwich bags of a hundred grams, Monty was thinking that Alex ain't have shit on his guy Rudy.

Bullet couldn't believe all the work he saw on the table when he walked back through the door. Just like Monty couldn't believe the ground work that the team had put in during their three-day absence. After connecting thoughts, the two of them stood over the stove watching as the last batch of the first kilo cooked slowly. Without agreeing on it verbally, Bullet had silently passed the reins of the sleigh to Monty for him to head the team to the top. Just like some guy named Dwayne Wade would put away his pride many years later so his friend Lebron James could come over and lead their dynasty in the direction of history making. Monty had taken a bad situation and now made it a great opportunity. It was crystal clear that his team was simply rich with opportunity.

CHAPTER 9

The God was willing to bet that Monty wasn't expecting him to say it was time to reload when *he* picked up his phone. It was Sunday afternoon and it had only been four complete days since Monty and Bullet had dropped off the nine ounces on Wednesday evening. After not saying too many words during their one-minute call, The God had seen through Monty's attempt to conceal his excitement. Monty calmly told him that he'd be down to the Elm in an hour if that. He and Bullet had only been back from AZ for a day and everything had fallen right into place. It didn't take a rocket scientist to see that New Haven was about to be *a* gold mine.

God Body wasn't new to hustling or getting money on the blocks one bit. Just because Monty met him on a bid that he was doing for a failed robbery didn't mean he didn't know how to flip work. It didn't mean that The God just wanted to take other niggas plates. Nah, God Body was just an all-purpose gangsta who would get it by any means. You know, that thoro street nigga who would build an eightball into a bird. But would still take yours if he caught ya' ass slippin'. A certified dope boy to the heart, but The God had just grown an addiction to following niggas to their stash and taking their safes. It was the reason he was dead broke just a few days ago. He had a certain big fish on his radar and was looking to strike him right before the holidays. There was no way The God was letting Santa skip by Tootie's chimney this season. Not on his watch. But Monty had come through for him. Just like he said he would in the Bing, and now God Body was extra straight. Because not only did Monty come through on his word, but The God had also pulled the heist that he had been laying on. The stash house of a certain big fish was just too sweet to pass up.

The cocaine was like taking candy from a baby. The only thing to do now was lay low and keep playing his position with Monty, since he had looked out for him that much to let him reach his arm to New Haven and take some money that was in his hood. But now that the spot had jumped off in only a few days, The God was already thinking he should become a partner in Monty's program, and not just a lieutenant.

God Body had used his wifey's little brother, Bad Luck, to be second in command for his operation in the Hill. Luck was a fourteen-year-old hard-headed little muthafucka. He couldn't fight, but that boy would shoot the shit out'cha. Bad Luck ain't wanna do nothing but steal cars and smoke weed. He wasn't never gonna amount to shit. But the advantage of recruiting Luck was that The God knew Nikki's lil' brother would be loyal to him. The God had been fucking with Nikki since Luck was in the Third grade stealing lunch tickets out the teacher's desk. It was a step in the right direction to building the team that The God needed.

The God had agreed with Monty's system of bagging up a lesser amount off the ounces. The rocks in his bags were bigger and they made a bold opening statement to the fiends. He had wanted to get the block booming in record-setting time. So, The God actually bagged up a $100 less than Monty actually called for off the 0. God Body knew that he also had all the free coke that he stole from the house, so taking the hundred-dollar hit to get the spot flowing wasn't nothing to him. Once he got the block to start doing four or five Gs a day, that lil' money would come back ten-fold. What's ill is that The God's mind frame and dedication had paid off in only two days.

The God's system was a lot like Y.G. and the fellas had in the projects. Him and Bad Luck had chosen to post up around the corner on Ward St., where The God made the few traps meet him the first night that Monty had hit him with the work. He and Bad Luck sat in Nikki's Sentra which was now running pearly, and they posted one of Luck's lil' dusty ass friends in the hallway of the building. Instead of leaving in the Nissan to go pick up new fiends, The God just paid four of the most popular baseheads to run all the money to Ward St. And because they weren't fully designated to pump outta the building yet, they gave the number to the money-phone to everyone who smoked the rock. While settling into his new position as boss, God Body sat behind the wheel of the bucket and schooled his little brother-in-law. With an open ear, Luck took in all the lessons while gripping the bli˘cky, and watching for stick-up kids from the passenger seat. The lil' dirt bag stayed in the bldg., and made all the sales inside the hallway. The main reason that The God was building his team with young boys was because they were still juvies and couldn't be booked at 1 Union Ave. or given a bond.

They had been playing the Ward St. bldg. from early morning until a little after midnight. At that time, "Dirtbag" would be dropped off at home, and Bad Luck would post up on the couch at his sister's and God Body's crib. The money-phone had Jay-Z's song as a ring tone. And every time it would scream, "Money, cash, hoes. Money, cash, hoes - What!" Luck would grab the gat and meet the late-night money right around the corner on Ward. Fully dressed at all times, Bad Luck ain't wash his ass for four days straight. But I bet he never missed a call after they came in the crib for the night.

Playing fair with his two-man crew, The God properly blessed their pockets for the 96 hours worth of work. Monty had only told The God to bring back $8,400 off the nine ounces. Monty knew it would take time and a lot of groundwork to pioneer the spot and get it running like they wanted. Paying fiends for running the money and a bunch of other expenses had been taken in consideration. Also, when you realize that those same nine ounces were extra grams that came off the bird that Monty paid Alex $18K for, it was easier to understand that the $8,400 was free money at the end of the day.

When The God made the call to Monty in the afternoon, Luck and his little homie only had $300 in dime bags and $440 in twenties left of the work. As far as cash, The God counted twelve Gs and change in wrinkled up, funky money, that even had dried up blood on some of the bills.

Eighty-four hundred was put to the side and rubber banded for Monty. Thirty-eight-hundred of the smallest bills were left stacked on the coffee table. Using mostly fives and tens, with only a couple of twenties, The God piled a G-note so high that it looked more like five grand. He then slowly pushed it over in front of a grinning Bad Luck. God Body dapped his young brother-in-law and saluted him for a job well done. Doing the same thing for Dirtbag, The God had formed a bond with a wolf who would never bite the hand that fed him. This lil' filthy nigga ain't never have shit. He was now ready to go against his own father if The God pushed the button.

Taking thirteen hundred for himself, God Body then folded up the last $500 to give to his wifey. He was only looking to stack two Gs off the work for himself. And the last two bundles that the young boys had would put him right there.

About an hour and a half ago, Bad Luck and his little co-d had pulled up to Vernon St. in a sky-blue Chevy Nova. The two friends had gone half on it and copped it for $500. When they walked into The God's living room them lil' niggas was fresh as a muthafucka. Matching suede Timbs, Enyce jeans, and Columbia coats adorned them both. Luck had a bright red Guess sweatshirt under his red and black Columbia. And Dirtbag was just as coordinated wearing a Pittsburg Steelers jersey and a matching skully. His coat was all black and he wore a black thermal underneath his black and yellow Jerome Bettis jersey. And even though he might rock his outfit for five days straight, Bad Luck's bestfriend's days of being a dirt bag were now numbered. He flashed his fresh gold fronts for The God and displayed his new name. Three shiny teeth on the top, and five on the bottom, spelled out "New Money" in white-gold bubble letters that stood out from the fronts.

Nikki had been out shopping for Tootie's Christmas gifts all day. And she had just checked in with The God to let him know that one of the Africans at Sue's had agreed to come in on a Sunday to braid her hair. Nikki wasn't getting the extra-small micro braids that took five hours to do, but the style she wanted was only a notch or two above. So, she told The God not to expect her home for maybe two and a half hours. She would pick Tootie up from her mom's on the way in, and they would order grinders from Empire Pizza for their dinner tonight.

The God was pleased that he had been able to make his wifey smile lately and appreciate the finer things in life. Nikki's potential to be a dime had been breaking through. The little shopping sprees The God had taken her on had transformed her into a honey that you would see on a low-budget film like *Soul Plane* or *State Property*. Her face was always pretty. And her body was ridiculously toned and curvy. But the glow from her high school years at Career High had suddenly returned full-fledged. The fire between Nikki's thick brown legs had also been rekindled. And her and The God's love making had been smoking hot lately. She was back to wearing sexy nighties to bed and wouldn't wrap her long, layered doobie until right before she knew they were going to sleep. It would be pulled into a ponytail or even cascade down to her shoulder blades while she pranced around the bed room in a sexy gown, playing house with her man. Tootie had been being put to bed rather early over the last week or so, and Nikki had been spending a lot of quarters at the laundromat on Howard Ave. washing her sheets. Every episode of their wet sexcapades had been like those of Latin newlyweds, but the fuck faces and love making had taken the cake.

While job searching and posting her resume online, Nikki's mind couldn't stop wandering off to riding her man's dick. The God was busy handling his business around the corner on Ward St., but would come in every other hour and dump stacks of cash inside one of her Nine-West shoe boxes. Nikki tried to catch him at the door a few times for a quickie, but The God was too much into the block. He was putting that dirty green cream before her sweet polly pure bread. A quick kiss and a thunderous smack across her fat ass was all Nikki was able to achieve. She had been feeling so good about herself, and Nikki wanted to fuck her man real bad, so it was no surprise that she wet two pairs of panties when he was finally in her presence later that night.

It was 12:30 a.m., and The God and Bad Luck had just called it a night on Ward. After a hot shower, God Body thought he was gonna bust Luck's ass in Madden 2000 for a couple of hours but Nikki didn't hide the fact that she wasn't having it at all.

From the middle of her bed, dressed in a black sheer teddy, Nikki sent a threatening text message to The God's phone. In all capital letters, she told him that he had five minutes to come to bed or else. So after scoring another touchdown three plays later with the Broncos running back, Terrell Davis, The God walked into their bedroom in his New York Knicks gym shorts. He had on black house shoes and no shirt.

A quick five hundred push-ups every morning had kept The God's chest beefed up like his first day home. Nikki was laying on her side with her round ass exposed in the see-through nightie. Knowing he was behind her she arched her ass up even more. Nikki's brown body was oiled up and her pretty toes were painted in a French pedicure. She put her hand on her hip and looked back at The God as if she didn't call him and was wondering what he wanted. His stiff hardware was plain to see in the shorts, and Nikki wiggled her ass at him when she noticed the state of his dick.

It was the only invitation he needed. He slid right out of his shorts and came up from behind on his girl. After lightly pushing her over onto her stomach, The God slowly stroked his dick a few times. Pushing one thick brown leg towards the head of the bed, he helped Nikki arch her ass up in the air, and was rubbing her soaking hole from the back in a circular motion. All the wetness made a rhythmic light smacking sound. Nikki was busy fuckin' her man's hand by rotating her hips. She was so caught up in the moment that she didn't realize that she was humping the air after he pulled his hand away from her. Nikki's lover was licking her love from his fingers.

Nikki kept moving her hips in a circle. And before she knew it Nikki was panting as The God alternately slurped then flicked his tongue, devouring her pussy from behind. The God knew exactly what usually drove his girl wild. He wasn't holding nothing back. He rubbed around her ass with his finger while tongue-fuckin' her pussy. Spitting, nibbling, and humming between her legs. Being a total freak in the dark, Nikki loved to get her pussy and ass licked, but she would rather be in a position where she could return the oral favor. She had been hot all day for her man and Nikki's mouth was watering to suck his dick, so while late-night re-runs of "Law and Order" illuminated their room, the two freshly-showered bodies switched positions to engage in a sixty-nine.

"Money, cash, hoes. Money, cash hoes-What!" could be

heard shouting from the living room.

And Bad Luck's construction Timbs stomped back and forth down the hall. Nikki and The God had quickly came in each other's mouths and she was now slow-riding his dick, that wasted no time in getting instantly hard again after a nut.

Twirling her hands through her silk doobie, Nikki's perky C-cup titties bounced lightly on every hop. She locked eyes with her man and her mind and body was in another world. Nikki was staring into The God's soul. Her heavy breathing began to match her pounding heart rate. Nikki was cumming again. But the convulsions in her body had told her that it wasn't an ordinary nut. As she grinded down her hips and took all The God's dick in her tight pulsing pussy, she could hear Luck's Timbs stomping by with DMX still shouting through the speaker. The money-phone was off the muthafuckin' hook and it felt like The God's dick had stretched an inch longer from motivation, punching on Nikki's G-spot and pushing her over the edge.

She dug her hot pink manicure into The God's chest, and made her love rain down all over her man's bottom half. The God knew what this all meant, but was still shocked nevertheless. He knew Nikki was a squirter, but it had been years since she let it go. It only confirmed that he had been making her feel really good about herself. Nikki was never the gold-digging type that was checking for niggas' pockets, but being financially situated could be the reason for a lot of happiness inside a household. The God knew his lady was now very happy indeed because for the first time in years, it felt like she poured a warm cup of water between the crack of his ass when she came.

Spooning in a dry spot that they found toward the left of the bed, Nikki and The God's conversation began to travel on unfamiliar ground over the next half-hour. Through it all, the money-phone wouldn't go five minutes without ringing. The God had always been popular with the ladies, and he never found himself being jealous since being in a relationship with Nik. And although times had been financially tough for him up until two weeks ago, The God never in his life would stay down for too long. He was always known as a go-getta around the way. Even back in their high school days he was known to keep his girl laced. He bought Nikki a black shearling, and also another cream one freshman year. And he copped bubble-link chains and bamboo earrings on his dime all the time back then. Nikki never wanted for nothing since fuckin' with The God from the time she was sixteen. Not to mention that he was the first one to ever fuck her until she came. Her nose was wide open for as long as she could remember. And she was down to thug it out with him through both the good and the bad times. But taking hand-outs from Bullet and Monty had sort of brought her man a ton of insecurities. A nigga who had chips would always seem to be able to fuck the next man's girl. And Bullet was caked up, so The God knew that Monty was sitting lovely on the strength of his man.

After trying to figure out a way to say it, The God told Nikki that it seemed like she wanted to give Monty some pussy. She was automatically sensitive to her man's insecurities, but had still laughed at The God's ridiculousness. Nikki was cracking up until seeing the serious expression written on The God's face. She cupped her right hand behind the back of her man's neck, then looked straight into his eyes while keeping it completely 100 with him. Nikki easily admitted that she thought Monty was very attractive and his swag was through the roof. Upon hearing the actual facts, The God's stomach instantly started turning. He thought he would throw up before she could say another word. However, Nikki swore on Tootie that she only had eyes for him and that it had been that way ever since freshman year. She told him that she had begun to wonder if he was getting jealous from the way she showed love to Monty with compliments whenever he came around. But Nikki explained that the reason was simply because Monty wasn't see-through like all the other guys she had met through him, yet he was still easy for her to read and his sincerity poured from his eyes. She told Germaine that she never got such a loyal vibe from any of his other friends. And she would be very hurt if he showed Monty anything less in return. A woman's intuition was usually right about things of this nature. And even though God Body was all ears, he still chose to approach the situation from a different angle. He had to be sure that no part of Nikki's body yearned for Monty's touch while he came and sat in their living room playing with their daughter.

The God knew his lady was down for him and would play any position he needed her to. So he came with a Bonnie & Clyde scenario to try and penetrate her story. He told Nikki that he knew where Monty and Bullet kept their safe, and he needed her to fuck Monty and help rock him to sleep. He went on to add a little more spice to the pot. Before he could say how much cash was in the safe, Nikki's hand that wasn't cupped behind his neck had come from near her ass and slapped the Wu-Tang Clan outta The God. That nigga's face was on fire. And The God would've thrown a sleeper hold on anyone else, but Nikki's verbal riffing that came with the hand check had proven that she had no hidden interest in the handsome gangsta, Monty.

Tears fell down her cheeks as Nikki asked The God how he could want her to do such a thing. She fought to get out of his hold and leave their bed for the night, but God Body begged her to believe that he was only testing her loyalty to him. Nikki punched, and The God kissed. Then he bit, and she squirmed. And before any of them could say another word, The God was on top of her, long-dicking her down from the missionary position.

Germaine continued to fuck his girl real good until about four in the morning. She erupted in three more intense rainshowers from having her pussy stuffed with his swollen muscle. DMX was still rapping well into the wee hours and it was secretly The God's inspiration for his crazy fuck game. And bright and early this morning Nikki had woken him up to some warm head, hot turkey sausage links, and scrambled cheese eggs, before promising The God that he was all she needed in this world of sin. Nikki also made a mental note to herself to get off Monty's dick.

Monty had hit The God on his cell when he and Bullet were about to get off the downtown New Haven exit. God Body had left Luck and New Money on the block by themselves while he walked around to his crib on Vernon St. He put Monty on to using the downtown exit instead of getting off on the hot ass

Kimberley Ave. ramp. Downtown was literally seconds away from Vernon St., so Monty and Bullet were pulling up in a red Chevy Tahoe as The God walked up to the front of the crib. With a lot of strange things happening in the past week, still, everyone's smiles seemed genuine and the hugs were still tight. There were no question marks or ill-feelings in the air towards anyone at all. It was 6 o'clock in the evening and light snow flurries had been coming down for at least twenty minutes. So, the three jetted upstairs to handle business before the storm really hit.

As The God ran down the details of how he completed his mission, Monty was pulling out a fresh nine ounces, while Bullet fingered through the eighty four hundred dollars. They both knew that there was always a lot of money in New Haven and that The God knew how to get it, but neither Monty nor Bullet thought nine ounces would move so fast without any real promotion or blueprint like they had made for Bridgeport. The God told them about the bldg. around the corner on Ward and how they only been working from out the hallways. But he spoke about being "this close" to having a lady named Rose agree to letting him set up shop in her apartment. Unlike most cities in CT, New Haven was definitely known for having 24-hour trap houses for the fiends to get served. So, it sounded all too familiar to Monty when The God was talking that talk. The God told them that he couldn't wait for them to meet his lil' homies, Bad Luck and New Money. He told them that they were the only two he needed for the moment to take over the whole hood. The God went on to claim that he could see himself being king of the Hill as early as the upcoming new year. And a 50/50 joint-venture between them would only be right. God Body explained to Monty how he came up on a nice piece of change from doin' a check-scam with one of Nikki's friends. He told them he was ready to go half on a bird for a new spot around the corner on Ward. Of course, there was no scam with any of Nikki's friends, and he had really gotten the money by selling some smoke-coke he stole to a dopeboy that he knew from Ansonia, but why would The God want to put that stick-up shit in their heads. So, the check scam was his story and he was sticking to it.

Bullet wanted to smoke The God right there on the spot. And Monty could see it all in his homeboy's face. But Monty shot his man the eye for him to relax and fall back. Monty had felt all the vibes from The God's bullshit, but he hadn't truly convicted him of the heist yet. He knew it would take more investigating and for the nigga to really expose his hand. But all the talk of the 50/50 venture had been expected from the start. It's just that Monty didn't think that The God would be feeling himself so quickly and letting his nuts hang low. But still and all, New Haven's pie was a delicious dessert Monty had to have, especially the Hill side, with it being the biggest neighborhood in the city. And if it took being partners with The God for them to eat out of town, then that's exactly what they would have to do for the moment. With busting the pie three ways, he and Bullet would still get the majority by having two slices. But what The God said next threw them both for a loop. God Body intended for the partnership to be 50/50 and only split two ways. Meaning, he would take a complete 50% half for himself. Then the two of them would be left to slice their half right down the middle. Yeah, Monty and Bullet had extended their hands and put food on The God's table a couple weeks ago, but this was business. And technically, The God wasn't saying anything wrong. He was a boss in his own right and was still anticipating having to bust his gun for the takeover. Not to mention that niggas would pop his top if they knew he had out-of-town niggas eatin' in the hood. And The God wasn't planning on calling his P.T. crew to handle any beef he accumulated. Him, Luck, and New Money would have to push back any nigga's wigs themselves. The God had his young wolves to feed, so nothing less than 50% of the net profit was negotiable. Bullet was vexed, but Monty still saw the plus in the whole situation. The God would control the entire program and they wouldn't be required to do anything but supply the work and keep their eyes on the profit. And by supplying the coke, Monty saw another way for them to get ahead on the strength of The God's labor.

The God had no right to know about Rudy, or Arizona period, for that matter. As far as God Body knew, him, Bullet, and Monty would still be scoring locally from Alex, at nineteen thousand a ki. And when the drought really hit in a couple of weeks they would definitely knock The God in the head by charging themselves twenty- eight to thirty grand a bird. But the whole time they would eventually earn back the money for the twenty kilo's that Bullet swears The God robbed them for. And as soon as they made up for the loss and profited substantially from Ward St., they would have Y.G. make The God put his mouth around the pistol. Chess was Kwame's expertise in the joint. And Monty had quickly learned his every attack. He understood that life was a lot like chess.

While in the middle of agreeing to their partnership with daps and hugs, Nikki had walked in the crib and into the living room. She had a bundled up Tootie hanging from one arm and an Empire Pizza shop bag in the other. She lowered Tootie to the floor for The God to pull his daughter out of her snow suit. With both hands now free, Nikki came out of her butter-soft leather and pulled the scarf from around her head. She had the same style braids that Janet Jackson rocked in "Poetic Justice." Nikki's slightly chinky eyes made her look like Lee-Lee from the R&B group SWV. A pair of form-fitted black jeans clung tight to her every curve. And thigh-high leather boots arched her fat ass from the small heel. Nikki had gotten her brains fucked out of her last night and it showed all in her smile. Monty had known she was a bad bitch behind her tacky ass wardrobe, but the shopping spree and braids had Nikki straight shining. Monty had silently wondered what it would be like to fuck her doggy-style before pushing her scalp back. He found it quite strange that she wasn't jocking his new leather and Vasquez Gore-tex. Nikki dryly said hello to Monty and Bullet before heading to the back of the crib. The God was highly pleased with his lady's attitude as he placed a warm kiss on the tip of Tootie's nose.

CHAPTER 8

Monty's State of Mind...

O ne thing I could credit my pops, Free, with was that he schooled me at a very young age how to recognize mistakes and not make the same ones twice. When I damn near sliced my ear off trying to shave with his razors at five years old, it was guaranteed that I would never fuck with his Gillettes again. And the time we were at Toys 'R Us and I got caught with a Macho Man Randy Savage doll down my pants had taught me that someone was always watching you in the department stores no matter what.

Even learning from the mistakes of others was just as good as them being your own. Like the time when we were seventeen and Hard-Headed Sammy collected everybody's money before going to see his connect. Bullet and my whole project gave up their chips in advance for the ghost grams. At the time, I had been dry and out of heroin for three days, but I ain't give Hard Headed Sammy a penny of my cash. I preferred to hold on to mine than for him to bring back some garbage dope or possibly nothing at all.

Well anyway, Hard-Headed Sammy took the train to meet his cousin in East New York. On their way uptown they got lured into a thick dice game. Nothing was celo on the three dice, and you couldn't roll to a six or triples. Those were the set rules. Seventy-five hundred was in the bank and niggas had been dying to the deuce all day. But you couldn't tell Hard-Headed Sammy that the nigga holding the dice ain't have a weak arm. Sammy felt there was no way Son could out-roll him on the dice.

The first bet Sammy made was to stop a buck, throwing down a crisp hundred-dollar bill. Dude shook the dice and let 'em go after kissing them, making everybody losers by rolling a six. Two hundred dollars was then stopped and another six prevented everyone from even touching the dice.

After rolling yet another dick on the dice, then back to back triple squares, Sammy was down thirteen hundred and everybody in the projects' grams were looking to be short. But without even touching the dice one time, Hard-Head believed he could come up once he got them in his palm. There was no way Son was going to keep winning with no rollers. So, after feeling his left eye twitch, Sammy jumped out the window and stopped two stacks. He wanted to get his bread back plus a couple hundred of Son's money. The three dice bounced around on the cracked curb and a deuce was the number. Feeling cocky, Hard-Head Sammy was the first one to jump from the curb to smack the deuce on its ass. He even laid another stack on the ground claiming that he'd roll a three or better. Sammy's celo arm was usually strong, and rolling a tray was nothing to him. Plus, being his first roll of the day, he knew he could throw a big number. Sammy shook the dice and blew over them before letting them hit the ground. One, One, and after the last dice winked on a six, it landed face up on a two. Sammy didn't throw a three or better, plus he died to the deuce. He lost his whole project's money, and Son from Brooklyn sold the bank for $50 and bounced.

When Sammy slid back to the projects later that night, he ain't have not one gram of dope for niggas. But he did have about fourteen nickel bags of blue funk skunk. He told a sob story that he got stuck up for the bread then stole somebody's bundle of weed from the trash. The skunk was the real deal and niggas got high as a giraffe's ass in stilettos. But when the flame on the last blunt was put out, Bullet and two other niggas who had lost their grams literally beat Hot-Headed Sammy's ass like he stole something. So yeah, I learned from Bullet not to use another niggas' connect unless I was dealing directly with them myself. You gotta limit the liabilities on your cash. The fewer losses you take, the quicker you could reach the top. It's all easier said than done in this game of hustle we play. Everything's a gamble when you're depending on that flip. You win some and you lose the rest. But a dedicated hustla was gonna get rich or die trying. As long as you were free and alive, you had a legitimate shot to strike a million cash. My boy Bullet was well on his way before I came home and we took that hit. But I already told you that my determination wouldn't allow me to lose. It was all about making adjustments and how you reinvented yourself after you fell. In a perfect world, I would have told you that my team's reign was a walk in the park. But the robbery in West Haven already showed you that nothing's guaranteed in this shit. Yeah, I ended up sitting on a few mil and was able to get out the game before Tarahji smoked me, but there's still many answers to a whole lot of questions you may still have. So, let's cheat and fast forward a little bit so I can tell you how that bitch of a wife did me dirty. But it's only right that we start with the fetti situation with Alex.

CHAPTER 7

The 21 bldg. in P.T. had become an overnight success. And about a week and a half after opening up the spot, the coke drought had finally hit full-fledge in the city. Out of nowhere, all the hustlas were scrambling for coke when they woke up early one morning. Very little work was available in the city. And the few Dominicans that were holding a little coke had a price on the powder that a lot of part-time dopeboys couldn't afford. Niggas like Miguel and Jose were hitting niggas for thirty dollars a gram. And they weren't letting anyone buy a whole kilo to try to knock their price down.

Alex had called for his cash a few days after Monty and Bullet touched down from AZ. They had his complete forty racks on deck like nothing had ever happened. Y.G. and the crew had the $7,800 when Monty came back from out West. And The God's eight and a half stacks put them a little over sixteen thousand. From the time Y.G. had kicked Turtle square in the ass, the 21 bldg. did exactly eleven Gs in the next 24 hours. They quickly rubberband twenty-four more thousand and hit Alex with his cash. Now designated as Bullet's old connect, the fat Dominican, Alex, was also feeling the pressure of the drought. His shipment had been cut down to twenty-five bricks and he had thirteen left. Alex just knew that Bullet and Monty were going to jump on them for twenty-seven Gs apiece. He couldn't believe the shit they were saying - not wanting to cop even one of the birds. And what Alex did next let Monty know that there was truth to what Kwame had taught him about the droughts. Kwame had said that the prices never fluctuated for none of the true suppliers. And even in a drought when their shipments might be scarce, they wouldn't be charged a penny more. The connects knew the block workers would profit thousands more on breaking the grams to dimes. So, they simply seized the opportunity to charge more for the weight. Alex then dropped the price to twenty-four thousand, then stalled out at twenty-two, before realizing Monty and Bullet were good and must have found something better. It meant nothing to Alex because he'd eventually get the whole twenty-seven thousand and maybe a lot more depending on how long it stayed dry. Alex had his set people and didn't try to branch out to new places. It would just take him a lot longer to finish now because he lost two good men in Monty and Bullet.

With their $40K bill out of the way and minimal competition on the street, Monty was able to put all his focus on maximizing the come-back cash on five ki's from Rudy. With the prices on cocaine skyrocketing because of the drought, the few hustlas that did have work were stretching the shit out of it. Not only were they loading the coke up with a ton of baking soda, but niggas were bagging up about $3,500 off an ounce. Monty knew the rules of the drought, but he considered it a sin to be stretching three Gs off an Oz.

All the kilos that they had gotten from Rudy had continued to put up Shaquille O'Neal numbers. They got all the extra grams that niggas were now beating the work with Arm n' Hammer to get. But the straight drop was like that '80s crack that had ammonia in it. That shit was frying the wigs off all the baseheads.

But Monty really fucked the game up by still stuffing their bags with jums. So, all the block huggers who thought they were smart and kept their work fire for the fiends to smoke had to go back to the drawing board. They may have matched the crew in quality, but they couldn't fuck with the quantity that was stuffed into the bags. Going against everybody's grain, Monty was only bagging up $2,500 off an ounce, so the 21 bldg. had the fattest twenties in the city. Everyone else was paying top dollar for the powder so they would lose out trying to compete. But for them boys in the projects, it was like having their debut album go diamond. Ten million sold. And them boys ate fast.

Monty and Bullet had paid a total of sixty-six racks for the five kilos, which was 5,000 grams. By the time they finished dropping all the birds in the bath, they had 7,895 grams of straight drop crack. That was almost three ki's for free. Those were the perks of having a direct line to the raw cocaine. That meant Monty's formula on the stove had brought back two hundred and eighty-four ounces altogether. When you times that by the $2,500 they would chop off every O, you got $710K. But don't think that's what Monty and the crew would have after every gram was gone. Nah, the drug game ain't work like that. You gotta factor in shorts and all types of expenditures; like bills, living expenses, and money for the team to build their own personal stashes. Plus, the system with The God had gone down just like Monty predicted. So, with that New Haven pie being sliced two ways, that would further shorten up that seven hundred large.

Bad Luck and New Money were basically responsible for turning Ward Street into a million-dollar block. They used the same formula as Monty getting only $2,500 off an ounce. But there were more Dominican connects in Bridgeport than New Haven, so the Elm City was a lot drier than Monty's hood.

The baseheads in the Day St. projects couldn't find a rock to save their lives. And when they did, they were better off putting a Jolly Rancher inside their pipe. A lot of niggas in the Hill, Ville, and Fair Haven had straight garbage and had literally resorted to putting pieces of sheet rock inside of bags. The lil' scam artists made thousands off the dummies. So, when the word got out that two little boys had that '80s base on Ward St., crackheads from every hood started walking, taking cabs, and riding bikes in the snow to cop the work.

In no time, Bad Luck and New Money had that shit doing nothing less than fifteen Gs a day. The God set the record last Friday clearing an even twenty in one night. He began to brag to Monty afterwards, claiming his mission was to break down a whole bird in one day. Monty knew his boy was just talking to be talking, but still he amped The God up to try to make the shit happen.

With cutting the Ward St. pie two ways, the profit on the bricks that The God moved was not as substantial for Monty as the ones that Quan and the team pushed through 21. They only paid thirteen thousand for kilos from Tucson, and had made up a little of the lost profit by telling The God that they were buying the bricks from Alex at thirty Gs apiece. The ticket in New Haven was thirty-three points a joint, so God Body ain't really know no better anyway. With him fronting half the buy money as a 50/50 partner, the fifteen Gs that The God put up was more than enough for the whole ki that they went half on. Then they would bust the come-back cash down the middle, which was about sixty stacks apiece after paying Luck and New Money's little asses. It was Monty's way of making The God pay back the money from the twenty missing kilos whether he had taken them or not.

Christmas time had been unbelievable for Nikki, Tootie, Tyshanna, and everyone affiliated with these niggas. And some time in the third week of January, Monty was ready to go back to Arizona. Him and Bullet left the projects and Ward St. with half a kilo apiece. And this time they flew with sixty-something thousand in all $100 bills. The bulge underneath their clothes was no bigger than the bulge from the first flight with all the smaller bills. They were going to get twenty bricks and planned on having ten mailed back to two different spots in Bridgeport. So, in just one month, Bullet and Monty were back where they started, times two. It's how real champions performed when playing from behind in Game 7. You left everything on the floor and put all the other bullshit to the side. And so far, Bullet ain't have no problem at all with playing Robin to Monty's Batman.

Rudy's apartment in Tucson was decorated and laced like a bachelor's pad would be. He had brightly colored furniture, a built-inside-the-wall shark tank, and big screen TVs everywhere. Even a stripper's pole was off to the side area of the entertainment room. And a marble-top wet bar was stocked with only top-shelf liquor. It turned out that Rudy had stuck to his word in securing everyone's safety. They now had private places to do their business instead of in public hotels, so no one had to rush or worry about unexpected guests popping up at the door.

Still geeky looking, the only change in Rudy's appearance for the new year was the fact that he cut off the little peach fuzz of a goatee he had under his chin. Rudy's preppy get-up still reminded

Monty of Cliff Huxtable. And he still couldn't believe that the cornball was really the plug.

Rudy knew the up North duo weren't the average hustlas from the very start, so he wasn't surprised when Monty told him that they came for twenty birds. The grind had shown in both of their eyes from the beginning and Rudy knew that the sky was the limit when fuckin' with them. Rudy was so connected to the drug lords that he was able to tell Monty and Bullet how badly their whole city and state was in an uproar for coke. He told them that it would be nasty for at least a couple more months and they should really "milk the cow" for as long as they could. Rudy couldn't believe when they told him that they moved the ki's on the block in all dimes and twenties without selling any weight. He knew right then that they had to have made a crazy profit off the flip. And quite naturally for a hustla, Rudy quickly tried counting their pockets. He was wondering why they didn't come for more than twenty kilos if they had seen so much cash back from the last flip. Playing mind reader, Monty spoke up and said that they had to get their safes back right after almost losing everything. But he assured Rudy that this was just the start of the beginning. Monty told him that his goal was to one day come and get a hundred of them thangs. All Rudy could do was laugh when they asked if he would be able to cover the order. After assuring Monty that he would be able to, Rudy admitted that it was the type of order that he had been waiting to see from them. And although he was dead serious, he wasn't just stroking their egos when saying he knew they were more than capable of doing it.

Rudy double-counted the sixty grand by hand, and just like the first time, it was all there. Not a dime more or less. There was still a little resistance on Monty's end when Rudy got set to take the bread until he brought back the coke. But Bullet's attitude was relaxed and calm, so Monty also fell right in line after a few minutes. Plus, Tara's sexy ass was there and still used as collateral. And having Rudy's baby sister would always guarantee their coke.

Give or take a few minutes, it was the same exact process with the cornball. As Tara heard the dual pipes to her brother's

Shelby Mustang pull into the yard, she hopped her thick ass off the pole and slid back in her jeans. The strip tease had gotten a little hotter this time around, but still neither Monty nor Bullet had gotten a sample of none of that southern pussy.

Rudy understood that the relationship with the two was still forming its bond, but he was trying to do everything he could to show Monty and Bullet that he was the absolute truth. He knew they didn't have to open or cook up none of the work, but the business side of things ain't work like that at all. Still, he kept repeating to them that they'd only be wasting time with having to repackage the work. However, after choosing thirteen random kilos to slice open in different parts, and then cooking grams from three of those, a satisfied Monty had given Bullet the nod that he felt everything was copey. The birds were then rewrapped and resealed, then taken to the post office to be sent in regular postal mail. No same day super express was needed this time. And once again, the fellas enjoyed a second night of ballin' at Cheetahs on Rudy's dime. Monty and Bullet woke up with hangovers the next morning before flying back up North.

The year 2000 started out on a great note! It marked the rise of a young crew who would take the game to a level that nobody in Bridgeport had done since Free, Manchild, and all the Freeman boys back in the eighties. The 21 bldg. in the projects had continued to rock and roll. And although Ward St. would never match the twenty-grand day again, as far as Monty would know, it remained consistent with doing seven to ten grand a night.

The spot had seemed to slow down a little and The God blamed it on a surge of cocaine brought into the city by a new group of Mexicans. But Bullet believed God Body had started filtering in the kilos taken from West Haven. He felt The God was lying when reporting that the block was only doing eleven stacks when all the checks came out on the first of the month. Bullet believed he was doing ten to fifteen thousand more with his side hustle. But even when The God popped up with a new black Benz on Valentine's Day, Monty still wasn't convinced that the bread came from the caper. Shit, if that was the case, then Monty felt that Ro-Ro and Lord were also suspect. Them niggas bought twin 540 Beemers with the tiptronic shifter and sport packages.

Even though the whips were two years old and 1998s, them shits were mean and ready to go, and had cost a grip. Monty's whole team was eating so purchases like that were destined to come. Y.G. had the big Q45 Infiniti and Quan copped a Lexus LS. By Memorial Day, every one of their personal safes had over a hundred thousand in it. And you could argue that Monty and Bullet were about to split a million between the two of them. But they were at the top of the totem pole. They were the captains of the ship. Those two were the very cause of all the success from the start. Ro-Ro was comfy in his position. And Live was the happiest he had ever been in his life. Y.G. got his dick sucked every night by some of the baddest bitches in the state. And you couldn't tell Lord one bit that he wasn't hood rich.

Even Bad Luck and New Money had gotten out the Nova they shared. Them niggas were pushing Honda wagons and Acura Integras with racing pipes and 18" wheels around the potholes in the hood. Both of those little boys were quickly sitting on over thirty thousand. And grown women were fucking them for bedroom and living room sets from Bob's. And yeah, The God was definitely being slick and double juggling from Ward St., but Monty was still seeing his share from the spot, plus taxing him on the bricks. Bullet was mad about the whole damn situation and was just waiting to push the button to release Y.G.

The warm spring months came and led the way to a scorching hot summer. The coke prices started coming back down by the end of April. The twenty bricks from Rudy had held the crew over until the middle of June. And Monty couldn't believe the cash they had on deck when only thirty ounces of base was left.

After all the shorts, taking care of the crew, and only getting 50% from New Haven, he and Bullet saw nine hundred and twenty thousand come back off the flip. And when you added the quarter million dollars that was still sitting - left over from their first trip to see Rudy - these two childhood homies now had a million-dollar friendship. But there were a few things that needed to be discussed before going back to Arizona.

Bullet was in more of a rush to get a couple million to the head, so he wanted to go back and get maybe fifty or sixty ki's. And since the drought had eased up and the prices were pretty much back to normal, Bullet thought it would be a good idea to come back and wholesale most of their order. Selling at least forty bricks to outta town niggas in Waterbury and Hartford was an easy way to get a quick $320K. Monty knew that Bullet's figures were on point, and branching out to those cities was something he also had on his radar, but Monty didn't think it was the right time to start wholesaling and he just wanted to first secure their stash. He was against going out West and risking seven or eight hundred thousand through the mail at the moment. Monty felt that they should double back and get the same twenty kilos as the last order. They would have a million dollars apiece when they ran through it all. And once he broke it down to his partner, Bullet fully understood Monty's logic. At that point, they would then be in position to risk more through the mail.

Regardless of how many birds they copped, Bullet knew that about half of them would get run down through The God on Ward. Although The God's numbers no longer matched those of the projects, Ward St. was still consistent enough to clear a kilo a week. Monty pointed out the fact that the last twenty kilos of powder kept them from needing to fly out to AZ for about five months. He reminded Bullet how much fewer trips out West meant to all of their safety. He thought the best thing for them to do now was to split a million cash down the middle then stash five hundred Gs a piece in the wall somewhere. Since the prices had dropped back down Monty was going to tell The God that Alex wanted twenty-two a ki. That meant that God Body would have to put up a hundred and ten stacks to go half on ten of the twenty bricks. Because they were really getting them from Rudy for thirteen a pop, he and Bullet would only have to drop a buck fifty for twenty kilos. Monty still wasn't sure if God Body had really taken their coke, but he started realizing that it would be much cheaper to keep The God around. The God was basically buying his own bricks, moving the work, then splitting the profits with them.

After seeing it like this, it all started to make sense to Bullet. He shook his head then asked Monty how did he come up with some of the shit that he did. Monty went on to explain that together they would still have a million in cash between the walls of their cribs and after only putting a buck fifty towards this flip, there would still be about a hundred grand to play with. Monty figured they'd keep it real with Rudy and handle the bill this time at Cheetahs. Plus, Monty was digging the new T-Rex bikes that the Ruff Ryders had in their videos. He wanted to be the first nigga in Bridgeport peeling off in one of them shits at the upcoming Puerto Rican Day parade. Last year a Puerto Rican nigga named Pichon had shut it down with a purple and orange Can-Am Spyder. But the flamboyant Puerto Rican with dreads wouldn't stand a chance this July.

The fall came and went, and the winter brought the prices back up just a little. Dick Clark hosted another New Year's Eve party in Times Square and 2001 started off on an incredible note. However, it would eventually veer off track a little down the line.

First, the lovely R&B princess, Aaliyah, passed away. Then a couple of weeks later a few U.S. planes were hi-jacked and flown into the Twin Towers. Families lost thousands of loved ones, but more importantly to Monty, was the beefed-up security at all the airports - not to mention the inflated prices on coke. Keeping the number the same on a man-made drought was one thing, but the September 11th attacks even forced Rudy to go up on the birds. Importing and distribution in the U.S. had suddenly become an obstacle for the cartels.

After hours of negotiating, Rudy set the new price at sixteen a ki. Getting into the Tunnel nightclub in Manhattan was now suddenly easier than getting into a major airport. Only a fool would try to fly with more than nine thousand dollars in cash. Monty had started mailing the re-up money out West a couple times like he mailed the coke back East. Even all the new steps at the post office were becoming too big of a gamble. Because of all this, they were forced to completely change the game by 2002. But he and Bullet were both millionaires and could afford to do it of course.

They purchased a 1999 stretch limousine and secretly installed a sliding floor. It was a Lincoln Town Car and older family members were trained and hired as personal drivers. The hidden compartment was built to easily hold fifty bricks and a chopper Army gun. They arranged two trips out West that year - in '02 - with the stash box filled to capacity on both rounds. Changing with time, Monty had begun wholesaling bricks only to niggas from outta town. He and Bullet paid for Rudy's lesson on re-rocking the blocks and it became just another way to beat The God in his head.

Tara had finally proved that she was just a jump-off by letting Monty and Bullet gang bang her while Rudy would take the bread and come back with the coke. She would take one dick from the back while the other one would be humping her face. It's crazy because all three of them would always seem to cum right before her big brother returned. It was a big change in how things used to go down in 1999 with just a strip show. But other than that, everything was the same for the most part.

Bad Luck and New Money were still eating and finally became hood rich. They were now seventeen and had more paper than the average grown man. Thirty-year old women cooked them dinner and punched holes in condoms before riding their young dicks. Them scandalous hoes were trying to secure their futures with babies.

The boy God Body had bought another Benz. But this one was for Nikki to congratulate her on finding a good job. Tootie was doing awesome in kindergarten but was starting to get a little grown.

Monty's sister Tyshanna graduated from the University of Bridgeport and was becoming a social worker. She was already conjuring up ways for Monty to get out of the fast life and start investing his money.

The team was on top of their game by the end of 2002, and everyone was in a good place, with the exception of Y.G. While going against his own rule, the young gunna had caught a raw deal after deciding to fuck a jump-off in her second-floor apartment down in New Haven.

Quita was a super thick, twenty-six-year-old hood rat who used to dance three nights out the week at one of the many strip clubs in Bridgeport. She was almost on the chunky side, but not quite – with a very pretty face and a big 46" ass. Y.G. had paid for a private dance the very first time he saw her making it clap at Terry's. Right there in one of the back rooms, he melted in her slippery pussy for a measly $60.

After leaving the stage to pursue a new career in check fraud with the slickest nigga in New Haven, named Kurt, Quita's crib was suddenly laced with new living room sets, TVs, and washers & dryers. Her three little boys all had race-car bunk beds. Quita was balling. She still had Y.G.'s number stored in her Nextel under the name "Prime Choice". When she wanted some beef, he never failed at knockin' Quita's pussy out the box after poppin' a blue pill. Nobody could seem to make her cum as much as the tall lanky Y.G.

On a hot summer night in July of '02, Y.G. was on the second floor at 592 Button Street. He was sweating like a runaway slave while digging a new hole in Quita's big ass. It was only the second time she had tried anal sex with him and the new-found orgasm was head-spinning.

Ray-Ray, Jr., and Lil' Daddy were full of Nyquil and knocked the fuck out, while their mother had her mouth stuffed with a pillow and her ass in the air. The new posturepedic mattress, that was courtesy of a scam at Rent-A-Center, had them feeling like they were fuckin' on a cloud. Avant's new album knocked lightly in Quita's dimly lit room. And Keke Wyatt told everyone that there was "nothing in the world she wouldn't do for you, boy."

The song was Quita's jam and the only reason she stole the album from Walmart in the first place. The lyrics always made her think of Y.G. She had been wanting to handcuff him to her headboard and wife him up for some time now. He plunged in and out of her tight spot and they both moaned loudly with pleasure.

Neither one of them heard Quita's baby daddy stumbling

through the dark crib.   That bitch ass nigga had skillfully climbed up the back porch onto the second-floor balcony. From there, he slid through the open kitchen window with ease. When the night stalker busted into Quita's room, her brand-new CD started skipping, and KeKe kept saying "boy-boy-boy," while her baby daddy tried to bull charge Y.G.

The condom was filled with cum and after quickly getting out of a headlock, the rubber slipped right off Y.G.'s dick. With Sugar Shane Mosley speed, he caught her baby daddy with a hard right and knocked his ass out for a hot two seconds. It was just enough time for Y.G. to grab the hammer from under his Polo boxers and click the safety off. Quita's baby daddy was thinking they was gonna grind out a fair one, hand-to-hand, but Y.G.'s skinny ass wasn't trying to fight shit.

With a slug already in the chamber of the four-fifth, Y.G. squeezed three times on the trigger and lifted the nigga right off his muthafuckin' feet. While Quita was barking into the Nextel, Y.G. had just enough time to get dressed and peel off in the Q45. And even though she wanted to wife him, Quita was still in love with the father of her youngest son, Lil' Daddy. She didn't know Y.G.'s real name, but she had enough information for a warrant to be drawn up on him for attempted murder.

When Y.G. got bagged, his bond was court set at $350K. Although he had plenty of his own cash, the whole crew came together and put in three Gs apiece to come up with twenty-one stacks to spring him. Lord, Quan, Live, Ro-Ro, Bullet, and Monty all dropped change from their own stashes. Bullet was surprised that The God had even come down on the bond. For all of his own reasons, Bullet still believed The God was a snake in the grass. But for the time being, Y.G. was home and his case had been put on the trial docket. But for some reason no one seemed to be worrying about trial. It was like they depended on nobody being around to testify. These niggas had too much paper. And we all know that money is power.

On Memorial weekend 2003, Monty was flying to Arizona to handle the business side of the deal with Rudy. Bullet had gone down to Miami Beach with Live and Quan. So Monty took the trip alone for the first time since meeting their connect.

Quite naturally, the relationship with Rudy was remarkable by this time. Technically, Monty didn't really need to be present for the trip at all. The limo driver was set to drive out West, so Monty could have arranged for the deal to go down in his absence since the cash would be on deck. However, these decisions are what separated the boys from the men. Monty manned up and put Miami Beach on the back burner to see the fifty-ki deal go smooth.

While waiting at the Delta terminal in Bradley Airport, Monty sat next to a very sexy woman who was boarding the same flight to Phoenix, then Tucson. She traveled in professional attire; black pumps and a matching business pantsuit. The red blouse underneath her jacket had the top three buttons undone. The opening showed a nice portion of a smooth, round brown-skinned cleavage. On her couple of trips to the refreshment vendors and restrooms, Monty became mesmerized by the way her plump booty swayed in her fitting pants.

The woman was slightly bowlegged, exposing a small sexy gap between her inner thighs with every step. She was absolutely stunning. The sweet pea fragrance she was wearing, shortened Monty's breath when they crossed paths at the register. The lady's long black hair was pulled back in a ponytail. Mac lip gloss made her lips look enticingly wet. Her exotic features and skin tone made it hard for Monty to put a finger on nationality.

Unafraid to approach her, he went over and sat directly next to her inside the terminal. When she told him her name, Monty immediately started thinking of the sexy black actress who was fairly new on the scene. The butter and caramel smell from a Worthers' Original made her breath smell inviting. Her big smile and the sparkle in her eye told Monty that she wasn't at all annoyed by his presence. Monty had never been next to a woman who made him catch butterflies before. Like the up and coming actress from the movie "Baby Boy", this sexy brown honey's name was Tarahji. Ms. Tarahji P. Valentine.

CHAPTER 6

Monty's State Of Mind...

It's no secret that I was just running game when I asked the sexy stewardess, Angela, if she believed in love at first sight. Yeah, I had bumped back into her on that first return flight from AZ and she was amped up about all that "everything happens for a reason" bullshit. I mean, it wasn't love at first sight at all for me. However, I did end up knocking her fine ass off a few times. I was getting money, so you know flying and meeting up in places like Vegas was nothing for me. Plus, with her position with the airlines, I wasn't paying much for the tickets at all. Angela started catching a few feelings but it was strictly lust for me. The thrill of fuckin' a sexy older woman gave me the ultimate rush.

It was the same way when I saw how Tarahji moved through the airport in her business suit. I wanted to undress her right there in the terminal and press our bodies against one another - maybe fuck her a few times then change up all my numbers on her ass. But it was a totally different story by the time we separated at the Tucson airport.

Me and Tarahji sat directly next to each other on the not--too-crowded Delta airline flight to Phoenix, Arizona. We were even able to continue our conversation on the small connector plane to Tucson. And in six hours we told each other almost our whole life stories. Well, at least evrything we wanted each other to know at that point. The fact that she was part of a cartel who was looking for an East Coast contact, and me declaring that I was him, was never mentioned at all. Tarahji told me that she was simply a director at a medicine company. I claimed to be an up-and-coming music producer who was highly inspired by the Bad Boy record movement. As far as our trips out toward the deserts, well Tarahji said she was going to drive across the border to see her

Mexican side of the family. And me, oh, I was going to lay down some tracks for a hot new rap artist named Rude Rudy. We both found it a coincidence that we lived just mere minutes apart in Stratford and Bridgeport, yet, had never come across each other until flying cross country to the same city. We knew it was a small world, but still, we couldn't help but laugh at how strange life could be.

As with all my flights, there was a very sexy stewardess flying with us yet again. And Tarahji and me took full advantage of being able to drink on the airline. We laughed and toasted to things like the lost lives of the 9/11 victims, Beyonce and Jay-Z's relationship going public, and even Tom Brady winning the Superbowls. Tarahji had moved from New York and become a huge New England Patriots fan. She grew up liking the Dallas Cowboys only because of her father's loyalty to Tom Landry's team. The closest thing the airline had to Hennessey was Crown Royal, so I put the brown liquor on a few rocks and got a little bent. Tarahji sipped on Absolut and cranberry juice the whole time.

Tarahji told me she was thirty-seven and had a nineteen-year-old daughter who was a Freshman at Howard. I thought maybe the alcohol had started kicking her ass and she was misjudging shit. I knew she was a grown woman from the start, but I was willing to guess she was merely five years my senior at thirty. Her skin was tight and wrinkle free and Tarahji took pride in the fact that her jet-black hair was her natural color without a strand of gray. She was a natural beauty like Selma Hayek but much thicker in the ass and thighs. We exchanged numbers before landing, then went our own separate ways with different business to handle out West.

My stay was always a day at most, so there was no reason to try making any plans while across the coast. Tarahji was staying in Mexico for a week and said we'd go out as soon as she was back up North. A knowing smirk suddenly came over her face like she was hip to my bullshit, as if a music producer really flew all the way out west to make tracks in one day. Before hopping in her cab, she wished me good luck with Rude Rudy; then while shaking her head from side to side, she told me to be careful.

Not only did I take Tarahji out as soon as she returned home, but I was the one who insisted on picking her up from the airport. She was prepared to pay a $100 cab fare from Bradley International to Stratford, but as a gentleman, there was no way I was letting it go down like that. I was on time for her landing and even carried her light luggage to my rented Chevy Lumina. Our conversation picked up from where it ended in Tucson: we didn't need any music to fill the space at all. Our chemistry together was evident from the very start. She was actually the one who suggested we go out to eat later that night. And like somebody just waiting on that special someone to pop the big question, I gladly accepted.

Our first date was to a Hibachi restaurant in Greenwich. It was cool and we ended up seeing one of the actors from "The Sopranos" and taking a photo with him. We treated our bellies to a wonderful meal and shared laughs over a bottle of red wine. I entertained Tarahji with stories of playing running back at Central High and the excitement she showed for the sport made me wish I had stayed. We both agreed to take a couple of trips to Gillette Stadium in Foxboro, Massachusetts the upcoming year. Then she told me how her company gave out tickets to the Knicks games all the time. I didn't want the night to ever end, but when it did, I couldn't ask for a better conclusion. Tarahji invited me inside her crib to have more drinks and hang out for a while. Before we knew it, we were engaged in a soft wet kiss. We weren't ripping each other's clothes or anything. It was quite grown; sensuous and slow. I didn't try to advance at all, and I think that went far in Tarahji's assessment of my character. I could tell that she was doing certain things as if to test me. It didn't bother me because I was already convinced that she was the woman of my dreams. Very beautiful, smart, and independent with a career. I started thinking that she would be sure to lose her interest once she figured out that I was knee deep in the cocaine and not a music producer.

It didn't help that I started fumbling when she inquired about the music biz. She just chuckled and finished her wine while shooting me a crooked smile. When she walked me to the door about 1 a.m., she said something that wouldn't make sense to me until about a year later. After a friendly punch in the chest, she told me that I seemed to be very street smart. She then laughed and said I was exactly what she had been sent to CT for.

Days passed into weeks, then weeks turned into months. The Spurs had gone on to beat the Detroit Pistons in six games for the NBA title, and now the NFL rookies were showing what they were made of in the preseason games. Tarahji was souped on what Bill Belichick did with the Pats in the off season. And she jumped into my arms when they were predicted to do a three-peat. Our late-night kisses were now steamy but I still hadn't so much as sniffed the pussy yet. Every time our hands were all over one another it seemed like it would abruptly end with both of us just giggling. I was trying to play my cards right and wait for a sure sign that she wanted the dick. But after a 37-0 New England blow-out over the Bills in Week 1, Tarahji took the initiative to show me just how flexible she was at forty years old.

Dressed in a ladies' Patriots jersey and boy-shorts, Tarahji's pretty, bare feet stepped towards me during the post-game show. She sashayed over and stopped right between my legs. There was a look in her eyes and a smirk on her face that I had never seen from her before. However, I would become very familiar with it after this night.

Tarahji's body and stance was so ridiculous that I was able to see highlights from the *GameDay* through her bowlegged gap. I had on a white Nautica T with red and yellow water craft on the front, and my blue Nautica sweats were already sticking up in the middle. My all white Air-Forces were by the front door, where she made me put all of my footwear since day one. Only Tarahji's kitchen, bath, and dining room weren't covered in wall to wall cushion-like beige carpet. No, she wasn't stuck up at all nor did she think she was better than anyone else, Tarahji just had a lot of class and her home was her sanctuary, it was also becoming my place of refuge.

Pulling me up from the sofa, she asked me to raise my arms as she took off my T to expose my chest that was still stocky from my push-ups in prison. We came together for a passionate kiss and her soft mesh jersey felt good against my bare chest. The swollen muscle between my legs poked Tarahji's stomach and I had her fatty cuffed in a firm grip. I had noticed some time ago that she got turned on from having her juicy ass squeezed and rubbed. Tarahji began to melt in my arms, barely able to wrap around my broad back, she gently pushed off of me and ran her hands over my chest, then down to my abs. She finally rested her fingers inside my sweats and around the shaft of my dick. She took her left hand and started pushing my sweats and boxers down and around my ankles, never taking her hand off my throbbing gearshift.

Of course, I complied and stepped out of them one foot at a time. With the exception of a pair of white Nike ankle socks, I was standing ass naked in front of one of the baddest women I had ever seen in my life. Tarahji then pushed me back down on the suede mint-green sofa and fell between my legs with her knees planted in the 1 1/2" carpet. Her soft wet lips worked around the head of my dick while her delicate pretty hands just held it from the base. After a few strokes up and down, and in circular motions like cranking a motor cycle throttle, Tarahji took me deep in the back of her throat. She applied so much spit to her epic, ocean-wet blow job that my balls were soaked. My head fell towards the back of the sofa and my body was taken over by the heat from her mouth.

Tarahji moaned softly, getting pleasure from the oral herself and the only break she took was to come out of her Tom Brady jersey and let her braless perky titties make a guest appearance. Me and this woman had almost led to having sex on a few different occasions, but we would always seem to snap out of the moment as soon as my dick started to leak. But she now had her titties out for the first time and 80% of my dick rammed in her head for the moment. A part of me was just waiting on her to say that maybe it was time for me to leave. However, what she did next let me know that Tarahji was finally ready to be fucked.

Like magic, Tarahji pulled out a special non-latex condom from thin air. 'Til this very day, I believe she had that shit stationed under the sofa or somewhere. She was allergic to regular brands and would become irritated from the material. I honestly ain't give a fuck where she pulled it from, what brand it was, or even if she had one at all. I had wanted that pussy since being in the Bradley Airport terminal and wasn't trying to waste another second once I had the green light.

After about five minutes she got up from her knees and slid the boy shorts from over her hips and down to her ankles. Her Brazilian wax exposed a pretty pink pussy with a swollen clit that seemed to automatically protrude from its hidden spot. Man, this woman sat on my dick and rode me so slowly and seductively that I almost lost my damn mind. She leaned in and let me taste a titty a few times, but for the most part she wasn't trying to break her stride. Tarahji rode my dick like a mechanical bull until we both shouted from our orgasms. It was only our first round, and that night set the tone for a monogamous relationship filled with hot, spontaneous, sense-exploding sex.

Over the next couple of months, I would bring Tarahji grilled chicken salads for lunch and fuck her on the desk inside her office. We fucked inside the truck in the parking lot of Foxwoods Casino like we were both young and in heat. Tarahji even rode my dick for five minutes inside the last cart of the haunted house mansion at the Big E. I was only the eighth guy to fuck her, and it worked for me because the limit for my future wife was always set at ten. Our sexual attraction was crazy and we weren't able to stay away from one another for much longer than her eight-hour shift at Bayer

Before I knew it, the 2003 X-Mas holidays were around the corner and I felt it was the perfect time to introduce Tarahji and her daughter, Lala, to my family; my sister Ty and my moms. Tarahji had also suggested that I cut my cornrows for the new year. But before anything, me and Bullet had to finally make the long-awaited trip that was planned to last us about a year.

Before I left for AZ, I ended up telling Tarahji the half-truth about my profession. I came clean about not knowing anything about making a beat, but admitted to doing grown man business in Tucson with Rude Rudy. Yeah, I kept his stage name alive for my testimony, but that was the extent of the information

I gave her about my connect. I confessed my love to Tarahji, but I told her, "God forbid there would ever come a day when it would be better for the both of us that she didn't know exactly what I did for a living."

She took my truth on the chin, then made a joke by saying if I did what she thought I did for a living, then I'd be surprised about the things she could teach me. She did her impression of a B-Boy stance and we both cracked up laughing. I took her to be such a prankster and found her professional ass trying to B-boy anything to be funny as hell.

As soon as me and Bullet walked through the doors of Rudy's crib, he handed us both chilled bottles of Rosé and saluted us on accomplishing our goal. It's what I had promised him when we first established our relationship exactly four years ago this time. I had vowed to build an empire and one day come and cop a hundred bricks. We could've dumped our hands and bought the buck two years ago, but there are methods to hustling, and strategic planning went a long way in this game. Instead of dipping into our safe, me and Bullet let the flips build and reach a hundred blocks on their own. And we still tucked away crazy stacks on every re-up. Now with $1.3 million in cash set to reach Tucson inside three cars in a couple of hours, we were two and a half weeks from 2004 and becoming multi-millionaires on individual levels.

I had called Rudy in advance and used minimal words to make sure that he was able to cover our order. He answered my question by simply telling me that he couldn't wait to see me. So, after careful planning, me and Bullet paid for three Chrysler Town & Country minivans to get outfitted with stash boxes. All the vans were going to be outfitted the same gold color and equipped to hold forty bricks apiece. A three-car dolly and two drivers were then hired to haul the vans out to the West Coast. We scanned car dealer forms and placed them in the windows of the used, but mint conditioned vehicles to give the impression that they were going to a car lot. But the vans would transport a hundred ki's back to Connecticut on the dolly with no reason to be searched at all.

Rudy owned the home that we were in and we had

actually used it to do our business on the last two trips. The 1,800 sq. ft. home was usually laced from top to bottom with name-brand furniture and electronics, but Rudy had recently put it on the market and it was now cleaned out. No large sofas, paintings, or projector screens in the house at all. Just cold pizza in the fridge, three fold-up chairs, and a 19" flat screen sitting on a milk crate. Rudy said he was looking to make a substantial profit after the closing. I made a mental note to talk to Tarahji about investing in rental properties as soon as I got home. I wasn't really trying to sell cocaine for the rest of my life.

Like always, Tara showed up to the crib to hold up her end of the deal and be held as collateral. She had on a sweat suit with red and white Air Max and it was the first time I had seen her out of designer jeans and heels. It was a real good look because the soft cotton material couldn't contain her ass from wobbling like crazy. I suddenly couldn't wait for Rudy to take off and go get the coke so I could pound out his little sister. Last time Bullet had become greedy with the pussy from the back while I was limited to fuckin' her mouth. The played-out strip teases were no longer the choice of entertainment and we usually pounced on her as soon as Rudy's engine came alive outside. And with the dolly on schedule to pull up at the residence in another ten minutes, my dick had already begun throbbing.

Rudy's crib was situated in the middle of two huge acres and sat about forty yards back from the road. There was a long narrow driveway in the front yard. L.B. was behind the wheel of the dolly and Rudy met him out front to tell him to pull it around to the back of the house. So, if anyone happened to pop up they wouldn't peep our layout. Me and Bullet went out and climbed up into two of the vans to retrieve the cash from the compartments. Both drivers, L.B. and Tex, came inside to take a piss and took their asses back outside to sit in the truck. The exchange usually took an hour tops to count the bread and get the work, so them niggas were straight with sitting out in the dolly for a few.

Changing his style, Rudy was prepared to count the cash with a money machine for this re-up. By having all hundreds and fifties, the mil and change took about forty-five minutes to run through. A DVD player was hooked up to the small 19", and the movie *Paid in Full* was playing on the screen. Rich Porter had just come home and "A" tossed him the keys to a new cherry-red drop-top Bimmer. Rich's man holding it down for him reminded me of Bullet holding it down for me while I was away. Man, they just don't make niggas like that no more.

Rudy's frail ass struggled to carry the two duffle bags out to his old-school '87 IROC. As soon as the dual pipes barked on the Chevy, I was tugging on Tara's Juicy Couture sweatpants. I had to get the jump on Bullet before he tried to hog the pussy again. Tara kicked the Air Maxes across the empty living room and wiggled out of her sweats and top in no time. I beat Bullet to her backside, so he already had his dick up in her face while I was unbuckling my Gucci belt.

I tore open a Magnum, then rolled it on while Tara gagged on Bullet's dick for a few sloppy slurps. With lust in her eyes, she said she needed to pee before getting filled with dick from both ends. Tara's freaky ass wanted to fuck just as bad as we did. She quickly dashed for the bathroom to hurry up to get ganged-banged for every minute that her brother would be gone. We heard the toilet flushing and the sink's faucet running to wash her hands. On the DVD, A.Z. was lured to the crib by the Kermit the Frog-looking Calvin and before you knew it he was popped in his nugget for fronting on opening the safe.

As Calvin had his goon turn the music up to drown out the gun shots in the movie, our own living room became crazy loud. I grabbed the remote and turned the volume down and heard the water still running from the bathroom's faucet. At that point, my spidey senses started tingling.

With my pants hung around my ankles and dick still rock hard, I hopped to the bathroom and busted in the door. The bathroom blind was pulled up and the window was wide open. When I leaned over the tub to look out, I saw Tara's round ass bouncing around in the wind. The idling IROC was waiting at the end of the dirt road. When Tara reached the passenger door, she jumped through the window before Rudy kicked up dirt in the

THE BACKSTORY

Chevy.

Man, you couldn't pay me to believe this shit was really happening. I turned around to jet out the bathroom and tripped over my jeans and almost broke my dick. Bullet must've already known what time it was because I was staring directly at his backside while he bent over to pull up his pants. Then he shot out the front door as quick as lightning.

It turned out the nigga Rudy had been laying on us from day one. Popping off Gs at the strip club because he knew it was all an investment anyway. Rudy's corny ass was the only child and Tara wasn't his sister at all. But she was his bottom bitch and he had loved her just the same. He had been fuckin' Tara for years and she would do anything for him. Can you believe I let this country muthafucka rock me to sleep? See, I told you there were no limits in the con-game. Remember? Well, I was now prepared to live out in AZ 'til I found this fool.

CHAPTER 5

While everyone was waiting on Lala's arrival to enjoy Christmas dinner at Monty's mother Lakiya's house, the sex-addicted college sophomore was busy committing another one of her most scandalous acts. After fuckin' one of her favorite side-flings to sleep, Lala posed in front of his camera phone while she snapped a picture with every inch of his soft dick stuffed inside of her mouth. She had been fuckin' Mook ever since her Senior year at Stratford High. And the slightly older auto mechanic had been in a serious relationship with another girl the whole time. Lala had never met Hook's shorty, but she respected his situation from the very start. That is until the nigga slipped up and let his wifey find text messages that Lala had sent him while in class in D.C.

Mook's girl then got Lala's number and was calling her a side show, plus threatening to whup her ass. The 1/3 % Mexican mami had no problem with being called a homewrecker, whore, or nasty side-piece. Shit, Mook wasn't by far the only woman's man who she was fucking. And Lala felt if bitches couldn't keep her man's bone buried in their own asses, then they ought to expect him to stray out in the streets and try to piss on every hydrant that he saw.

Lala felt that Mook's wifey had the game fucked up. She should've been checking his ass instead of calling Lala's phone to the point where Lala had to change her number. So, for that, Lala had captured time with a clear image of her committing her deliciously lewd act. It's exactly what niggas did to chickenheads anyway: secretly recording bitches on their cell phones while they came in their faces or while fuckin' them from the back. The only difference here is that it was Lala who went through Mook's call log and sent the picture message to the name labeled "wifey."

While Lala slipped into her jeans, Mook was slumped across his futon in the basement of his mother's house. His chest rose and fell, up and down, and Mook's mouth was gapped wide open. It was another stellar performance by the good girl turned nymph. Lala had fallen in love with the feeling of being fucked hard and deep, having her squirting pussy drip between the crevices of her thick inner thighs. She was infatuated with the way a man's dick pulsated in her mouth right before he came. But Lala didn't think she was a whore, no, she was just single and hardcore with her mingle. She didn't care about fuckin' somebody else's man to feed her own sexual hunger.

By the time Lala tied the laces to her four-inch, Jimmy Choo heels, and slipped into her leather jacket, Mook's phone was vibrating from an incoming call. The name "wifey" was flashing across the little clear screen. Lala felt joyful as she tossed the thin, razor-like phone across Mook's chest. She then strutted to the cellar door to see herself out the basement. With a silly dazed-ass look on his face, Monkey-man Mook pressed talk and immediately knew he had fucked up.

Over the past couple of days Monty and Tarahji's relationship kept proving that it was built to last. Monty had come clean with his girl about his situation and the million-dollar loss in Tucson. Before he let his guard down further, it took time and a lot of promises from Tarahji not to place judgement on his choices. Tarahji had rubbed his back and repeated numerous times that he could trust her with anything. She also admitted to the fact that she might even be able to help. Her compassion was cute, but Monty was no longer in the mood to laugh at her subliminal shots of acting like she knew something about the game. However, Tarahji was now his lady and she was the only person he felt comfortable telling how he had been conned.

Tarahji acknowledged that the loss was tremendous, but she assured her man that it wasn't the end of the world. She pointed out the fact that at least he didn't take his last to Arizona, and so Monty was still in a better position than 98% of other hustlas. She promised her king that better days were to come.

While watching the NFL countdown on ESPN last Sunday morning, Tarahji had stepped out onto her balcony in the cold to place a call. After a ten-minute conversation, she came back and took her seat next to Monty on the sofa. Playfully pressing her freezing cold hands into his broad bare chest, they began to wrestle after Monty protested her actions. While T.J., Jimmy Johnson, and Boom made their early game picks, Tarahji ended up riding her man's dick right there on the sofa. Just like the very first night they made love. The difference this Sunday morning was that Tarahji had decided not to roll one of the special condoms on her lover. It marked the first time that they ever had unprotected sex, and Monty shot his warm nut in her welcoming womb in a matter of mere minutes. They were instantly drained, and would both go on to miss the first half of the early games. But before dozing off, Tarahji told Monty that, like him, she too was ready to introduce him to her family. She said he would love the experience of traveling to Mexico, and had promised that there would even be a surprise for him over in her country.

Monty started wondering if he unwittingly had the connect right under his nose for the last seven months. But as quickly as he considered it, he shot the idea down even quicker. He knew she was half-Mexican and had to at least have a cousin who was in the game, but Monty figured his lady was the most squarest of the square. Tarahji told him not to worry about anything, and she was booking their flights for right after New Year's. Until then, they would go meet his family and have dinner with them for X-Mas. Then go across the border to meet the Mendozas in the first week of January.

At Monty's mother's house, the Christmas turkey had been deep fried, the yams were cooked with marshmallows, and the homemade stuffing was fresh out the oven and still steaming in its pot on the dining room table. Ms. Lester's home had the holiday spirit all throughout. Tarahji and Monty exchanged a nice kiss underneath the mistletoe in the hallway. Lakiya and her male friend of three years, Hop, laughed at a personal joke while he spiked the glasses of egg nog with Henny XO. Patti Labelle's version of "Silent Night" played softly from the living room's surround sound system.

The only one who seemed to bring their stress to the holiday season was Monty's sister, Tyshanna. Ty was seen moping back and forth throughout the house with her face hanging low. When

Monty finally asked his sister what was bothering her, she admitted to being fed up with her job. Ty had a bachelor's degree in psychology and figured she deserved a higher salary that better reflected it. After four solid years at the DCF building, she felt really underappreciated in her government career. After immediately clicking, since meeting two hours before, Tarahji and Ty had talked and shared opinions on a number of different things. After she found out that it was work that was bothering Monty's sister, they exchanged email addresses and Tarahji promised her a wonderful position at Bayer. She told Ty that the degree would also guarantee a better salary than most of the women who had already been there a few years. It cheered Monty's little sister up a lot, but for some reason her shoulders still hung low.

Fresh off a nice nut, Lala finally decided to show up at Ms. Lester's waltzing in around 5:45 p.m. The stuffing was still very warm and everyone's stomach seemed to thank Tarahji's daughter with a growl for finally coming. The presence of a girl closer to Tyshanna in age had sort of cheered her up as she lost most of the slouch in her back. As introductions were made, Lala hugged Monty's mother tight for a warm greeting. She then turned and shook Hop's hand with a big smile. Lastly, she reached for Tyshanna's hand to exchange a girly-girl hug, but Lala was met with an open hand that smacked fire out her ass. Everyone stood up from the table, like *what the fuck just happened.* But Lala responded like a pit bull and already had a fistful of hair.

Tyshanna came with an overhanded right and squared up on Lala's nose, instantly drawing blood. A dazed Lala staggered backwards and Tarahji caught her before she could hit the floor. Monty had Ty slung over his shoulder and was carrying her into the kitchen. Suddenly, loud shouts for explanations exploded from five different people. From the dining room, Lala yelled that she never met or did anything to Tyshanna. And Ty yelled back from the kitchen calling her a dirty side-bitch. Lala fucked a lot of women's men, but this name kind of rang a bell and her facial expression twisted into an apparent question mark. To clear up any misconceptions, Ty pulled out her phone and went into her text messages. Right there on the touch screen was Lala trying to muster up the best smile that she could with a soft dick in her mouth.

Tarahji and Ms. Lester couldn't believe their eyes. Hop's silly ass was sort of bent from the Henny and laughing about the whole shit, and Monty realized that his initial perception of Lala was true after all. Ty and Lala both stood up with their arms crossed and their eyebrows almost meeting. Their noses had the same wrinkle in it that even Monty's nose had when he got pissed off. Both mad, and looking sexy as hell, Lala and Tyshanna almost looked like identical twins.

The day after Christmas had come with an urgent request from Tarahji's people in Mexico. They had planned to meet Monty right after the new year, but something had come up. Tarahji had to drop whatever she was doing and bring Monty directly to the old man. And even though they had sort of divided and taken sides at last night's dinner, the new couple had rather easily communicated through it and Monty ended up cumming deep in Tarahji twice while making love late last night.

The flight from BDL to Phoenix was on time, departing and landing without any issues. Once they arrived in AZ, the cartel sent a driver to pick them up and the Town Car quickly made the short ride to Nogales. Nogales was a small city that had half of its territory in the state of Arizona, and the other half belonged to Mexico. With a border to cross, Nogales, Mexico was a thirty-minute drive from Tucson.

In the back of the Lincoln, in a hushed tone that the driver couldn't pick up, Tarahji and Monty held hands and confessed their love for one another. Tall fruit trees were still green and steep hilltops were in plain view on the ride. A newly built McDonald's and two gas stations were right next to each other by the border. Tarahji knew the short journey like the back of her hand. As they passed different parts of the city she gave her man a quick history lesson of her country. Monty made sure he paid close attention to the details she decribed with pride while he tried once again to reach Bullet on their new prepaid jack. Monty's homeboy had a large-scale transaction to make, and he was just checking to make sure his friend was good. Although Monty found it a bit strange that Bullet's phone kept going straight to voicemail, he didn't trip about it too much. He just figured that – as of late - his boy was putting a lady before business. Monty casually tucked his prepaid away and focused his full attention back on Tarahji's tour.

The Mendoza estate sat on five acres of land that were slightly sectioned off in its own area. There were a couple miles of woods until the next hidden estate. As the Lincoln cruised down the paved driveway that led to the mansion, Monty could see a group of kids riding ATVs and go-karts in the big open field. There were both boys and girls with long ponytails flying in the wind. The temperature was 64° in the winter's sun. Tarahji had already started smiling as she could recognize her little cousins and other family members enjoying what was most likely their Christmas gifts. Twelve-year-old Mikey even noticed his favorite older cousin in the back seat of the Town Car. Mikey rode alongside the Lincoln on a shiny, red four-wheeler.

Tarahji and Monty made it under the overhead drive port when they saw her grandfather standing in the doorway ready to greet them. As soon as they were within arm's reach, introductions were made and welcoming hugs exchanged. The old man welcomed Monty with a firm handshake and a kiss on both cheeks. The 5- horse powered buggy could be heard kicking up grass. And the two-stroke ATVs screamed as the old man escorted his favorite granddaughter and her guest inside.

The place was immaculate, with red carpet covering the staircase, and gold chandeliers hanging down from the ceiling in every room. A large oakwood grandfather clock stood against one of the walls, and the marble floors were so shiny that you could see your reflection.

After showing Monty around the home, the old man took them into a small conference room that had red leather furniture and a tank full of piranhas built into the floor. The glass was four inches thick and the room felt like they were standing on top of an ocean. There were rocks, reefs, and things of the sea placed under the water. Monty couldn't hide his amazement at the under-floor tank, and the old man was glad to explain his unique creation in more detail.

There was a 3 x 3 ft. metal chess table with light weight metal chess pieces placed between two of the leather recliners. From Tarahji, the old man already knew that Monty played chess, so after pointing and directing him to sit on the other side, Monty involuntarily became the opponent. Tarahji sat in one of the loveseats that was off to the side, but still very much in eye view of the game.

An African American butler entered the room carrying a polished silver tray that held a silver-looking thermos pot and three shiny matching mugs. A very sexy Brazilian, or some type of Latin woman, walked by dusting the hallway in a black and white French maid outfit and heels. The way the short skirt exposed a sexy pair of thighs was the exact reason that Monty would have Tarahji get the exact same outfit a couple weeks later. But it would be for role-playing purposes only, not dusting.

After the hot cocoa was poured, the old man came out with his white knight to start the first chess match. Each skilled strategist analyzed then attacked, moving to penetrate each other's defenses on the board. After an hour and ten minutes the score was 1-1, with the final game ending in a stalemate. Tarahji had warned her grandfather that Monty was good, but Mr. Mendoza still went into the game underestimating the young man's vision. After being impressed with each other's skills, they opted out a fourth game and settled for the tie with the promise to play a tie-breaking game in the near future.

There were no TVs, radios, or any other entertainment besides chess in the small ocean room. So, it was dead quiet; no one had to raise their voice in the slightest to be heard. The old man hit a few buttons on a small round remote, and a thick glass door, with a one-sided mirror slid across the doorway entrance. They were now secluded and no one else was welcome to enter or could see inside. A bright red light that matched all the furniture illuminated the sea under their feet. After Mr. Mendoza pressed another button on the remote, a few pieces of flesh suddenly appeared in the middle of the water and dozens of piranha devoured it - all within seconds. The big-mouthed fish then swam around mean mugging, looking for whatever fleshy morsel was next. The old man broke the silence explaining his belief that the piranha was the most serious creature under the sea.

Tarahji had heard her grandpops theory a million times, but with keen listening and comprehension skills, Monty was all ears. Mr. Mendoza told Monty that only piranha ever win in the drug game. He believed that sharks were too unpredictable and shiesty. With their eyes positioned on the side of their heads, sharks had no real direction in life. But the piranha was different. They were intelligent. Always hungry. Always loyal. From the direction the conversation was taking, it wasn't hard for Monty to confirm that he was correct in thinking that Tarahji had brought him there to be a part of the family, meaning the cartel. Her grandfather's drug empire. He now thought it was silly that it had never even crossed his mind, that she may have been connected when he first realized she was half Mexican.

After a few more minutes passed, the old man was ready to make his proposal. The conversation turned to the war on drugs that the United States president had proclaimed in the 1980's. From there, he covered the topic of transportation and the distribution process. Next came the fact that everything was going to be on consignment followed by a commitment to the set prices. And last, of course, was the fact that Monty would be held solely responsible for all errors.

All the news had Monty pumped. He now knew that he had taken a minor setback for a greater comeback. Trying to send his lady an early thank you, Monty placed a small smile on his face when Tarahji's eyes fell upon him. But while he expected her to blush tremendously, she had a face made of stone. She knew her grandfather's business was as serious as cancer. With a slight head-nod, she silently told Monty to pay attention. He felt a little sensitive from her subtle yet clear cold shoulder, but what the old man said next really pushed him over the top.

Monty had been all about that paper ever since he was turned out that night in Terry's, but he honestly had fallen madly in love with Tarahji. He was ready to spend the rest of his life with her. However, the old man busted Monty's bubble when he stood up to hug and congratulate his granddaughter on a job well done. He told Monty that Tarahji's mission was to find somebody between Boston and Jersey who was more than capable of running the family's business on the East Coast. His words took Monty back to the time when Tarahji had joked saying that he was the reason she was in CT. Monty felt his stomach twisting in a knot from Mr. Mendoza's hammering blows. Tarahji had fallen in love with Monty also, and she had warned her grandfather to tread lightly with the situation. But it was obvious that the old man was letting Monty know that business was going to be first and foremost. The old man then got out of his seat and walked over to a huge book shelf. Pulling his hands from his pockets, he took a minute fumbling around with a few books. Monty found this the perfect time to join Tarahji on the loveseat and pick his bone with her. But Tarahji quickly grabbed his hand and sort of told him to hush. But first she whispered that she was totally in love with him and it was nothing like her grandfather had said. With a lot of love in her expression, she told Monty that she'd explain everything to him later. Trying to switch the subject, she then asked him how he liked his surprise so far. After he answered affirmatively, she told him to sit tight because there was more.

When the old man slid the hard-covered novel back in its place, the book shelf opened up slowly and revealed a hidden room. Right there in the middle of the small area, tied to a leather swivel chair with wheels, was none other than Rude Rudy. The old man wheeled him slowly across the glass floor and stopped a few feet away from the metal chess table. When the blind fold was removed) and Monty's face came into view, he saw the fear of God creep quickly into the pupils of Rudy's eyes. Surprise!

CHAPTER 4

Monty's State Of Mind...

T he first drug shipment arrived in Bridgeport exactly seven days later by 18-wheeler. January 1st had marked the start of a new year, but the second day of the month had officially certified my place in the drug game. The big rig had transported the work in the company of a large furniture haul that was headed to Springfield, Massachusetts. The truck driver first made a stop at the discount furniture store on Lordship Blvd. in Bridgeport, then Alberto, the manager, called Tarahji and set a time for when her TVs and dresser drawers could be delivered. I had basically moved in with her, so I was actually there on the morning the furniture was dropped off. Two bulky Mexicans came in and set the things up in the empty living room area off to the right of the kitchen. As soon as the furniture truck left from in front of the Stratford home, Tarahji grabbed a Phillips screwdriver and started to remove the back of the TV. It was a huge 50" floor model, and a number of kilos were neatly stacked in the back of that bitch.

She then went and pressed down on the top of the dresser and it slowly opened up like magic. More bricks had been placed neatly throughout the entire middle of the red-oak furniture. I knew right then that my team was back like we had never left. With fifty ki's in total, we didn't have as many bricks as we would've had if the hundred birds from Rudy had landed, but trust me, this situation was better than any other one before it because twenty-five of the ki's were raw, uncut, Mexican-mud heroin. You know, that straight potent, knock-down-a-buffalo dope. The shit you couldn't find in the states any more.

The cock-diesel Mexican movers acted like they didn't know what time it was and like they had never met Tarahji a day in their life. I silently wondered if they were a part of the cartel and knew exactly what they were delivering. I was kind of curious but I stayed in my lane. I ain't bother to ask my lady about nothing she didn't voluntarily mention. I was the king at saying, "Everything ain't for everybody." It was just a couple months ago when I told Tarahji that it was best that she didn't truly know what I did for a living, so when the same two Mexicans came and took the furniture the next morning, I acted like it was normal shit, like it just didn't match the carpet and two of the other dressers. For a tip, Tarahji handed them both a five thousand dollar brick of cash that they quickly tucked away. And just like we were all supposed to do, no one said a word or asked any questions.

The coke was the same Grade A premium work as what we had been getting from Tucson - jumping out the gym like Jordan - with hundreds of extra grams after the cook. This was only more proof that the cocksucka Rudy was really giving us the birds uncut. But it was the heroin that would enable a nigga to get rich on the street within a month.

Busting the packages open and cutting the dope was a job that everyone wasn't built to do. There were a lot of methods and safety measures to be taken when fuckin' with that shit. We labeled dope "Boy" out on the strip; however, that game was strictly for grown men; it would take a weak boy and chew him up, then spit him out after becoming strung out on the drug. This brown powder was a monster that could bend you over so far that you'd be able to suck your own dick. That dope fiend lean was something serious. Ask heroin-head Troy.

The first shipment was worth $1.7M to the old man, but that was just his cut. Trust me, my whole team would go into the next tax bracket after this one flip. By now, me and Bullet had the re-rock game mastered when it came to the "Girl", which was coke. But it took for us to fuck up dozens of grams of "Boy" to get our cutting skills where they needed to be with the heroin. See, the heroin that the old man sent to me was so raw that it would be a problem to put it right out on the street the way it came. The fiends wouldn't respect its power and would try to bang it into their veins for the ultimate high. But the dope would be so potent that it would travel straight to their heart and pop it like a red Valentine's Day balloon. I stepped on it two times, then Bullet gave it to a dope fiend that he knew to try out. Twenty minutes later we saw the ambulance hauling ass through the projects trying to save that boy. It took four levels of cut to calm the dope down enough for it to not take a life, and it was still better than any other smack on the street. So, that meant Bullet could take one kilo of heroin and hit it four times to make five ki's, then break it all down into fingers to be sold to the young boys in the hood. But we weren't trying to smack every ki of dope that hard. We would hit some of the bricks of heroin just once then compress it back into two bricks. These would be set aside for the true dope boys who were looking to buy the whole squares and not just a couple of fingers. We would hit them cats up for sixty stacks for the whole thing. After spending that much, they had a right to be left with the benefit of being able to do the Harlem shake on them shits – to step all over the ki of heroin a couple times themselves. So, we would leave them enough room to dance on a few songs.

Bullet had convinced me that it would be a bad idea to involve The God in the dope biz to put down in the Elm. He said God Body wasn't worthy of getting a dime more than he was already getting from our relationship. Bullet felt it wasn't worth splitting another pie two ways when we could eat the whole thing ourselves. He said it would probably complicate our situation even more. Bullet would rather give our immediate crew more responsibilities and let Quan and them enjoy all the fruits of our success. I realized that The God did have a lot of shit with him and I was finally seeing my boy's vision. I mean, I still didn't think he was the one who stole our coke, but it was obvious that God Body was definitely double-jugglin'.

Me and Bullet had decided to chill with him a little longer than usual the last time we dropped off a bird for Ward St. The God's spot had been raided about a half-dozen times in the past four years. The Ward Street trap was actually a group of six apartment buildings that formed its own little projects and parking lot. And it's a known fact that trap spots in housing projects were built to last. After a raid, you'd simply put the front door back on the hinges when the jake left and got back to work like it never happened. Out of the seven times that the building was raided, someone only got bagged and went to jail twice. Luck and New Money had been promoted to lieutenants a long time ago, so they didn't have to pump bundles in the buildings any more. They were now eighteen and definitely old enough to make it to 1 Union Ave. So, they went out and recruited a fresh group of adolescents to stand in the spot and serve the fiends hand to hand. Poodie, a jug-headed fifteen-year-old went down for interfering, and sixteen-year-old Froggy got caught trying to stuff a G-pack in his ass. Froggy had just gotten the bundle, so it was fresh and the size of a softball. The youngster was tall and lanky, wearing size 28-slim in most of his jeans. Froggy's teenaged ass cheeks were the size of two raisin bagels, and the Ds looked at him like he was crazy when he tried to cuff the bundle right in front of their eyes. They took Froggy's ass straight to detention, where his mother had to wait thirty days before she could sign him out.

The night that me and Bullet went down to monitor The God's block was a Wednesday, in the middle of the month of August. It was hump day and the money from all the state welfare checks had already been smoked up. So, we weren't expecting The God's block to put up numbers like Nelly's debut album, *Country Grammar*. But while sitting behind the dark tints of God Body's black 500 Benz, we watched as fiend after fiend hopped out of moving vehicles to get served.

We sat on the low and polished off a fifth of Remy VSOP from plastic cups. After three hours inside the V we were listening as The God boldly bragged about how we ain't seen nothing. According to him, it was a slow day. He said the weekends and the 1st of the month were off the fuckin' hook. New Money had pulled up on a brand-new Helix scooter, and after running up in the building to play his new position, he dropped $2,400 through the window into The God's lap. He also reported that the niggas in the building were starting their fourth bundle. That meant Poodie and them little bastards had rocked three G-packs while I sat my black ass in The God's Benz for a couple hours. Doing the numbers in my head, I concluded that it was safe to say that The God's spot was doing a little better than our 21 bldg. He was probably seeing at least fifteen stacks a day to our ten or twelve.

Bullet must have read my mind, because from sunk down in the back seat, he mumbled, "about twenty", in a low voice.

The God was bent off the Remy and didn't quite catch it so he asked Bullet, "What you say?"

On point, my main man just told him that we had to be sliding back to Bridgeport in "about twenty" more minutes. And when it was time to leave The God's spot that night, me and Bullet both kept our hugs tight with him. Ever since that day I saw why Bullet wasn't trying to include God Body in this "Boy" thing of ours. Nah, we would just keep smacking him in the head by boosting the price up on the "Girl".

In the next couple of months my whole team had doubled their safes. The coke and dope we were getting was always fire, so it easily sold itself. We never had to rush to do shit. Ro-Ro said it was definitely the dope money that bought the chromed-out Harley he was now riding with no helmet. I had to agree because I couldn't believe how fast I was counting most of the money that was to go back to the old man. I had $1.2 million dollars wrapped up in under four months. And this was after we all took half of our profit up front. My whole team was rich and rugged and we could buy our way out of any problem.

Through a mutual third party, Y.G. had pushed up on Quita and offered to give her and her baby daddy twenty-five Gs apiece to not get on the stand against him. Although she was now getting ridiculous money by fuckin' with Kurt, the quarter sounded nice to Quita so she agreed to talk to Lil' Daddy's father about recanting his statement. Quita then requested a little bit more from the bribe. She sent the message to Y.G. that she would definitely make it happen if he fucked her in the ass the way he did before clappin' her baby daddy. But as fat as Quita's booty was, Y.G. passed on all the drama. Because he knew he would have to murk her and her baby daddy the next time some shit like that went down.

As far as Lala, she was still riding the dicks of a few select men on her roster. But in a very rare move she decided to take Hook out of her line-up. After Tarahji talked some sense into her, Lala stepped up and apologized to Tyshanna. She told her aunt-in-law not to take it personally, and that she was just standing up for herself. Tyshanna didn't understand how sucking a dick for the camera meant that you were standing up for yourself, but at the end of the day they had squashed the beef and were now laughing about it because Ty had ended up leaving Mook a few weeks later over yet another bitch. She now says she's staying single for a while. But one thing for sure, she's now making $8,700 more on her salary by working at Bayer.

Me and Tarahji's relationship continued to soar. We were talking to a few real estate investors and planning to make a splash in their world by the beginning of next year. I was ready to make a portion of my cash start working for itself. My lady knew all the steps to protect our assets as best as possible. Mentally, she was getting more rest at night, but would still wake up from her sleep sometimes sweating, suffering from post-traumatic stress. However, Tarahji had elected to deal with it on her own and not go see a shrink. Y.G. once told me that he wasn't able to sleep for months after seeing his first body drop before his eyes, and after what happened to Rudy, I could totally understand how my baby was feeling.

Monty may as well have been the Grim Reaper himself, the way he made Rudy's cunning ass get the look of death on his face. Monty was sitting next to Tarahji on the loveseat and she had her thick golden legs crossed like the perfect sophisticated lady. The old man's hands were gripped around the back of Rudy's scrawny looking neck. Mr. Mendoza was just staring at Monty with no emotion whatsoever written on his ageless face. Clearly, Tarahji's grandfather was a stone-cold killer.

It turned out that Rudy had gotten in over his head with the cartel. He had fucked up a truck load that was worth $3.5M to the old man: eighty ki's of coke, and another forty of heroin. From all his years of hustling, Rudy's corny ass had only been able to stack up about two million in cash. He owned the deeds to a couple of cribs and the titles to a few of his muscle cars were in his momma's name. However, the 427 block engine in the '72

THE BACKSTORY

Stingray wasn't worth shit to the old man. He wasn't taking no collateral or personal property at all. The head of the Mendoza Cartel wanted his payment in straight cash. Rudy had become a bad businessman by stepping all over the work, then selling it to all of his life-long customers throughout Arizona, Texas, and Louisiana. It was more than just a coincidence that niggas from three different states had all decided to beat him at the same time. They had all spent a few dollars and copped a few birds apiece, but Rudy gave out a total of forty-five ki's of coke and twenty of dope to his people on consignment. By the time they decided to burn him, he was left with nine kilos of coke and only two bricks of heroin. This was after subtracting the number of ki's they actually paid up front for.

In a desperate move, Rudy tried to re-rock the drugs to make up for the loss. He stepped on them shits so much that they wouldn't even hold together and were falling all apart. The work was garbage and Rudy couldn't have moved the birds if he was giving them away. He didn't grow up with the country boys from New Orleans so he didn't give a fuck, but Rudy's reputation was now on the line in his own home state. He even went to Cali for a couple days trying to find new buyers. But when all options failed, he knew there was only one thing left to do.

Rudy had been saving Monty and Bullet for a rainy-day jux from the very start. His bottom bitch and a couple of her girls had called Rudy and told him there were a couple of live ones who had checked into the hotel. This was the very same day that the two city slickers had arrived in town. They were easy to spot, and Rudy had his eyes on them the whole time while at Club Rolex. And he was mad as a muthafucka when he lost sight of them on the dance floor while he mixed his Michael Jackson routine with Smokey's dance from *Friday*. He called it the "Billy Snake". So, when he got the call the next morning from Tara, all of Rudy's excitement from the night before had rushed back into his body. The crowd had claimed him as the winner of the dance competition with the Billy Snake, and Rudy even scored a threesome with two of the hottest niggas in the club that night. They had gone and rented a Jacuzzi suite in a lavish hotel. It was the reason why Rudy had showed up to Monty's room in the same outfit from the night before. The stench of nuts and butt were all on his breath. And just think, Bullet had thought it meant that Rudy had a little bit of hood in him. Sheeeiit, that boy was as sweet as a candy apple. However, Tara was still his bottom bitch.

Rudy knew his East Coast boys would be calling soon and they would spend at least six or seven hundred thousand whenever they did. He knew once he snatched that and put it with his two million and change, he would only be short a couple hundred large of having the old man's cash⁻. The old geezer took that shit seriously, but Rudy was confident Mr. Mendoza wouldn't trip. He just knew he'd let him work it off. But being short a cool million would definitely cost Rudy his life. He would've left the West on the run from the cartel instead of trying to negotiate. Talking wouldn't have done anything to spare his life which is why he almost busted a nut when Monty called and asked if he could cover the goal that he and Bullet had mentioned some while back. Rudy knew that Monty was referring to a hundred birds because it was exactly what he'd been waiting on them to order before robbing their asses. But now there was only one problem. Everything he had worked so hard to build them up to would now go directly into the hands of the old man.

Rudy had driven across the Mexican border to Nogales with a fortune hidden inside the compartment of his Range Rover. He had hand delivered $3.5 million dollars on the nose to the bid man. Mr. Mendoza had been hearing whispers about Rudy's bad business affairs, but the young man that he had known since a kid had always brought him every dime that was owed. So, Mr. Mendoza figured Rudy was just fine. Therefore, it was business as usual and Rudy had expected his tractor trailer in a couple of days. This was a few nights before Christmas and the old man wanted to relax with his family in peace for the holidays. That is until Sunday morning on Christmas Eve when he got a call from his favorite grandchild who made him aware of her situation.

After putting two and two together, Tarahji had figured out a while ago that the rap artist, Rude Rudy, was none other than the lil' homo thug that worked for her grandfather. She told her papa that she was positive that she had found the right guy to run the East Coast division and Tarahji admitted that she had fallen in love with the dude. She watched Monty handle his business with his friends for months and he was always the one to make sure things went according to plan. He had boss written all over him. Plus, Tarahji really admired the fact that Monty didn't pillow talk. He sincerely abided by all the laws of the street. Tarahji had assured her grandfather that Monty had passed every test. And before their lines went dead that morning, Mr. Mendoza had put a plan in order. That was the morning when Tarahji told Monty she was taking him to meet her family after the new year because that's when her grandfather had said he'd have Rudy captured.

However, after waking up on Christmas and no longer in a jolly spirit because of Tarahji's problem, Mr. Mendoza placed a call to Rudy and summoned him to the mansion. All bills had been paid, so Mr. Mendoza knew that Rudy would have no worries at all. He then placed a call to Tarahji telling her that there had been a change of plans. She and Monty were to get on the first plane smoking and be at the mansion in Nogales as soon as possible. The old man knew the whole story of Rudy's foul behavior. He was aware that Rudy had given up all his cash to pay off the last bill and he was now waiting on the next shipment to get himself back in order. He knew Rudy didn't have any more cash on hand, just ten garbage kilo's of dope. The sixteen ki's of coke were so wacked up that they weren't even worth mentioning. He couldn't even get five Gs for them shits in any of the hoods in Phoenix or Tucson. And a nigga from up North would body Rudy's ass after cooking a few grams.

Since the old man hated robbers and bad businessmen more than anything, he felt like the most honorable thing to do was give Monty back his million plus that Rudy took. This now meant that Rudy had fucked Mr. Mendoza for close to $1.5 million. These circumstances definitely guaranteed his death. Thinking back to the twins, Corey and Cameron, the old man was proving that no one was exempt.

After pulling out a nine-millimeter Beretta that was hidden in the small of his back the entire time, the old man laid the warm barrel right between Rudy's eyes. A gag still covered his mouth so no pleas could be heard. This happened to be Mr. Mendoza's style. Begging only made it worse. The armpits of Rudy's argyle sweater were soaked and wet. His honey-brown shoulders were slumped, low and Rudy's bird chest was deflated. And just when the old man was about to pull the trigger, he thought that maybe Monty would rather put in the work. Besides, it was him and his best friend who Rudy had truly robbed. And if not for Tarahji, he and Bullet would be out of a connect, plus an amount of cash that the average drug dealer only dreamed of.

Now waving for Monty to come over, the old man placed the pistol in his hand and gladly gave him the honor off getting some get back. Monty had been having dreams of murking Rudy, but now given the opportunity he was having second thoughts. Monty wasn't scared to get blood on his hands, but he wasn't really a killer. Bullet's gun was very hot when he was younger but had since cooled down. Y.G. was the only real gunman on the team, but Ro-Ro⁻ would also shoot the shit out of you. It's just that Monty felt some way with having Tarahji around to witness something like this. It was the same thing as when he told her it was a good idea not to know what he did in the streets. Obviously, for purposes of her ever being called to testify in court. But this was all before Tarahji had involved herself in his drug dealings by introducing him to the head of a cartel. Yet, he still couldn't bring himself to let his lady see him pull the trigger.

With the same never changing, blank expression, the old man stayed to the side and observed everything. Tarahji had kind of picked up on Monty's vibe and quickly came to his side. She knew it wasn't that Monty was soft or squeamish. She knew first-hand that he would let his hammer go because she had already witnessed him bust off when he was backed into a corner. While out on a date a few months ago, some young teenagers were fronting like they were scheming on Monty's chain. Once her and Monty were inside the car the young goons must've thought it was the perfect time to strike. But when the short, filthiest-assed one, reached for the driver's door handle he caught a big surprise. Monty had the banger out and was already dumping while switching the gear into drive. The goon took two to the abdomen and one to the leg before his partner tried to squeeze off a few shots. Monty's Benz was untouched and he and Tarahji made it back to Stratford in one piece. The inexperienced stick-up kids thought they had caught a smooth nigga slippin', but a smooth nigga had licked them. So Tarahji knew her man would protect her from any danger lurking her way, like an attempted home invasion or something, but her grandfather may have asked too much for him to kill in cold blood.

Feeling more pressure since his lady had come and stood by his side, Monty placed the now cool barrel back in the same place on Rudy's head where the old man had put it. His finger brushed against the trigger but Monty's hand couldn't come to a squeeze. Rudy was now crying and wailing under the gag. The old man just continued to look on from next to the book shelf. In a low voice, Tarahji told Monty that it was okay. She didn't want him to make a mistake he couldn't live with. So, reaching slowly for his hand, she peeled the Beretta from out his palm. Feeling like he was spared, Rudy was mumbling something that sounded like, "Thank you".

It was ironic, because Mr. Mendoza could see no fear in Monty's eyes, and he knew that Tarahji's man was playing mental chess with the situation. The old man realized that Monty must have really fallen in love with his granddaughter, but it was also obvious that Monty didn't know his lady was trained to go. With no hesitation, Mr. Mendoza's grandchild put the barrel to Rudy's temple and blew his wig off. The hot shell casing spit out the chamber and bounced three times before sliding across the glass floor. Rudy's head was slumped to the right and sprinkles of his blood had splattered on Tarahji's sheer ruffled blouse. Monty wasn't frightened at all, but he was totally shocked at what he just witnessed his girl do. The old man just stayed put. He watched as Rudy's stomach exhaled for the final time. He knew his granddaughter had never murdered, but was sure that she had it in her blood. Her father, the Corey twin, had taught Tarahji how to shoot when she was just a lil' girl and Mr. Mendoza knew that his favorite grandchild could murder again if she had to.

The old man made a call on his phone and three little Mexicans in white masks and jumpers came into the room. The glass door slid closed as soon as they entered. They all wore gloves and carried bags, seeming to know exactly what they had been summoned to do. One of them immediately took the smoking gun from Tarahji's hand, while another one went and tracked down the hot casing. The last one occupied himself with untying and taking the gag off Rudy.

The body was then stripped naked and Rudy's wack-ass argyle sweater and outfit were placed in one of the bags. The old man then pushed a button on the remote and the entire 3"x3" chess table slid left, revealing the same size hole in the glass floor. The loyal piranha crowded the opening like they did this all the time. Two of the little men grabbed Rudy by his lifeless arms and feet while the other one was thoroughly cleaning the blood and disinfecting the floor. Rudy's body was then dumped inside the hole and as soon as he touched the water, a hundred and one piranha swarmed his ass like a California gang set. An exceedingly rare albino piranha with razor-like teeth seemed to be the hungriest. In a matter of three minutes, they had torn through his flesh and left nothing but bone. One of the men then used a long net to fish the skeleton from the indoor ocean. What was left of Rude Rudy was thrown into a bag and taken out back for the final procedure.

In a 1000° outdoor oven, Rudy's clothes were burned and his bones were cremated. It was sort of Mr. Mendoza's way of following his tradition. Stuck in his ways, the old man had a habit of killing anyone that crossed him, by means of three deaths. He had contemplated letting the fish eat Rudy alive, but then he would have only been able to kill him twice in that way.

CHAPTER 3

The remainder of '04 had gone by in a breeze without any major issues for the crew. The "Pats" had ran through their opponents in the playoffs and in the fifth week of 2005, Feb. 3rd to be exact, they had recaptured the top spot in the NFL. After being knocked off in the season before, Brady had led the team to its third title in four years by routing the Philadelphia Eagles. Tarahji was very proud of her African American heritage and she saluted Donovan McNabb's courage. T.O. even showed his determination by playing with a fractured ankle. But a fresh and revived Tarahji, who was now able to sleep past her Nogales nightmares, had won the bid on two tickets to the Superbowl and had taken the man of her dreams. The trip had turned into a mini-vacation and it was really that moment when Monty knew he didn't ever wanna be without his lady. So, he started shopping for rings as soon as their plane landed back home.

Monty's relationship had sort of grown into one that best friends usually share. During dates the two of them would clown and laugh at all the funny-looking people. And when a bad bitch in a mean pair of heels walked by, Monty was able to look at her from head to toe and silently approve. He was allowed to appreciate a woman's beauty without his own lady turning green and throwing a fit. In Monty's eyes, he truly had the baddest bitch in the world so there was really no comparison. It's just that Tarahji was very secure and didn't see anything wrong with her man enjoying the view of a fat ass.

Tarahji had played queen for Monty and in turn, she worshipped the very ground that he walked on. He never had to ask twice for anything and most of the time he didn't even have to open his mouth at all. For instance, she served his favorite dishes daily for breakfast, lunch, and dinner and when he left dry cleaning receipts on the night stand, his designer wear would automatically pop up inside the closet later. These were just the little points of chemistry that were supposed to naturally develop over time. On highways, behind dark tints, Monty never had to ask to get head behind the wheel of any of their Vs. In skin-tight leather Dolce & Gabana pants or short Prada summer dresses, Tarahji would give her now signature look before seductively leaning over the center console. Cruise control would be set, then Monty would ride the middle lane while his lady spit-polished his pole. So yeah, he got everything he asked for, even the shit that he didn't. And after the near robbery experience with the young boys, Tarahji even did as Monty asked and went and got her pistol permit. She sort of felt empowered after legally being able to keep the steel close by. And Monty would occasionally joke that it was just a license to carry, not kill. But now deep down inside he wondered if poppin' Rudy had given his lady a thirst for blood. Her temper had sort of darkened and Tarahji was now suddenly ready to dump on cars for simply cutting her off on the highway.

Monty had definitely grown mentally and made a lot of changes for Tarahji. When being with someone almost your mother's age you tended to learn how to really treat a woman. He stopped addressing Tarahji with "yo", and had become a great communicator. Monty's sense of fashion had long since caught up and he was definitely considered a fly gangsta. He let go of the fatigues, snap-backs and flopping Timberland boots. He picked up more Gucci loafers, Ralph Lauren slacks, and Cavalli sweaters. Monty no longer hauled around stacks inside the sleeves of zipped up Avirex leathers. No, Monty now carried a black leather wallet with a valid driver license and bank cards in the slots. He even honored Tarahji's request to chop off his long corn-rows for a short Caesar. The one against the grain had left just enough hair to show a razor-sharp line-up. However, he kept his goatee - dark to match his thick eyebrows. Monty was always considered handsome but the lily-white women at Bayer now teased Tarahji by labeling her man "a hunk". Shedding the ruff-neck look for a grown man cut had made Monty more of a heartthrob in every sense of the word.

As far as the sexual chemistry, clearly, it was out of this world. Tarahji's waterfall between her thighs was always flowing and Monty had loved it since day one. By running through his fair share of women, Monty was no stranger to things like eating pussy and sucking toes, but Tarahji had taken time to show him all the things that a grown woman really liked. More specifically, things that she personally loved. She taught him the importance of foreplay and preparing her mind just as much as her body before sex. She loved to have soft kisses planted on her forehead the same way Monty did on her lips. She taught him to be sensual and how to suck her titties soft and delicately instead of acting like a nursing puppy. Monty's fingertips had soon become just as dangerous as his tongue. Oral sex was an art and Tarahji wanted Monty to be more like Michaelangelo. He made shapes, wrote phrases, and traced the whole alphabet on her clit with his tongue, to the point where she couldn't take it no more and demanded his dick. And Monty would know if his lady wanted to make sweet love or be fucked like a slut in the streets.

Different days would call for different things behind the closed doors of their bedroom. But regardless of what day it was one thing would always remain the same: Gone were the days of the young boy routine of passing out right after a nut. Monty had started getting ridiculous with that shit until Tarahji had kindly checked him. She told him she wasn't looking to spend every second of the day with him and didn't need him for his money, but as a grown ass forty-year-old woman, Tarahji demanded that Monty be a bully in the pussy every time they fucked. She wanted to have to tap out and put an icepack between her thighs when they finished. She didn't get all insecure with questioning him about why was he always so tired when coming in for the night. Tarahji was willing to bet that Monty had some side pussy, but none of that shit ever came up in her face or got back to her. Not ever. And she wasn't about to start playing herself with snooping through his shit. Nah, Monty was always respectful and took care of his home. She just told him that she wasn't about to stand for letting whatever he was doing in the streets start affecting how he fucked her. Tarahji simply suggested that Monty do a better job with planning his day. So, with the fair warning,

Monty went back to the drawing board and did what no nigga in the street would've been able to do. That nigga changed all of his cell phone numbers and stopped cheating. Well, maybe not completely stopped, but his couple of side-things were now limited to out-of-state bitches when he would go on vacations three or four times a year. They were long distance with no strings attached. Monty came home one night and fucked Tarahji until she jumped up and had to lock herself in one of the guest rooms to keep him off the pussy. It was exactly what she asked for, but Monty was being a lil' ridiculous with it. This nigga had already bust four nuts and she had to get up for a mandatory meeting in a couple of hours. Tarahji quickly came up with a way to prevent that from ever happening again. If for some reason he ever beat the pussy up in a similar manner, she would just suck his dick until he was drained and passed out. So, at this point in her life, Ms. Valentine had everything she ever wanted in a man. Just a little rough around the edges still, Monty had become her king.

As planned, one of Tarahji's real estate friends started overloading them with MLS listings of great investment opportunities. This was right after the 2005 new year, the exact time that Monty had predicted they would start buying. They decided to stay low-key and keep residing at her home in Stratford for at least another year, then together they would buy something bigger in the same neighborhood. Until then, any property that they dropped money on would be for investment purposes only.

The first deal they closed on was the multi-apartment building on Albany Avenue in Hartford. It was an old building in need of a major electrical makeover. Besides that, all the windows in the bldg. had to be updated. The rewiring had cost a grip, but the investment was well worth it. All the repairs had added another thirty-five stacks to the $345K purchase price, but the twenty-unit bldg. had quickly filled to capacity four months after the Hartford Courant listed the vacant apartments. At a range of eight hundred to a thousand dollars a month for two and three bedrooms, the power couple of Monty and Tarahji stood to make their money back in three years at the most.

In a chain reaction, they masterfully succeeded in

purchasing a whole block of abandoned houses on the South End of Bridgeport. Foreclosed and bank-owned homes had become their point of interest. Tarahji had Mexican carpenters and plumbers on speed dial. Them dudes would do a hell of a job for ten bucks an hour. The corporations and LLC's had been set up in their names and then the "company cars" had started to come. In the middle of the spring, Monty copped the new Range Rover sport. He was thinking of waiting for the '06 to drop in the fall, but the '05 was also cocky and he hadn't seen one yet in his city. Well, at least not one owned by a dopeboy.·

Carl's Custom Cars, had switched all the yellow reflector lights and black trimmings to match the truck and its white leather interior. In the middle of June, he pushed the all-white Sport through PT knocking the *Can't Band the Snowman* mix-tape. With about $2.7 million in cash for himself at the time, Monty had truly made it in the game. And he owed it all to his partner in life, Tarahji which is why he was ready to make it all the way official.

Tarahji was a huge R&B Soul fan and being in her early forties she loved guys like Luther Vandross, Gerald Levert, and Charlie Wilson. A cat from Jersey was also making a name for himself, and she always respected what Usher and Kells were doing. But if Tarahji ever had to crown somebody, then Luther was surely that dude. Monty's mother, Lakiya, had kept Luther's classic in the 8-track when he was a little boy, so his soul was also old and he would dance with Tarahji all the time when they were at home. Monty's favorites were the Chi-lites and the Isley Brothers. He pulled up in the Range Rover knockin' the Stylistics at a cookout in Seaside Park and all the older women were suddenly on his dick. They ran up on Tarahji like they were indulging in girl talk, but all the ladies from her book club were really trying to steal her man.

On June 2nd, tickets went on sale for a concert at Foxwood's Casino for a tour called '80s Babies. Johnny Gill and Al B. Sure were on board to bless the mic, but a trimmed down Luther was headlining the show. Monty had gotten wind of the event through Hot 94.3 FM and he knew Tarahji wouldn't be able to forgive him if he didn't take her. So, being thoughtful, Monty went out and bought a total of six tickets. He was inviting Lala, Tyshanna, his moms, and Hop to join them in hearing Tarahji's favorite singer of all time blow the house down. Monty booked a white H2 Hummer limousine for the event and asked everyone to please be dressed in all white. All the women wore long summer dresses and white sandals. Instead of gold or silver jewelry like the rest of the ladies, Tarahji had capped off her dress with a white pearl necklace and matching bracelet. Monty and Hop had on short-sleeve linen suits and white V-necks. Hop rocked white Stacy Adams and a Kangol. Monty was flossing crisp white Forces and a sharp razor's edge on his Caesar.

Al B. Sure was a little off-key, but Johnny Gill was like foreplay to all the women; he had gotten them nice and wet. By the time Luther was into his third song all the ladies had already cum in their panties. Wet spots had already soaked through the back of all their thin layers. And no longer "waiting to exhale", the women all seemed to be able to relax, sigh and finally breathe out through their mouths.

From the middle of the row, Tarahji shouted to Luther that she was his #1 fan. She knew it was impossible for him to hear her but it didn't matter. The rest of the group was laughing at her but Monty was all smiles. He was basking in the fact that she was loving her night out. Tarahji just wanted the singer to know that she thought he was simply amazing. But when Luther called from the mic for Tarahji Valentine to come to the stage, Hop had to fan her with his Kangol to keep her from passing out. After realizing that this was really happening and not a dream, she immediately looked at Monty and asked what the hell was going on. Shrugging his shoulders, Monty pointed towards the stage and told her he thought she should go and see.

When Tarahji made it to center stage the singer gently took her by the hand and kindly introduced himself. It took everything Tarahji had for her legs not to give out. After Luther asked her if she liked his music, he put the mic in front of her face to hear her response. Tarahji's mind told her lips to say "yes", but when she moved her mouth she couldn't get anything to come out. Surely she was star-struck. Luther and the whole crowd understood, so he then went on to ask her his second question while still gently holding her by the hand.

The man with the healing voice then asked her if she knew Monty Lester. And when he put the mic back in front of her mouth, the same thing happened again. Her voice was trapped inside her body. Tarahji just nodded her head "yes" and couldn't seem to make it stop bobbing. Her back was to the stage steps and the crowd suddenly went wild.

"Well sweetheart, Monty's here and he has something to ask you," Luther said while spinning Tarahji around.

Right behind her in his gleaming white was Monty holding a dozen Juliet roses in his hand, the most expensive rose known to man. He gave the flowers to his lady, then he told her he loved her. Luther had the mic in between their faces so the whole crowd responded with "Awww's". Then, pulling a black box from out of his pants pocket, Monty had slowly gotten down on one knee. Tarahji's heart had started to skip and tears were flowing down her cheek in an instant. Monty flipped the top of the box open and 3.5 karats sat in the middle of a platinum engagement ring. Another karat and a half was sprinkled around the sides of the band.

With the mic held directly in front of his mouth, Monty looked Tarahji in her eyes and asked her to be his wife. Although she was no longer star-struck, Tarahji's voice still wasn't ready to work. Nevertheless, she still couldn't make her head stop nodding "yes" as Monty slid the ring around the fourth finger of her left hand.

When the pianist from Luther's live band began to introduce his next song, Monty got up from one knee and took his wife by the hand. Though he would've been willing to pay anything, it only took for Monty to offer Luther ten Gs through his manager to pull off the stunt. While still holding the bouquet of roses, Tarahji wrapped her arms around her man's back as they danced to Luther singing his classic, "The Power of Love". And Tarahji fell even deeper in love with Monty when she heard Luther say, ♫♪ "When I say good-bye, It is never for long" ♫♪

CHAPTER 2

You would have expected The God's wifey Nikki to become as cocky and arrogant as her man, but no one could truthfully say that was the case at all. However, Nikki honestly had a reason to be on a high horse if she wanted to. Verizon Wireless Communications in Wallingford had plucked her application along with a half dozen others from off their company's website. She was quickly hired and trained by another young black woman name Iesha who had been there for years. Nikki's starting rate was $15.75/hr., and for someone whose employment history wasn't the best, a $33K salary was a huge step in the right direction.

Although her man, Germaine, was now sitting on top of the world, Nikki was able to become independent and bring something of her own to the table, too. She got on her feet and canceled all her state assistance benefits like welfare, and SAGA medical. However, Nikki was blessed to be able to retain partial assistance from Section 8. Now instead of the state giving her nine fifty towards her thousand-dollar rent, the program only fronted her a buck forty-five after making adjustments for her pay rate. Nikki thanked the Lord every morning for what He had been doing in her life. God forbid anything ever happened to Germaine, but she was now in a position to help others get hired.

The God had put her in a Benz a few years ago, but Nikki had just bought a brand-new Acura MDX for herself. It was the middle of September, so the '06 truck had just come out. Last year's model had experienced some issues with transmission problems – forcing a recall - but the parent company, Honda, had corrected all the wrongs. The new MDX was stockier, with a slightly better gas mileage per gallon rating. While doing a buck in the fast lane, the tranny on the newer model would shift without the slightest jerk. Nikki's checking account was set up to automatically deduct the car note on the first of every month. So instead of waiting on a check to be funded to her EBT card, the around-the-way girl was now cutting them herself.

THE BACKSTORY

Within months, the three credit bureaus were reporting that her score had risen dramatically. Dozens of agencies were offering her cards with wild limits. Nikki was never a dumb chic, she just used to bullshit on applying herself. But now with a new attitude, she set a lot of short and long-term goals for herself.

The most important short-term one was buying a home for her family and stop renting someone else's shit. She took a pair of orange kitchen shears and sliced all the credit cards in half except the one from Capital which had the best interest rate. She began using it to pay monthly bills and would then get the balance back to zero by the middle of the month. This way she was able to repeat these steps the following month. Capital saw her responsible habits and quickly reported it to all the credit bureaus. Nikki's score was starting to show a huge increase every four to six weeks. This was all a part of the plan that she had made for herself.

While paying all of her bills on time, Nikki had begun the second step of her blueprint. By attending a first-time home buyers program on the weekend, she became qualified for all the help and benefits from the foundation. Great interest rates with pre-approved lenders, first option on bank owned homes, and minimum down payments were just a few of the perks.

Having a Benz that was paid for and just recently financing a new truck, most people would say that Nikki was hustling backwards with her planning. You would've thought that the home would come in her first couple years on the job. But there was a method to Nikki's madness and it all made sense. After building with The God they came up with a plan that was perfect for the both of them.

Although not quite as filthy rich as Monty or Bullet, God Body was now sitting on some change himself. He didn't have multiple spots like P.T. Barnum, the Terrace Houses, and the North Side, and he damn sure wasn't munching off none of the heroin that they kept hidden from him, but The God was doing quite well for himself with just the Ward St. building and selling a lil' weight to a small select few.

The prison-converted 5-percenter was now thirty-two

years old and had just over a million in cash tucked in his safe. He and Nikki's Benzes were both paid for and The God was now making monthly payments on an '04 Audi A8 that he had put in Nikki's name. He beat up the city streets in an all-black used Prelude with a twin-cam engine. Plus, to switch up on the jack-boys, he always kept different rentals on deck.

Monty didn't give The God any knowledge on the real estate investments that he, Tarahji, and now even Bullet had made happen. They ain't want that boy to have nothing more than he deserved. But unbeknownst to them all, The God was sharp as a tack. He would read or take courses on anything he wanted to branch off into. And if he didn't have time to gain the knowledge, then he would give the duty to Nikki, who with her upper-management position, had more than enough time to use the internet service on her computer. Between the two of their mind frames, power moves were being made.

The God had moved his family from the corner of Vernon St. and Davenport Ave. back when the Ward St. bldg. had first started to bubble. Niggas on the North Side of The Hill knew The God was starting to eat, so he had to pick up and get low from out the hood. For fourteen hundred a month, Nikki took out a five-year lease at the Seramonte condominium complex behind Hamden High School. The three-bedroom condo came equipped with a sliding balcony, a washer and dryer area, and two-car garage. There was a bullshit gym onsite that consisted of mostly treadmills. A three-court tennis area with a 15 ft. fence was on one side of the complex and the blue water in the 8 ft. pool always smelled of fresh chlorine.

Nikki's mother always tried to convince her daughter to buy instead of renting such an expensive place, but The God had trained his wifey to always follow his lead and his lead only. He was nearing a six-year run without taking any major spills. It was his largest consecutive span by far with him getting real money. He moved carefully and very wisely as if the Feds were on him from day one. But being realistic The God knew he had to get out before getting caught up. His girl now had a career and the million in change was more than enough to set his family up for life. He wanted to move and open a business in one of the up-and-coming cities in the south. Charlotte was ideal, but Nikki was leaning more towards Columbia, S.C. The cost of living was fair and there were plenty of great colleges, like USC and Benedict, for Tootie to attend.

After a little more research, The God had set his eyes on Greenville, S.C. There was a lot of new development in Greenville and he knew there was great potential for a small business to thrive. What sealed the deal was when he discovered that Verizon had another communication center there in the city. Nikki might lose her assistant manager's position, but a regular transfer was a bank-shot. She immediately set up an appointment with the HR director in the Wallingford bldg. To Nikki's surprise she was made aware of a lead manager's position there in Greenville. The HR woman had made a phone call and told Nikki that she could almost guarantee her the position. With seniority and the fact that it was basically a lateral move, she said the company would see it as a plus transferring Nikki to the Carolina office.

The stars had aligned with the moon and a Higher Power had blessed Nikki with the position after submitting her resume online. She would lose ten thousand with the regional difference in salary, but with the small promotion from assistant to lead, Nikki would gain back roughly twenty-four hundred to her yearly pay. She was to report to the Greenville bldg. for her first day of work on January 5th, 2006. It was exactly one and a half months away.

So, this was the reason that The God wouldn't let Nikki be persuaded to let Nikki take out a mortgage in the constitution state of Connecticut. He had been off probation for two years and didn't want to be tied into CT for any longer then he had to be. In fact, The God was ready to wash his hands of New Haven and the drug game completely.

On Schomes.com, he and Nikki found a newly built split-entry, four bedroom, and two and a half bath home on the market for $190K. An acre of land was included in the price. After negotiating with the agent, Nikki had secured the deal at $175K plus closing fees. With help from the homebuyer's program, she acquired the complete loan with a rock-bottom fixed interest rate.

Nikki was only required to drop five thousand dollars from her own pocket for the beautiful home in South Carolina.

Planning ahead, The God took Nikki down to a Bank of America branch in Greenville. Using two forms of I.D. and a paper document that showed she was a resident, Nikki set up a safe deposit box in only her and Tootie's name. Alone in the secured room, she put two hundred and twenty thousand cash inside the box and then locked it. Then she casually walked out the bank to where The God was parked out front in a rented Dodge Charger. God Body had done this just in case anything ever happened to him or his safe with the million in cash. Even though Nikki was gonna be making good money at Verizon, he wanted them to be able to pay off the mortgage loan without struggling or ever having to worry at all. Full ownership of their home would be the best asset ever.

Another Christmas was coming up in a few weeks and Tootie was eagerly waiting. She was now nine years old and was as smart as a high school freshman. The Hamden public school system had done great for her education. Tootie talked proper, like all the kids on the Disney channel, and for now she thought all the fresh lil' boys had cooties. She acted so much like Nikki, but looked just like her father. With long black hair and a welcoming smile, Tootie made lots of friends living right there behind the Hamden Plaza. She paid complete attention in school and would ace all her tests. Crossing off a diamond bracelet for a pair of diamond earrings, Tootie made five different rough drafts of her Christmas list. And just the other day she came home with a final copy for The God.

Nikki was busy preparing for her job transfer and their relocation down South. She wasn't planning on bringing any of their used furniture from the Seramonte condo. So she was spending a lot of time and money ordering things online for Greenville. Her and Tootie were set to move two days after Christmas, then The God would come down and join them right after New Year's. Nikki was happy and she printed a list of new resolutions off the computer. The God only had one change in mind that he wanted to make, so he had no need to print out a list. Tootie and Nikki would already be down South, but when the ball dropped at 12 a.m. on New Year's morning it would mark the last day he would touch a gram of coke. The last day he would resort to selling any drug for that matter. No more shoot-outs, plus he would be done with all the capers forever. The God was ready to square up for his wife and baby girl. Maybe even have three or four more kids instead of the two they were now planning. The bottom line is he was tired and was now ready to live a regular life. He planned to tell Monty and Bullet in a couple of weeks that he was giving them the Ward St. spot as a way to pay homage to them for always keeping it real with him. And he wouldn't ask neither of them for nothing in return. No monthly allowances, kick-backs, or nothing. He wanted out and he was determined to show niggas how to leave the game forever and never get the itch to come back. He had really caked up from fuckin' with Monty and Bullet these last five-plus years. Now all they would have to do is supply the work and let Luck and New Money run the block.

On the morning of December 27th, 2005, Nikki was doing her last-minute rounds and saying good-bye before her move down South. The furniture people in Greenville were able to deliver the living room and bedroom sets in her absence. Nikki's plane was departing at 5 p.m. and landing in S.C. at 6:25. Her E350 Benz had already been left in the garage at the new home so once they got down South, her and Tootie would be all set to make a quick trip to Walmart for a few groceries which would be the only thing they would need. The God was on his way to Bridgeport and he would take them to the airport as soon as he returned. It was only 12 p.m. so they had plenty of time.

With four days to his retirement date, The God now had a tough call to make. Bad Luck had informed him that there were only three G-packs left. And that lil' bit of work would most likely be gone before nightfall. The God had thought about walking away from the game a couple days early, but he hadn't really had the chance to talk to Monty or Bullet yet. To make things even more complicated, Monty was in Aruba with his fiancée. And although Bullet was good people, The God personally wanted to run things by Monty first. It was Monty who he had done his time in prison with, so it was with Monty where The God's loyalty really lied.

Monty and Tarahji were due back in the states in two days, and that's what made The God lean towards flipping one more ki on the block. It would take six days at the most to move the entire bird, but God Body only had eighty-four hours before the ball dropped and he'd have to honor his word. There was only one solution to the small problem at hand. The God would take his cut from the work first and off top, then Monty and Bullet would have to come down and deal with the block lieutenants on their own time to pick up their chips. The God figured he could have his own portion of the cash in his palm in two days flat. Because once the ball dropped he didn't want nothing to do with the game whatsoever. He wouldn't be bagging up grams, or even sitting on the block playing lookout from the V. He wasn't even trying to let his fingers touch the bloody money after the new year which was why he was going to tell Bullet that they'd have to deal with Luck directly when the paper for this last kilo was ready. Then they would run it down to Monty once he arrived back from his vacay.

Bullet was busy doing a little late X-mas shopping in Trumbull Mall and he told God Body to call him once he was out in the parking lot by the Macy's entrance. Bullet had a bad-ass Filipino chick named Kia with him inside the stores. After three months of wining and dining, Kia had finally fucked him just the night before after a failed attempt on their lives. Yeah, you read that right. It was the near-brush with death that made the little Filipina come alive. For a good girl, dating a nigga from the streets, that action movie scene shit turned her freak factor all the way on. It had all happened so fast. Sunk in the butter-soft leather seats of Bullet's whip, a wild rush of adrenaline ran through Kia's amazing frame after a small hail of slugs couldn't penetrate her new boo's car doors. She and Bullet were sitting idle inside the Olive Garden's parking lot on Boston Post Road when three very short masked men approached the vehicle with guns drawn. Always aware of his surroundings, Bullet instinctively slapped the curved gear paddle into D-sport and screeched up the wrong way through the entrance sign to the restaurant. Small hard objects could be heard slamming into and pinging off the doors as Bullet made what looked like three little kids part like a double-wide ass crack.

The attack surely had to be a case of mistaken identity, however, the adolescents underestimated their mark. Bullet had been doing a lot of suspect shit lately and had felt the need to bulletproof all the doors and windows on his V. Unbeknownst to everyone, including Monty, he had shipped his car to Nevada and had the reinforcements done. It was just one of the things on the sudden list that he kept from his partner.

That near brush with death, ironically turned out to be the wind to lift Kia's DKNY skirt and make her finally give the goodies to her modern-day Nino Brown. Kia performed well, and it was the reason she was now getting a late Christmas there in the mall. Bullet had about five Gs on him, but he had given her a fifteen hundred-dollar limit. While she was laying in his apartment this morning, naked, Bullet had blown over to the new stash spot and quickly cooked a whole bird. Of course, Mr. Mendoza's cocaine came back to a bird and a half. He then put it in the secret compartment of one of the gold Chrysler minivans and drove back to his crib. Once there, Bullet had fucked Kia again, this time doggy-style, until they both came, then took a shower together. They lathered up and rinsed in the hot morning water, then Kia sucked his dick under the shower head for a few minutes before they dried each other off. While Kia put back on last night's outfit, Bullet popped a few tags before heading to the mall.

It was no coincidence that Bullet was already in Macy's, in the shoe dept., when The God hit him on his cell. Kia was in the mirror posing with a black Chanel boot on her left foot, and a dark suede Steve Madden boot on the other. She had three hundred dollars left in her budget and both shoes had a sticker on the bottom that read a little over two hundred. Bullet thought about how beautiful Kia's ass looked from behind this morning and he figured it was okay to increase her budget a little bit. Plus, for some reason, meeting The God had him in a very good mood. So, Bullet told Kia to grab both pairs of boots because he wanted her to keep them both on when he fucked her later. He then gave her the green light to look for a bag to match the black ones while he ran outside for a minute. Yeah, The God really had this nigga feeling pumped.

Bullet immediately spotted the black Honda Prelude parked next to the gold Town & Country in the still empty parking lot. The God hopped out his little race car and gave Bullet dap and a tight thug-hug. Like any other time, Bullet gave the same tight squeeze back in return. God Body and Bullet weren't the closest friends but the love was clear as day. The God had begun telling Bullet the basics about him walking away from the game and leaving them the bldg. on Ward. He told Bullet that it was more to it but he'd wait for Monty to get back and explain everything at one time. Bullet tried to register it all but he was a lil' confused. But he had to admit that the news had made him even happier then he already was.

Bullet assured The God that they could wait for Monty to come back so they all could sit and make some sense of it. He then gave his boy dap and told him he had his blessings either way. Bullet then gave The God the keys to the Chrysler, so he could push the minivan to the Elm and transport the work safely. It was the only van that The God knew the sequence to make the compartment open. Bullet told him he'd drive the Prelude down to New Haven in a couple hours to switch back. But The God told him not to bother, and they could bring it down when they came to pick up their cash in a few days. Of course, he'd still be around to talk to them and make sure everything was copey, but it would be Luck or New Money who would give them the bread. Bullet couldn't believe that this was the last time he'd see The God in the game. So, with one last hug, Bullet told him to hit his cell when he made it safely to the Elm.

The God pulled out the mall parking lot behind the wheel of the Town & Country and Bullet sadly watched him go until the Chrysler was out of sight. He always knew The God was a smart dude and Bullet could totally understand why he was ready to get out. In Nikki, The God had a great wife, and Tootie was a smart and beautiful nine-year-old. But at the end of the day Bullet knew that The God had clipped them for those twenty birds, so he ain't feel too sorry for his black ass. From a brand new pre-paid phone, Bullet called the local number on the card in his hand. A deep groggy voice picked up and tiredly grumbled that he was Agent

Morley. He then asked the anonymous caller how could he be of any assistance. Bullet walked back inside Macy's and saw Kia's sexy ass smiling at him. He then disguised his voice and quickly spoke his piece before Kia came up sweating him.

"DEA Agent Morley, there's a gold colored 2001 Chrysler Town & Country van, license plate 392-CKI, on I-95 northbound with one and a half kilos of crack inside a hidden compartment. There's also a hundred-shot chopper concealed in the stash too," Bullet rattled off matter-of-fact, referring to the AK-47 army gun that would definitely seal The God's fate.

In a foul move that he thought he was justified on, Bullet also told the agent the sequence to open the stash box. When Agent Morley asked who was calling, Bullet quickly hung up just as Kia had snuck up on him and shouted his name. He didn't know for sure if the agent had heard her, but Bullet now wanted to knock Kia's ass out. He made her put all the shit from Macy's right back on the shelves. And if he hadn't already paid for the stuff she had in her bags he wouldn't have gotten her funky ass shit for Christmas. Bullet turned the phone off, then threw it in the trash on his way out the door. Kia dropped the items on the shelf closest to her as she tried to keep up.

CHAPTER 1

Sunday, June 16th, 2006

B efore anyone could take a breath and relax, the day that Monty and Tarahji had done so much planning for had finally rolled around. Their wedding had begun at 4:30 p.m. and the ceremony had taken place at Kingdom Love Center Ministries in Hamden. The day was blessed with clear skies and last week's heat wave had packed up and headed west. The temperature was 84° in the late afternoon and everybody seemed comfortable in the attire each had chosen for the occasion. About fifty cars and SUVs had pulled up inside the parking lot and there was an even split between the Valentines, Lesters, and even the Mendozas. The guests had attended in all sorts of colors and different arrangements. It was a beautiful crowd and everyone was happy to see the two tie the knot. It was amazing because that wasn't the case in every single wedding.

About 3:20 p.m., Monty showed up at Kingdom Love Center inside a silver Benz-limo with his Best Man and the rest of the groomsmen: Bullet, Quan, Live, and the entire crew. And to everyone, but the crew's surprise - fresh off an acquittal - even the Young Gunna was there. Bullet and the whole groom's party was dressed in light grey, three-piece linen tuxedos by Saint Laurent. Like their ties and linen dress shirts, they all wore black low-top Air Force Ones. Everybody had fresh manicures and facials to complement their crisp haircuts. The entire inside of the stretched Benz smelled like money.

Monty's tux was made of silk fabric by Gianni Versace. His all-white jacket, pants, and vest were wonderfully complimented by a soft pink shirt and tie with all-white, fresh out the box, low-top Air Forces. The leather Nikes were the only thing on the groom not woven of silk fabric. His early morning fresh Caesar cut had been laced with a line of precision. Monty even had the barber leave the single gray hair that was growing inside his goatee. A very wise one, Monty was in love and had patiently waited for this day to come.

THE BACKSTORY

As the limo driver came to a stop in front of the temple, Monty felt ecstatic behind the dark tint while watching a number of cars already pulling up. The chauffeur had opened the back door and the groom and his men stepped onto the concrete under the sun's pleasant rays. They all looked like stars. The different fragrances of men's cologne quickly swept through the air. The couple dozen or so people who were already there began snapping away with their phones and digital cameras. Monty received applause and hugs from a few of the Valentine women and a couple of his aunts before making it inside the chapel. Kingdom Love Center was one of the fairly new churches and was still in great condition. The wall-to-wall crimson-red carpet was clean as far as the eye could see; the windows and walls were scratch-free; and all the rosewood oak furniture had been polished and still shined. Monty's grandmother, his mom Lakiya's mother, had moved to Hamden and joined the church five years ago. Tarahji felt honored when she was asked by her grandmother-in-law if she would marry Monty inside her Love Center church. It was only a short ride for Monty's Bridgeport side of the family, and it didn't matter to Tarahji's people because they were all coming from Houston and Mexico. Besides, Hamden was a much more peaceful place to get married than Bridgeport.

At 4:29 p.m. every one of the expected guests was in his/her seat. In the next minute, the first of the wedding party began its elegant, slow procession down the aisle. There were the cute lil' Flower Girls, the Ring Bearers, the Best Man, and Bridesmaids. Then there was Monty marching slowly, but confidently down the aisle with Ms. Lester on his arm. When Tarahji was standing in the door way and next up to bat it felt as though time had stopped for a moment in the Love Center Ministries. Cameras flashed and you could hear gasps as the guests held their breath for a second. The bride was absolutely stunning. She wore a very stylish, ivory silk dress by Vera Wang that stopped mid-calf. The bottom was cut at an angle which made one side of the dress almost touch the floor. Gold, strappy Gianvito Rossi stilettos tied gracefully around her ankles, and her French manicure and pedicure were both done with a thin matching gold stripe. Tarahji's long black hair was pinned up in a bun. The three freeze-curls that spiraled down and caressed the left side of her face had a few new blonde highlights strewn about. Her best "B", Shameka, had taken basic cosmetology classes and was responsible for the flawless light makeup that Tarahji was wearing. The Mac products had given the beautiful forty-year-old an incredible covergirl look.

A tuxedo-clad Mr. Mendoza had been given the honor of walking his favorite grandchild down the aisle for her first ever wedding. And when he passed her off to Monty he gave his East Coast boss a sly wink of approval before taking his seat. Then all the other guests went back to their earlier calm state as they expectantly waited for the ceremony to proceed.

Bullet, Shameka, and all the others in the wedding party were up front with Monty and Tarahji as the couple held hands while exchanging vows. Their platinum and diamond rings were exchanged and there were "oohs and ahhhs" coming from everywhere. When Pastor Kennedy asked for anyone who objected to the marriage to speak now or forever hold their peace, the whole Kingdom Love Center was as quiet as a library. So quiet that when the doors burst open in the back everyone quickly turned around to see who was contesting the marriage. Standing in the doorway, in a light gray tux like he was a part of the groomsmen, was Monty's father, Free. He had a cocky ass look on his face like he was Michael Jordan and he had just escaped a kidnapping to show up in time for the playoffs.

Quietly under her breath, where only Monty could hear, Tarahji asked, "Who in the fuck is that?"

Monty didn't hear a word, he was too busy giving Y.G. a look as if he was telling him to go and pop his ass in front of a sellout crowd. However, Free wasn't there to object to the wedding at all. Tyshanna had gotten the approval from Tarahji and she had secretly sent her father an invitation to his son's wedding. Free was just a supportive guest who happened to bust through the ministry's door at the wrong damn time. So, through the madness, Pastor Kennedy proceeded on and successfully pronounced them husband and wife before Monty and Tarahji put on a kiss that almost set off the sprinkler system. After pulling away from one another, they joyously ran down the aisle with the wedding party and all the guests behind them.

The reception was off the hook and had turned out to be one for the ages. It was held at a new luxurious seafood restaurant that a young hustla-turned-entrepreneur had recently opened. The exclusive place had an enormous hall in the back that easily held the two hundred guests. Besides his current position as overseer, Monty was officially out the game and felt honored to be able to have his whole team present at the reception, with the exception, of course, being God Body.

Though their relationship had grown a bit stale over the years, Monty knew that dude was genuine and he still had a lot of love for The God. Unlike Bullet, Monty didn't really wanna believe that The God was behind the jux. When he returned from Aruba, Monty was truly saddened by the news of God Body's situation. He felt horrible for Nikki and their daughter, who Monty had nick-named Tootie Fruity. For failing to use his signal lights when getting off exit 10 on I-91 in North Haven, The God was pulled over and briefly detained by a state trooper from Troop F. The God never brought drugs to their condo in Hamden, but he had wanted to spend as much of the last hours with Nikki and Tootie as possible before driving them up to Bradley Airport. He was gonna park the Town & Country van in their garage, then use his new Audi when they were ready to start heading north to Windsor. He would then stop back in Hamden on the return from the airport. From there, he'd hop back in the van and take the work to the hood. However, fate wouldn't have it that way around 1:30 p.m. that day.

Expecting to hand over his license and registration, then maybe get a lil' ticket, The God was shocked when two more cruisers came to the scene and sort of surrounded his vehicle for a measly traffic violation. Officer Morrison summoned The God out of his vehicle and asked if any drugs or guns were inside. Knowing his rights were clearly being violated, The God called 911 and told the dispatcher that he was in fear for his life and asked that she please record the audio of the traffic incident in its entirety. Treading carefully in the shallow waters, the officer told God Body that he was being detained for DEA officers and the state-wide task force.

The God knew this shit could get ugly, still he played super cool, saying, "No, sir, "when asked if the inside of his vehicle could be searched.

In under ten minutes, a half dozen DEA and state-wide unmarked vehicles had joined the scene right off the exit. This was only five minutes away from the Seramonte Condominiums where Nikki and Tootie were waiting. A stocky albino agent with burnt-red eyebrows and a thick red Muslim-type beard had approached The God in a kindly manner and told him the situation was quite simple. DEA Agent Sean Morley said that he had reason to believe that The God was transporting drugs and guns. He said that after they looked under the hood, glove box, and a couple other places, The God would be free to go if he wasn't indeed riding dirty. God Body wasn't cuffed or put inside a cruiser; however, he was tightly surrounded by at least six agents and officers.

Agent Morley got inside the driver's seat of the minivan then strapped the seat belt around him. This was the first step that activated the stash box to work. With another DEA agent recording him with a small handheld Cannon camera, Agent Morley fumbled around with the radio buttons in a sequence that he learned from an unidentified informant - that at the time Agent Morley had no idea was the same confidential informant who had been working with the Feds ever since getting bagged with a half-ki of crack himself. **(Rewind this paragraph for full clarity)**

When the sequence was done, the top of the seat in the middle row had slowly opened up and ended The God's career. Needless to say, Nikki and Tootie missed their flight. Even worse, when Nikki went to go bail her man out she was given a rude awakening. Federal agents had been contacted and were salivating to take the case. A grand jury returned an indictment and a federal hold was placed on Germaine Mabry and he was detained without bail.

Now six months since the indictment, things were still unclear for The God. He was being held at the Donald W. Wyatt

Detention Center in Central Falls, RI, where the government was threatening to apply the ACCA (Armed Career Criminal Act) on him. Under the harsh penalties of the act, God Body was facing a mandatory sentence between fifteen years to life. In his first week of incarceration he had reached out to Monty through a letter and insisted that Bullet was his prime suspect as the informant. The God was told through his attorney that it was definitely an unidentified informant who placed a call to the agents, but because it was a hang-up, his discovery material wouldn't be able to place a finger on the snitch.

Monty responded to the letter by first expressing his understanding of The God's frustration, but he was unwilling to believe that his partner in crime was down with the Feds. Monty did however promise The God that he'd be there and would hold his family down for life. With the God taking the million-dollar hit that he had, Monty knew that his family could really use help.

Nikki was deaf, dumb, and blind to the way the Feds worked. So because she didn't talk to her man until the next morning after his arrest and was scared to lose her maternal rights when she was threatened, Nikki let the DEA have their way inside the Seramonte condo later that night. The agents easily located the simply-hidden safe and they had a professional on deck who had that shit popped open in minutes. Over a million in cash was sitting prettier than Julia Roberts. The money would first be used as evidence to help convict The God, then probably used afterwards to buy new spy equipment for the Feds.

Nikki had to cancel her promotion and relocation to the south so she could be close to the federal courthouse in Bridgeport where The God needed her most. The Verizon bldg. in Wallingford had simply deaded all the applications for the assistant manager's position that would have opened up had Nikki left. They accommodated their hard worker by letting everything remain the same as if she had never pondered a move. The home in Greenville was put back on the market at below value for a quick sale. Then Nikki used the money to buy something more modest, but still very nice over in Meriden. The price was $147K, so there would still be a nice piece of change left over from the safe deposit box after paying off the new mortgage. So even though The God was mad at Monty's response letter, there was no way he was gonna forbid him from holding down his family. But now The God was just convinced that Monty and Bullet were both working for "the man".

Y.G.'s availability for the wedding and reception was quite a different scenario. His trial for attempted murder had come around and Quita had still seemed optimistic about the incriminating statements being recanted for twenty-five thousand. However, she was still eating good off writing bad checks and her baby daddy had recently used a few dollars of hers to get on in the hood. Plus, he had not too long ago gotten hit from behind in a car accident and was expecting at least fifteen Gs in a settlement. Her baby daddy was doing the best he had ever done in his life. Shit, he was straight. That nigga went to the chiropractor three times a week faithfully to get the maximum check from his lawsuit. Quita's baby daddy had told her that Y.G. could kiss his ass, and that he'd talk to him from the witness stand in the New Haven courthouse. He had almost died that night, and twenty-five thousand wasn't worth all the surgeries and learning how to walk again. He wanted the Young Gunna to eat Ramen Oodles o' Noodles and mofongos for at least ten years. Besides, these days Quita could make twenty-five Gs over a weekend by taking a few checks into three different banks. So, her baby daddy advised her to shut the fuck up and just wait for their subpoena.

Quita and her baby's father decided to get back together and make it work on the strength of their youngest child, whom she called Lil' Daddy. A couple of days before they were due in court they had done a lil' shopping at the Tanger Outlets in Clinton. Donna Karan, Polo, Timberland, and Baby Gap bags covered the entire back seat of the rental. On the way back to New Haven, the re-connected/reunited couple had stopped for dinner at the Chowder Pot in Branford. Filet mignon, talapia, and wood-grilled salmon were their menu items of choice. All this was just last month in May, so the weather had already broken, and was hinting at it being an early summer. Quita had perfected a fat blunt for her man and she stuffed a whole eighth of sour inside a Vanilla Dutch. Fresh off a nice feast, they put a flame to the "L" before leaving the restaurant's parking lot. He made Quita get behind the wheel of the new-styled Camaro and she pushed the V to Button St. while her baby daddy got his mind right.

Dirt bikes and Banshees had already marked their start for the summer, and since the Freddy Fixer Day Parade, which was only a few days before, there had already been two young boys who had lost their lives on the bikes. They stopped briefly at the second-floor apartment, just long enough for Quita to take a shit. Her baby father had brought up all the shopping bags from the back seat of the whip. He was high as a kite, and a now-relieved Quita was ready for a Strawberry Blizzard from Dairy Queen. They were out the door in a flash and had every intention of enjoying this rare night without having any of the kids.

The little bad ass boys from next door were on the sidewalk shooting bottle rockets out of quarter water jugs. The M-80's and quarter-stick dynamites were setting off all the car alarms on the street. Those fucking eleven year olds on Button and Hurlburt Streets were known to tear shit up. Quita had put on over 40 lbs. in the past year and her big ass was now ready to relax, so she made her baby daddy slide into the driver's seat for the rest of the night. She was a lil' upset about putting on all the weight, but it still didn't take away the fact that she was cute as fuck and looked like Lisa Raye in the face. Now at 205 lbs. on the dot, Quita really had an ass like a donkey.

Her baby daddy turned the key in the ignition and the little hard-headed bastards next door let off a bunch of M-80's all at one time. But when the smoke cleared and all the fireworks stopped, Quita had two holes in her wet 'n wavy weave, and one lodged between her Victoria's Secret bra. A slug inside her baby daddy's fitted cap left his head blaring on the horn. Three more in the side of his Ralph Lauren short-sleeved rugby had his body deflated.

Y.G. jumped on the back of the R1 and Lord pulled off quickly, making a right onto Spring St. because the closest highway to get to Bridgeport was through the hot ass Kimberly Ave. strip. With no victim or witnesses, Frank Rosatti ate the case and the whole team popped bottles of Moet & Chandon. Quita and her man had nice memorial services and her three kids had been split up among different family members. Y.G. had wished it could've happened differently, but still, he felt no remorse. The only thing now tugging at his heart was what went down with Quita's youngest son, Lil' Daddy.

Lil' Daddy was now six and he was a beast for the Pop Warner Football League. If he didn't resort to drug dealing when he got to high school, he was a lock at getting a scholarship for a free ride to any school in the nation. But a future for him in football was not destined to be because Lil' Daddy was bad as fuck and nobody could tell him shit. Man, that little boy was ruthless; stealing candy from the corner store and fighting ten year olds and shit. Lil' Daddy had made the Bridgeport Post last week and Y.G. had read all about it. But it wasn't for scoring a touchdown against the Raiders nor for pocketing Laffy Taffys.

Apparently, Lil' Daddy had barked up the wrong tree and picked a fight with three neighborhood pit bulls. After trying to catch one of the strays to take back home, the three dogs attacked the little boy and tore him limb from limb. The dogs received lethal injections as penalties but Lil' Daddy had to have a closed casket like his parents did two weeks before him. The Young Gunna hadn't been acting the same ever since.

Over by one of the tables in the reception hall, Monty watched as Bullet and Tarahji shared a few words and smiles. It seemed that the two of them had gotten very friendly with one another over the past year, and quite frankly Monty had become a little insecure with it all. It wasn't to the point where he began questioning his fiancee in jealous rants, but he did make it his business to pay more attention to their relationship. Monty had been out the game for a couple months at this point and what he didn't know was that like he had tried doing, Bullet was also trying to get Tarahji to make her grandfather deal with him directly. But Bullet had also started letting a few slick comments leave his mouth from time to time.

Still in her bridesmaid dress, Lala was a little tipsy and had been flirtatious with all the guys throughout the evening. The dress's soft material had clung to her hips and exposed a shape that would give an old man heart complications. Her and Tyshanna snapped their fingers in the air and were amongst a vast amount of other American and Mexican beauties who attended the wedding. Lala had shot a few winks at Monty earlier and when it was time for Tarahji to throw her bouquet, Lala made sure Monty watched her ass wobble towards the middle of the floor. In a crowd of about thirty single women and young ladies, Tyshanna was standing in the right place to be able to reach up and snag the flowers from out of the air. She was instantly the target of envy by all the jealous women who had wanted the luck of being the next bride. The funniest shit in the world was when Monty tossed Tarahji's garter belt into the crowd of forty-two eligible bachelors. With his back turned, Monty flipped the belt high in the air and as it neared all the playboys, the crowd parted like the Red Sea. The ivory-colored garter belt sat like a grenade on the hall's floor.

The beautiful wedding cake had been cut and everyone enjoyed the succulent dessert after an exquisite dinner. The exclusive restaurant had done a wonderful job catering the food. The plates weren't kiddie-sized, and there was more than enough to go around. Finely aged wines and an expensive line of champagnes were perfect complements to the meal and gently washed down the delectable banquet. Monty rubbed seductively on Tarahji's thigh underneath the table the entire time they were eating. Whispering nasty thoughts to each other all night, the newly married couple couldn't wait to mess up their sheets now as "Mr. and Mrs. Lester". Tarahji's pussy had been wet since the pastor had granted Monty permission to kiss his bride. Underneath the table cloth, she had even rubbed her fingers between her own thighs and let her husband have a taste. To everyone that looked on it seemed like Monty was licking cake from his wife's fingers, but the couple was secretly seducing each other in preparation for later that night.

They shared their first dance together to R. Kelly's "Step in the Name of Love" remix, which was a classic. And oblivious to all the watchful guests, they were telling each other how much they wanted to fuck each other right there in the middle of the dance floor. Their bodies were hot, and at Tarahji's age, she was at the very height of her sexual peak.

Over the past several months she had grown a strong addiction to mostly being on top of Monty whenever they were fucking. Getting it from behind had even taken a back seat to the cowgirl position. And the way the silk wedding gown was now clinging to her pound cake, Monty wanted nothing more than for Tarahji to ride his dick. He had been begging her all night for the two of them to hop onto the Merritt Parkway and take the fifteen-minute drive to Stratford for a quickie. As horny as Tarahji was she was almost tempted, but instead she told her husband that the wait would only make it worse for him when she got a hold to his dick later on.

Free had finally made his way over to introduce himself to his new daughter-in-law although he was maybe nine years her senior. Monty watched with a disgusted look from the moment Free had greeted Tarahji with a light hug. Monty also made a mental note to check his sister and wife for the bullshit they pulled by inviting Free in the first place. But for the time being he decided to pose for a few flicks with family and friends.

Tarahji and Free were carrying on like they had known each other for years. Laughing and making a bit too much physical contact for Monty's taste. He could've sworn he'd seen Free look like he was storing a number inside his phone. And whatever Tarahji had told him had sort of made Free go pale in the face. Then they both bust out laughing and Monty had finally become sick and tired of Free's shit once and for all.

Monty hugged Grandma Lester tight for the last flick then made a beeline to where his wife stood giggling and shit. Monty snatched Tarahji's hand from out of Free's grip and slapped the taste outta his father's mouth. When Free looked like he wanted static he quickly checked himself when he saw Y.G., Lord, and Ro-Ro behind his son quick as lightning. Free's hands went up in the air like he wasn't looking for trouble, then in a low tone, he pleaded for Monty to bury their hatchet. Tarahji just stood aside watching. There was a look on her face like she was sort of feeling sympathy for Free and Mr. Mendoza was at his table with a bunch of wild Mexicans trying to figure everything out.

But when Monty told Free to make this the last time he ever showed up in his life, Tarahji knew from the tone of his words that her husband was dead serious.

Depleted, Free turned to Tarahji and told her it was nice meeting her, but he loved his son regardless of anything, and would rather leave than cause any harm whatsoever. With that, Free spun on his heels with the intention of walking out on Monty for the last time in his life.

The joy at the reception quickly returned and forty men and women were on the dance floor doing the electric slide. The liquor had everyone feeling nice and they all planned to party well into the night. Free had been gone a good forty-five minutes when Tyshanna and Ms. Lester ganged up on Monty for a "family affair" dance on the floor. He was in the middle of both of them like a sandwich. Bullet came over and whispered something in his best friend's ear while Monty kept up the rhythm with his family. Whatever was said had seemed to garner Monty's approval because they gave each other dap and tilted their heads in a "yes" nod. Bullet yelled over the music something like, "I'll be back in an hour tops." He stopped and said a few words to Tarahji before heading out, then gave her a high-five like they were homies from college. The dancing continued and a half-drunk Monty had once again felt at peace.

Ten minutes after Bullet left, Tarahji went over to her husband and told him she had a gift that she wanted to give him in the presence of everybody at the reception. The only problem was that it was at their home in Stratford. Monty had suggested that they skip out on the reception and go for the quickie that they rapped about earlier while picking up his gift, but a very tipsy Tarahji had persuaded him to stay and continue enjoying the party, saying she'd make the short ride with her bridesmaid and return in a flash. With that, Tarahji grabbed Meka's arm and shot out the door. More sober than the bride, Shameka jumped behind the wheel of Tarahji's Infinity truck and quickly dipped up the Merritt Parkway which was only two minutes up Dixwell Ave.

It was only a little after 9 p.m. so the party was going full throttle. Monty started thinking that it would be cool if he also grabbed one of the gifts that he was giving to Tarahji in Hawaii, and also present it to her tonight. Not one to be outdone, he quietly snuck out the door unnoticed and hopped in the Range twenty minutes after Tarahji and Meka had left. Monty figured they would have been to the house and long gone by· the time he arrived to sneak her gift back into Hamden.

Route 15's traffic flow was smooth and Monty was pulling up in front of his home in no time. He was a little surprised to see that Tarahji and Meka were still there. Tarahji's truck was parked in a position that blocked the driveway, so Monty parked the Rover right across the street. They had recently bought the new home and it was in a different neighborhood than the last one, but the area was still very peaceful and tranquil, as the whole of Stratford was.

As Monty got closer to the front porch a strange vibe overcame him. He wasn't really feeling the scenery and had suddenly started sobering up. Maybe it was the big S550 Benz that looked out of place a few houses down. From where Monty parked in the Range Rover the Mercedes looked exactly like the one Bullet just brought. Instead of going for the front door Monty. walked around the side of the house where he saw the living room light glowing through the blinds and sheer curtains. As he stepped in closer to the window, Shameka's voice became crystal clear as she encouraged Tarahji to "ride it faster".

As if this shit was meant for Monty to see, there was a small opening in the blinds at the very bottom of the window. The view almost matched exactly with Monty's eye level so all he had to do was zoom in. The words that Meka had moaned couldn't prepare him for what he saw Tarahji doing with her $3,500 wedding dress· hiked up over her round ass. Tarahji was in a straddle position, riding the dick like she was loving it. She was leaned forward like she was kissing the nigga in his mouth and Monty couldn't see his face because Tarahji's back was blocking the view. But two brown hands were squeezing on her golden ass, slamming her down harder on his dick with every bounce. Monty saw the pants to the guy's gray tuxedo down around his ankles and drooping over the black Air-Force Ones. He knew right then and there that his best friend, and Best Man at his wedding, was fucking his wife and had probably been fucking her for some time. And Tarahji had the nerve to be letting her nasty ass friend Shameka watch her get fucked on her wedding night by someone other than her husband.

With her finger in her own pussy, Meka had a front row seat. They all started moaning in ecstasy as Bullet was panting that he was cummin'. He pulled Tarahji off his dick just in the nick of time when he started to nut. Semen was shooting all over the sofa that Monty had just bought. Unable to stay out of all the fun, Shameka had leaned over Tarahji's ass and swallowed whatever cum that still oozed from the tip of the hard dick. Tarahji then collapsed forward into his chest, and wanting to see his dick get soft in Shameka's mouth, Bullet peeped over Tarahji's shoulder with a big smile on his face. But when Monty locked eyes on the guy's face, his heart had stopped beating for at least five seconds.

His father, Free, had one hand on Tarahji's ass and the other one was pushing on the back of Meka's head. Monty suddenly recalled Free being dressed like he was one of the groomsmen in a gray tux and black Forces. And the vision of him storing a number in his phone at the reception came back into the mix. Monty then realized that the plate on the Benz out front was white, and not blue like Connecticut tags. Monty was now sure that it was a Carolina plate and if he had ever had a reason to kill his father, then this was now the major one.

Monty gently slid his key into the door, but the newly-installed security system had alerted everyone that the front door had been opened. Running through the unfurnished dining room, that had been purposely left that way so the Mexicans could deliver furniture in, Monty took a short cut that had him in the living room in a fraction of a second.

Already aware of his presence from the alarm, Tarahji was smoothing out the wedding dress over her hips when Monty appeared in the living room. Free had just zipped and was buttoning the pants to his tux and Meka was using the back of her hand to wipe away any signs of cum from her mouth. Tarahji couldn't believe that this shit was really happening. She quickly yelled to Monty that Shameka had just wanted to get to know Free and that she was able to explain everything.

It was obvious that his wife didn't know that he was watching from the window as she rode Free's dick bounce by bounce. Trying to play it off and go with the flow, Free stepped next to Meka and pulled her in very close by her waist. Shameka did what she was supposed to do, kissing Free softly on the lips, but Monty had glided across the room like he was on a skateboard while they were smooching. With raw power that he had since taking hand-offs in high school, the twenty-eight-year-old gangsta had knocked the forty-nine-year-old playboy square on his ass. The blow was so staggering that Shameka had felt the vibration from Free's lips during their kiss.

As the middle-aged man fumbled around on the floor trying to get up, Monty dashed upstairs to get the tool that would finish Free forever. Taped behind the night stand on Monty's side of the bed was a stocky black .357 Glock that took ten Sig bullets. Monty ripped it away from the oakwood and basically jumped the whole staircase on the way back down. Tarahji and Meka were busy scurrying around and the front door was left wide open. In the night's silence of the suburban neighborhood, Monty heard a car engine come alive a few houses down. As soon as he made it to the porch the brake lights to the S550 went dim and the back of the Benz crouched low as Free stepped on the gas. The way Monty ran out into the middle of the street with the hammer in his hand was like a scene from the old-school movie *Ricochet* starring Denzel Washington. Free tried to run him over, but Monty jumped between the front bumper of his own Benz - which had been sitting parked in the driveway up against the garage – and the front of Tarahji's truck. Free shot past in a blur, but Monty was already back on his feet squeezing off multiple rounds from the tre-pound Glock. The Sigs shattered the back window of Free's Benz and knocked holes all in the trunk, but the big body V kept pushing up the block through the otherwise quiet neighborhood.

Before any nosy neighbors could come peeking out their

windows, Monty had already started the engine of the Range Rover. Tarahji was on the porch calling for him to come inside so she could finish explaining, but Monty ain't wanna hear that shit. Free had gone ghost, so catching him to finish swiss-cheesing his whip wasn't even an option. So, Monty dropped the automatic transmission into drive and headed back to the Merritt Parkway to rejoin the guests at the reception.

At 10:10 p.m., the party showed no signs of ending soon. The head of the Mexican cartel had a few glasses of champagne before him and Mr. Mendoza seemed to be enjoying the show of all the young women doing their best rendition of the booty dance that Beyonce had made famous. Lala spotted Monty walking through the doors and she met him with a playful dance routine of her own. She was clearly wasted, but she was handling her liquor well. Her dress seemed to be hugging her hips and thighs a little tighter than earlier that afternoon and she had a freaky look in her eyes when she was inches away from Monty. She had replaced her stilettos with a pair of pink comfortable flip-flops and her cute little pedicured feet were adorable. Lala left very little space between the two of them as she backed her wobbling ass up on Monty. The dance floor was crowded and everyone was under the influence of alcohol, off in their own world, so no one paid attention as Monty grabbed Lala slightly by her waist and whispered in her ear. He was telling her how sexy she was and how he had been wanting some of that pussy since the first time he saw her. The shit he was saying had caught the little freak off guard and she abruptly stopped popping her booty on his dick. Lala turned around and stared in Monty's face to see just how serious he was because the truth was that she had also wanted to dance on his dick since the first day her mother introduced her to him.

Tarahji was standing in the doorway looking over the entire hall, desperately trying to locate her husband. She had spotted the Rover outside, so it was obvious that Monty had returned to the party. Tarahji knew she had fucked up, but the two of them had way too much invested in each other. They were more than husband and wife, they were partners in every sense of the word. She was sure they would find a way to get past this turmoil.

Bringing her best bitch out of her stupor, Freak Meka tapped Tarahji's arm and pointed Monty out on the dance floor with Lala. From where Tarahji stood it looked like her daughter was a little too close for comfort on her husband. She knew Lala liked to fuck, but you couldn't have paid Tarahji to believe that her daughter had already set it up.

Prologue

Free's State Of Mind...

My name is Shaun "Free" Freeman and not only am I a rat bastard, but I'm also a piece of shit. Man, I don't need none of y'all to tell me I'm wrong, but there's always two sides to a story. So, don't be so quick to judge a muthafucka.

It's true that I received a 5k1.1 motion for assisting the Government in putting my brothers and cousins away for life, but man, they was trying to take all my momma's kids away forever. And I couldn't let them do it like that. So yeah, I told on everybody ass. I just wish momma's health could've held up a lil' longer after all that shit. And now none of the family fucks with me besides my baby girl, Tyshanna. But momma would've never turned her back on me if she was alive, no matter what I did.

I just wish me and Monty could've settled our differences because ain't no limit on what we could've done in the game on the whole East Coast. I know go-gettas down in Savannah, Georgia all the way up to Springfield, Mass that buy them birds by the pairs.

I was trying to tell Monty but his ass wouldn't listen. And no doubt, I was wrong for knocking off my son's wife on the night of their wedding, but technically I had fucked her first anyway. That's right, about twenty-three years ago I was on one of them blocks in Manhattan and ran into Tarahji's exotic-looking ass with a few of her friends. I told the bitch my name was "S-Class" because I had just copped the big-boy Benz. Me, Man-Child, and all the fellas were fronting like we were from Lenox Ave. I consoled the bitch about some jive-ass nigga that she was with from Brooklyn who was kicking her ass all the time. And you know I'm a smooth muthafucka. Sheeiit, I became her best friend in a matter of hours. And before you know it I was skeeting all up in that Latin pussy. I ain't give a fuck. I ain't have no plans on ever seeing her ass again.

When my daughter Tyshanna sent me an invitation, the name Tarahji didn't ring a bell because it had been so long ago. You know these days everybody be naming their sons Mekhi and their daughters shit like Farrah and Tavonna. Man, I ain't pay no attention to that shit. I just asked my daughter what colors the groomsmen were wearing. I wanted to show up ready just in case my son had a change of heart and finally accepted me back in his life. But Monty quickly made it clear that he wasn't fucking with me. Yeah, him and his boys was this close to going upside my damn head. And if I ever catch that damn Y.G. by himself and get the drop on him, I'mma shoot him in his ass. Somebody must've lied and told him he was the hardest nigga out. He thinks he's Styles P or somebody.

I was merely introducing myself to the bride in the middle of the dance floor. It was Tarahji who started saying a whole bunch of shit that ain't really make no sense at first. She said she had been staring at me the whole time I was there and it took for Tyshanna to make me smile before she realized we'd met before. Right there, while everybody was dancing to Usher Raymond's, "In this Club" remix, Tarahji admitted to being in love with my son. But in the same breath she confessed that she had never been fucked like the way that I fucked her in Manhattan many years back. Mind you, I had fucked more than a dozen women in Manhattan before, so how was I supposed to had remember her. Shit, we was gettin' money back then. But when Tarahji mentioned a few other details it all started coming together for me. How could I ever forget the way her long hair hung down to her ass when she rode me backwards? And the way that she came all over me in a downpour while in that position? I actually remember being mad at myself the next day for giving her the wrong number. Tarahji was someone I cursed myself for not holding on to. If not for anything else, at least to fuck her a few more times, you know.

Back on the dance floor, we had grabbed each other's hands and laughed as if someone had told a joke. To everyone at the reception it just looked like I was enjoying my new daughter-in-law. And no one seemed to be having a problem with that. No one except that stubborn ass son of mine. I saw him mean-muggin' me from a distance, so I pulled out my phone and acted like I was taking a call in the loud reception hall. But I was really typing Tarahji's math into my call log, then I quickly pressed the end button. I told her it was only to stay in touch now that she was a member of the family. Wanting me and Monty to restore our relationship, she saw no harm in it at all. However, little did she know, I was already scheming to fuck.

The way Monty and his corny-ass henchmen had run down on me in front of all the guests had only fueled the fire between my legs. I drove to Bridgeport and rode around behind the dark tints for a while in the Benz. I sent Tarahji a text, basically apologizing for my part in causing a scene. I saw a few niggas I used to run with hanging out in front of the liquor store and was very surprised by the speed with which Tarahji had responded to my message. But what had caught me even more off-guard was what she replied. I simply told her I couldn't wait for the next time we crossed paths. But she sent me a Stratford address and insisted that I meet her there in twenty minutes. Tarahji had asked me if I could fuck her once more for old times' sake. She promised me that she could ride the dick much more thoroughly than when she was just a young girl. Wanting to hurt my son now more than any other time, I agreed to our meet-up. Then five minutes later Tarahji sent me another text telling me that she couldn't come alone, and if she let her best friend watch, I had to promise that I wouldn't touch her.

Tarahji said that Shameka was a freak and I could possibly screw her later that night. But Tarahji wanted all of my attention on her for at least fifteen or twenty minutes. And if their security system hadn't alerted us of a visitor Monty would've seen his wife's fat ass slowly bouncing on my dick, and then her nasty ass homegirl bending under her to swallow whatever cum she could catch. I even caught my dick in the zipper trying to hurry up when Monty shot into the living room. He was always athletic, but I honestly didn't know that boy was that strong. It felt like my head had flown off my shoulders when he caught me with that right hook. And if he thought I was sticking around until he ran and grabbed the gat, he was out his rabid-ass mind. I almost ran his monkey ass over in the middle of the street, and a couple of slugs whistled pass my ear as I burned up the concrete. But if I knew that shit would have led to my son getting his life taken, it would've been a piece of pussy that I honestly would've passed on.

Apparently Tarahji clipped the security wire on the side of the house that morning she caught Monty fuckin' Lala. That's why he never heard the system alert that someone had entered the home. One of the neighbors in Stratford had called 911 and reported hearing multiple gun shots. Tarahji's crazy ass had bust the gun until she emptied the spinning chamber of the .44 revolver. When the Stratford police had kicked in the door of the home Tarahji and Lala were going room to room knocking shit over as they banged out like two grown men. Lala had taken one of the slugs to the back of her right shoulder, but it was a clean shot that had gone straight through and didn't seem to slow her down in the mix of their rumble.

The EMT paramedics were also on the scene immediately and had busied themselves with stopping Lala's bleeding shoulder, while a second all-Latin team seemed to discreetly race upstairs to my dying son's side. Most of the officers were preoccupied, having trouble trying to contain Tarahji, who had picked up the empty gun and was still trying to clap shit up. Two or three minutes passed and it may have been those precious minutes that could've saved Monty's life. Lala had started yelling that he was upstairs and badly wounded as the team of Latin first-responders stood at his bedside, witnessing Monty's chest exhale for a final time just a minute too late. The medical report proclaimed Monty dead on arrival.

In the following months things that that were getting revealed were quite shocking. For starters, Tarahji sat pregnant behind the walls of the York Niantic Women's Prison. Her bond had been set by the court at 2 mil cash, but for some reason the paperwork had gotten screwed up when a random furniture company came forth to drop the bread for the two-million bail. It was done on behalf of Mr. Mendoza and the Cartel. I guess the court's system and DA's office didn't know who they were fucking with by putting so low of bond on Tarahji for the murder. But after convincing the judge that she was a danger to society and even more, a flight risk, The Honorable Judge Allen Dubose decided to hold her without bail, pending the outcome of trial.

A hundred large was dropped to retain the top two

attorneys in Connecticut: Jake Williams out of Hartford and a mean lady name Diane Pollack out of New Haven. After extensive research and a few favors being pulled, the state's attorney's final offer was a rock bottom 20 years. Fifteen years for the murder to be run consecutively with an additional five for the assault in the 1st on Lala.

It was the best Mr. Mendoza could pull considering she shot more than one person, clearly showing she was rage and premeditation. . So Tarahji's now receiving prenatal care behind the wall where she's set to give birth to two twin boys in about seven weeks from now. And no, it's not what you think. Any drops of my sperm that didn't land on the sofa were guzzled down by Shameka's nasty ass. Tarahji had conceived while on her honeymoon in the islands. And my boy Monty was surely the daddy of them babies. So now I'm about to be a grandpa.

However, in a strange scenario, the few spurts of cum that my son had squirted inside Lala when Tarahji popped up in their bedroom that morning had been enough to also fertilize Lala's ovulating egg. And I'll be damned if she wasn't expecting twin boys of her own. Remember, Tarahji's father Corey also had a twin, Cameron. So it was no coincidence that twins ran in their family. And now out of the hospital and fully recovered from her gun wound, Lala, like Tarahji was also as big as a house. And she was due to give me two more grandsons in about eight weeks.

In an even crazier twist, the most surprising update came from Dr. Natalie Buress in the Paternity Testing Dept. at Bridgeport hospital. After getting a call from Shameka, who I had now been fucking for a while, I learned that Tarahji had added me to her visiting list and she needed to see me urgently. After checking out a few Oxycodone buyers in New London, CT, I decided to make the short trip over to the women's prison. I had to be in town for a couple days on coke and pills business anyway, so what better time to pay Tarahji a quick visit.

Tarahji was quite surprised to see me in the visiting room and her baby weight seemed to fill her out in all the right places. After bullshitting around and Tarahji asking me if I fucked Shameka as good as I had fucked her, her face got serious when she was ready to speak her piece. It turns out that she had blamed her first pregnancy on a Brooklyn cat from way back in the day, but she was actually 100% sure that Lala was mine. She joked that it had to be the reason our sex was so good that night in Manhattan. You know how women say that those are the times when they get pregnant. But Tarahji was dead serious and she put it on everything she loved. She was too embarrassed back then to admit that her baby was from a one-night stand. So, she told Jalen, her first true love, that the baby was his before his trifling ass strangely disappeared. Tarahji asked me if I thought it was a coincidence how much Tyshanna and Lala resembled each other. And when I pictured them both in my head I knew there was only one thing left to do.

I set up an appointment for me and Lala to take a paternity test. When it was revealed that there was a 99.999% chance that I fathered the girl, right then and only then, is when I felt the worse I ever had in my entire life. It's a very small world and fate couldn't have been any crueler. It turns out that Monty had gotten his little sister pregnant. So not only will the twin boys be brothers, but they'll be first cousins as well. If I ain't live the way that I lived, maybe this whole big mess would've never happened. I'm not just feeling bad because he was my son, but Monty was really a loyal and official dude and I'm honored to have produced someone so intelligent and raw. I don't regret doing the jux, but if I could turn back the hands of time and had never shown up at the wedding, I would.

Yeah, it was me who was responsible for robbing Monty and Bullet blind the whole time. I'm sure you can recall me politicking with him in his mother's living room. Well, that was me giving him the last chance to get money with me. We would've taken over the whole coast for real. You see, I had left my shorty in Jersey and had been in town for five days already. It wasn't hard to follow them niggas and scope their whole layout. Them niggas were young boys in the game and I'm a triple O.G. In a matter of seventy-two hours, I knew the exact crib and floor that them fools kept their bricks in. They weren't slick at all man. I even slipped up one time and was right behind them at a light in West Haven. But

Bullet's silly ass was too busy talking on the phone to see me in his rear view. I had my shorty's young teenage cousin with me to help carry the safe. I gave him ten Gs up front to not be concerned at all about what was inside. It worked for him, but he was definitely young and dumb. I ended up getting my ten stacks back once I sold him some of the weight. We even tried to go back to the crib and make sure we didn't miss anything else. It almost got ugly because Monty had suddenly pulled into the driveway. Parking a few blocks over and running through the woods was the best decision I could've made in my life. Because if not, then it would've definitely been a shoot-out in the quiet neighborhood. But when it was all said and done it was like taking candy from a baby. And trust me when I tell you, man, I ain't never look back. My S550 with the S.C. tags ain't a loner babyboy. I paid cash for that bitch.

For everyone that thinks I'm slime, it's funny how your boy Bullet turned out to be the biggest worm of all. He thought The God was behind the heist and ended up doing him real dirty. Although God Body was never able to get any paperwork to back up his claim, the long-time 5-percenter was sure that Bullet was a rat. The word had started spreading like wildfire through the city. Niggas were catching state and federal cases left and right and they were all blaming the kingpin for their sudden demise. It seemed like everyone who got knocked would just have finished talking to or copping weight from Bullet. He soon became the most dangerous nigga in the city, opening up seafood and pizza spots in a few different hoods. And with immunity from the Feds, all the coke, dope, and exotic weed came through him. But Bullet was so clever that no one could ever tie his name to a debriefing session with the agents. But everything about him said FBI and you just knew not to fuck with him. New Haven, Hartford, Bridgeport, and every major city and ghetto got a nigga like Bullet. He was even plotting to line Tarahji's grandfather's ass up. The Feds had made a deal to let Bullet keep half of whatever shipment they caught. But lucky for Mr. Mendoza, he never wanted to meet anyone but Monty. Bullet ain't know the first thing to tell the Feds about the old man. And once Monty died the cartel was back off the radar.

Y.G. and that wack-ass crew had left all the dime and twenty money to all the up-and-coming niggas in the projects. Without any paperwork to prove that Bullet was a NARC, he was once again their savior and his position as the head of the clique had been reclaimed. Word on the street is that a crew of niggas who had just came home from prison had formed a squad call A.R.M.E.D. It stood for All Rats Must End up Dead. The rumor is that The God's big brother Supreme had formed the crew. And since it's said that Bullet is responsible for God Body's downfall, it's understandable why the rich weasel had made the top of the A.R.M.E.D list. It's funny how Bullet rarely shows his face in Bridgeport anymore, opting now to spend most of his time in Atlanta and Orlando.

As for The God, the armed career criminal act stuck and he was smacked with 188 months. Fifteen years to be spent mostly in penitentiaries around the East Coast. Nikki ended up getting another promotion at the Verizon Bldg. in Wallingford and she's now designated to work 100% from home. So, wherever the BOP transfers The God, Nikki usually finds an apartment there in a matter of a month. Right now he's in Big Sandy and Nikki's living right there in Kentucky. The only disadvantage is that Tootie never establishes too strong of a bond with any friends. But she adores her dad and would trade any friendship to be able to have her weekend visits with him. I even reached out a few months ago and put $50,000 into a CD that Tootie wouldn't be able to touch until her twenty-first birthday. And if that ain't real nigga shit then what do you call that. I can't take away all the trife shit I ever did in my life, but hey, it's a start. I'm getting money like the '80s and that 50K wasn't shit to me.

The God was official the whole time that Bullet and Monty thought he was on some snake shit. Yeah, he was getting a lil' side money but shit, he was obligated to do that. He ran the program in New Haven by himself and felt like he deserved a bigger slice of the pie. He knew Monty and them were seeing double what he made after having to bless Bad Luck and New Money. The big fish that The God ended up clipping was a nigga from 'round Orchard St.

name Hova. And he only caught Hova for a brick and half, thirteen stacks cash, and a seventeen shot Ruger. But Bullet swears The God was sitting on their twenty birds. Still, The God kept it funky with Monty and made sure his money was always right. The God even cried all night upon hearing that Tarahji had murdered him. It ain't my fault, but it's fucked up that the numbers behind The God's name is 20758-014, which is his Federal I.D., with the 014 meaning a Connecticut inmate. Monty's is 6-24-2006, his death date. And me, well, mine is $2,254,000, my net worth. But I would give it all back to have my son with me again.

To be continued...

A.R.M.E.D !!!!
(All Rats Must End up Dead)

A Letter from the Author/CEO

I am the CEO and first author of One Wheel Publications, LLC. As a prolific writer of urban novels, I have pegged myself 'The Creator of Real-Life Fiction'. My stories are yours just as much as they are mine because I'm bringing forth a level of realism that's been missing in urban fiction to date.

Through my novels and publishing company I'll share vivid tales that will unfold like some of your favorite classic motion picture movies. I am very qualified to give you these stories. However, that's another story, one that I'll save for my auto-biography. In no way am I glorifying the street life through my work. I'm simply looking to entertain and enlighten based off of my own experiences.

During many trials & tribulations, One Wheel Publications was born in my head during the wee-hours of the night inside a Federal Detention Center. I am a trendsetter. I SEE IT, BELIEVE IT, THEN ACHIEVE IT. My motto is: IF I CAN SEE IT IN MY HEAD, I CAN HOLD IT IN MY HANDS.

Stay tuned for the arsenal of novels that I have written and will release over the next few months/years. My work is 'Medicine' for the avid reader and I will gladly prescribe small dosages to every patient I reach.

I am encouraging all aspiring writers to join One Wheel Publications as an author. Walk with me. Let's break the cycle. We all have a story to tell.

The Creator of Real-Life Fiction
Daniel "Boone" Mills

One Wheel Publications Brand

One Wheel Publications, LLC is a newly-formed publishing company geared towards delivering quality content to the literature and magazine world. The name 'One Wheel' represents INDEPENDENCE. It screams LEADERSHIP. It symbolizes being a BOSS. One Wheel Publications was formed in the mind of ONE individual; an individual who always been capable of standing on his own two and making his own way. The logo, a teenager doing a wheelie on his free-style bike, represents balance. The perfect balance of reality and imagination needed to create a new movement in the literature world. Even more, the boy riding on the back wheel represents the balance that our teenaged males need in leaning towards being positive, productive, young men. Daniel 'Boone' Mills, the CEO of One Wheel Publications, strives to encourage every young man to be their own wheel.

BOOK ORDER FORM

Please provide the following Information, so that your order can be processed.

Shipping Address

Name: _____

Name: _____

Address: _____

Address: _____

City, State, Zip code: _____

_____

Phone: _____

City, State, Zip code: _____

Email: _____

_____

QTY	UNIT	DESCRIPTION	UNIT PRICE	TOTAL
		The Backstory (Part 1 of the Trilogy)	$15.99	$
		A.R.M.E.D. (Pre-Order Summer 2017)	$14.99	$
			SUBTOTAL	
			SALES TAX	[6.35%]
			SHIPPING AND HANDLING	$1.90
			OTHER	
			TOTAL	$$

1. One Wheel Publications accepts Money Order **only:** Payable to **One Wheel Publications**, LLC.
2. Enter this order in accordance with the prices, terms, delivery method, and specifications listed above.
3. **Mail Order Form to:**
   One Wheel Publications, LLC
   P.O. Box 6661
   Hamden, CT 06517

Contact information for any questions:
Email: onewheelpublicatons@gmail.com

Please allow 7-10 business days for delivery.

Thank you for your business!

Made in the USA
Monee, IL
20 March 2022

93255353R00152